Forty Rooms

Forty Rooms

OLGA GRUSHIN

A MARIAN WOOD BOOK   Published by G. P. Putnam's Sons   *New York*

A MARIAN WOOD BOOK
Published by G. P. Putnam's Sons
Publishers Since 1838
An imprint of Penguin Random House LLC
375 Hudson Street
New York, New York 10014

The author gratefully acknowledges permission to quote excerpts from Anna Akhmatova,
"Requiem," from *Complete Poems of Anna Akhmatova*, translated by Judith Hemschemeyer, edited
and introduced by Roberta Reeder. Copyright © 1989, 1992, 1997 by Judith Hemschemeyer.
Reprinted with the permission of The Permissions Company, Inc., on behalf of Zephyr Press,
www.zephyrpress.org.

U.S. edition ISBN: 978-1-101-98233-4
Export edition ISBN: 978-0-399-57687-4

Printed in the United States of America
1   3   5   7   9   10   8   6   4   2

Book design by Chris Welch

TO ALEX AND TASHA

And it came to pass at the end of forty days, that
Noah opened the window of the ark which he had
made.

Genesis 8:6

Be thine own palace, or the world thy jail.

John Donne, "To Sir Henry Wotton"

Part One

Mythology

Moscow Apartment and Whereabouts

1. Bathroom

The Tree at the Heart of the World

THE BATHROOM IS THE FIRST PLACE TO EMERGE from the haze of nonbeing. It is cramped and smells sweet and changes from time to time. When the world outside hardens with dark and cold, the sky-blue tiles grow icy and sting my naked soles, but the pipes vibrate in a low, comforting hum and the water is hot and delightful; I dive into it with a heedless splash, rushing to slide into soapsuds up to my chin before the prickle of goose bumps overtakes me. Then the world swells stuffy and bright, and now the coolness of the floor feels nice, but the pipes lie chilled and inert; I watch the stream from a just-boiled tea-kettle hit the cold water inside the plastic bucket before I climb gingerly into the empty tub and wait for the sponge to dribble lukewarm rivulets down my back.

Most evenings the hands that touch me are the ones I know best, light and gentle, with a delicate ring on one finger and fingernails lovely and pink like flower petals. With the hands comes a voice, a soft, quiet voice that sings to me—though the songs themselves sound sad. Other times, the hands are harder, their fingers thick and blunt, the fingernails cut short, almost to the quick, one finger squeezed tight by a plain golden band that seems far too small for it; but these hands are never rough, and I like them just as much, not least because I am less used to them and I feel curious, and also because the voice of the blunter hands does not sing but tells jokes. The voice is firm at the edges, and the jokes are loud, large with mooing roosters and oinking cats, and a naughty gnome who comes only on Sundays to talk of messy meals and chamber pots and other things equally funny and gross, and I laugh and laugh until bubbles spurt out of my nose.

But sometimes, rarely, the hands are different—large, loose-skinned, and bony, smelling of smoke, their long fingers stiff, their joints like the bark of the old tree by the swing set in the courtyard. These hands move with an odd, crablike grace, barely touching the sponge, forgetting why they are there, emitting a faint clatter and jingle as they alight on the side of the tub; open-mouthed with amazement, I watch a bracelet of pink oval stones slide up and down the withered wrist, each stone carved with a pale woman's face, thin and elegant, glowing from within. And the voice, like the hands, is withered and straying; and it does not sing, and it does not laugh—it tells stories instead.

The passing of seasons, another winter giving way, another summer cresting, brings with it Grandmother's yearly visit. I find myself waiting for the stories above all else.

They never have the same beginnings—no matter how much I beg for some half-remembered tale, Grandmother will not repeat herself—but they all lead to the same place, a hidden kingdom of manifold marvels. The kingdom is reached in a hundred different ways, though few ever gain entrance to it. Some stumble upon it after a lifelong search, having wandered through treacherous forests and climbed snowy mountains, while others are plunged there headlong, without any warning, without expectation, having tasted of a strange drink or chased a chance shadow around the corner or stared for a moment too long into the mirror. (One little girl with the same name as mine arrives in the kingdom wet and wrapped in a towel: she is taking a bath when she gets swept down the drain.) The kingdom is home to amazing creatures and things—candle flames that have run away from their candles, warring armies of spoons and forks, flocks of traveling belfry bells, a beautiful blind fairy, a mouse who dreams only of dragons, a knight who has lost his horse—and all the creatures ceaselessly travel along the kingdom's many paths, some straight and simple, others twisted and full of dark adventure, all winding their way toward the kingdom's secret heart. There, at the center of the world, where all the paths converge, grows a wondrous tree whose branches touch the skies, and there, by its vast ancient roots, the creatures halt and wait—wait for the leaves to fall.

"And why do they want those leaves so much?" I ask, as I always do. "Are they made of gold?"

"They aren't gold," my grandmother answers, "but they are precious all the same. One side of each leaf bears a name, and only the person whose name it is can read the words on the leaf's other side. And only one leaf on the tree has your name on it, so if you aren't there waiting for it when it falls, you miss it forever."

"And what words are they, Grandmother?"

"The most important words in the world," she replies.

"Yes, but what do they *say*?"

Her fingers click with impatience against the tub's edge.

"They are different for every person, so I can't tell you."

I sink back in the bath. No matter how her tales begin, they always end this way: she will add nothing more. Whenever she starts, I hope that tonight will be different, that tonight she will tell me the rest. But she never does. She is a hundred years old, I think angrily to myself, and she is more stubborn than anyone I know; she likes to hoard her secrets. I sit in the bath willing myself not to cry, the skin of my fingers and toes puckered from being too long in the water. My grandmother has forgotten the sponge yet again; she is staring at the tiles above my head, and her pale red-rimmed eyes have that unseeing look I catch from time to time, like the blank eyes of the carved women on her old bracelet. And suddenly I think: Maybe she doesn't even know how the story ends, maybe she arrived there too late to catch her own leaf.

All at once I feel terribly excited. I look at the drain. Suds are being sucked into its whirlpool, and I glimpse a slice of my pink scrubbed cheek, a corner of my brown eye reflected in its silver curve, and something else too, a tiny elfin face grinning at me, beckoning me closer with a hand like a twig before vanishing in a splash of foam. I decide that right away, without losing another minute, I too will slip down the drain, and ride the soapy waters to the mysterious depths of the hidden kingdom, and brave its crooked paths alongside dragons and spoons, and reach the tree at the heart of the world—and when my leaf falls, I will be there to read the words and tell everyone about it. But immediately I grow sad as I remember that I'm only four years old—four years and three quarters—and I don't yet know how to read.

My mother sticks her head in the door. I feel a draft of cold air.

"Time for her milk," she says. "Mama, you're sitting on her towel."

My grandmother stands up with slow, injured dignity and sails out of the bathroom.

2. Mother's Bedroom

The Jewelry Box

ONE EVENING IN DECEMBER, I ENTER MY MOTHER'S bedroom to wish her good night, but my mother is not there. A mermaid is sitting on her bed instead. I know she is a mermaid right away, even though I am unable to make out the tail under the folds of her narrow skirt of the faintest gray color, the color of morning mist above the waters of our dacha pond. She is bending, her tresses long and pale, over my mother's jewelry box, which she holds open in her lap; I can see the silky fabric of her strange skirt stretched tight over her knees beneath the lacquered edge of the box.

I feel enchanted by the presence of the mermaid, but also deeply grieved. I love my mother's jewelry box. It is made of shiny black wood, and on its lid two pearly girls with wide belts and sticks in their hair fan a third girl, while all around them tiny trees twinkle with rosy blossoms in a walled-in garden. It is the one object in this room filled with wonders that I long to possess, but I am never allowed to touch it. On my last birthday, when I turned six, I begged and begged until, with a small, patient sigh, my mother pulled open a drawer, maneuvered the box from under the layers of folded nightgowns and stockings, and let me marvel at the princesslike sparkling for a brief minute; but she did not show me anything closely. It makes me sad to find a stranger— even if she is beautiful, even if she *is* a mermaid—handling that box as though she owns it.

I am about to tiptoe out when the mermaid looks up and beckons me toward her.

"Do you want me to show you?" she asks.

Her voice is like my mother's, but her eyes are not: they too are green, but their shifting depths lack the familiar misty softness; they glitter instead with joyous, hard brilliance, just like the brilliance I can already see trapped inside the jewelry box.

Now and then there are strange creatures to be stumbled upon in my mother's bedroom—it is my parents' bedroom, really, but I have always thought of it as my mother's alone—yet the mermaid makes me uneasy. She seems almost dangerous, more unpredictable than any of the others, not in the least like the kindly plump woman in the oval painting above the armchair who rambles about Brussels lace and satin slippers at teatime, or the two yellow-winged fairies who every spring morning slide down the sunbeams onto the dresser to splash in my mother's perfume bottles, or the man smiling with bright white teeth under a wiry mustache who used to pay afternoon calls the summer I was five. (I liked him best of all, because once or twice, just before he gently pushed me out into the hallway and locked the door behind me, he gave me a chocolate bar in a crinkly wrapper with unfamiliar letters on the side, and also because he possessed magic powers and was invisible to everyone but me. "That child has such a wild imagination," my mother said, laughing gaily, after I mentioned the visitor with the mustache one night at supper, and my father laughed too, though not as gaily, and ruffled my hair. I felt offended at not being believed, but more than that, I regretted letting go of something that had been mine and mine alone: I found that I liked having secrets all my own. After that, I never said anything to anyone about the things I saw in my mother's bedroom.)

The mermaid has already forgotten about me. She is staring into the box, moving her fingers over the velvet insides, as if remembering some tune she once played on a piano. I sit down on the edge of the bed, elated but wary. The mermaid begins to speak, but she is not speaking to me; she caresses this or that ring, this or that pendant, and tells long, winding tales I cannot follow.

"These cupid earrings," she says, "have been in the family for four generations. Your great-grandmother received them as a sign of special favor from the tsar's youngest uncle. He had them presented to her the night she premiered as Dulcinea. She had gifts from many men, of course, but this was the only thing she held on to when forced to sell off all her possessions in the civil war. One wonders why she kept them. She struggled so to feed her children, and the earrings would have brought in bread enough to last a month. But women in this family have always had their mysteries . . ." She pauses to take a sip from a nearly empty glass of dark red liquid on my mother's nightstand. "Of course, it was well

after her Dulcinea days that she married your great-grandfather
and had your grandfather and the twins. But could there have
been more to the Grand Duke anecdote? No one to ask about it
now—all that's left are two enamel cupids, half a rumor, and
maybe, just maybe, a thimble of royal blood."

"Is this my great-grandmother the ballet dancer?" I ask, confused. "And who is Dulcinea? And why is there blood in a thimble?" But she does not answer, only lightly trails her fingers over
the golden fire imprisoned in the box, and goes on talking.

"And see this ring? See how the emerald is uncut, rough and
enormous, like some green, misshapen bird's egg? This came
from an ancient icon, from one of those priceless frames set with
precious stones big as rocks. So many were vandalized in the revolution, hacked apart, hidden by drunks in rotting village coffers.
Your grandfather got the emerald at the end of the war, traded it
from another soldier for a length of smoked sausage and a box of
German sweets, then kept it for years in an empty saltshaker.
Eventually he had it set for Elena, your grandmother—a simple
pewter setting, he could afford nothing more."

"What does 'vandalized' mean?" I ask. "When was the revolution?"

In the circle of soft yellow lamplight the jewels inside their
dark nests shift with hidden, treacherous fire. The mermaid takes
another sip of the red liquid, tipping the glass into her mouth so
abruptly that some drops spill onto the blanket. In profile she
seems just like my mother, but every time she moves, every time
she speaks, every time she looks past me, not hearing my questions, I am filled anew with the knowledge that she is not.

"And this bracelet I've had since I was a child. It reminds me of all the mornings spent searching for bits of amber in the sand after the tide."

I am pleased to hear something I understand at last. My mother's family came from the Baltics; she grew up spending summers on the Latvian coast. It must have been there that she met the mermaid. I was wrong to ever find the mermaid dangerous, I think with relief. As I shift closer to her gleaming gray flanks, I am startled into pity by a sudden thought. "But isn't the Baltic Sea too cold in winter? What do you do if it turns to ice?"

She drops the bracelet back into the box and glances down at me, her metallic green gaze slipping over my face with a swift, cold touch I can almost feel on my skin.

"But that's enough, you are too little to care about the past," she says, and while her tone seems light, the chill of the faraway sea is there, underneath.

My pity abandons me, as does my relief. Once again I am nervous.

She stands up, balancing the box in one hand and the glass in the other.

"Come to the mirror with me."

Together we leave the reassuring circle of light and move into the graying dusk. The oval mirror over the dresser is curly and gilded. On evenings such as this, wintry and still, I like to come and look at my mother's room nestled into its quiet pool. The mirror room is smaller than the real one and has no angles, filled instead with a fuzzy, muted, familiar warmth, so much like my mother's soft presence. But now the two of us are reflected in it, me in my short white nightgown with green parrots, the mermaid a slim undulation of shadow behind my shoulder, and the mirror room seems different, cold and sharp-edged and mysterious, exciting in a new way, like something marvelous yet harmful, something forbidden, like—like a lollipop I once stole from the kitchen and devoured in crunching, glistening half licks, half bites in bed at night, under the covers, without brushing my teeth afterward.

"Here, let's try this on you, this was your father's gift when you were born, it will be yours someday," the mermaid says as she sets the jewelry box on the dresser and picks up a chain from which dangles a prim little cross of delicate pearls. But I have just spied something else—something I like so much more. Reaching out, I close my fingers on a necklace of small round stones, each kernel of blood-red glow in its own frame of darkness.

"This," I say. "I want this."

Something harsh and hurt flashes in the mermaid's eyes, and when she takes the necklace out of my hand, her movement is not gentle: she rips the strand through my fingers, scratching my palm, surprising me into a little cry. I expect her to throw the necklace back into the box, and slam it shut, and push me away; but a flush grows in her face instead, and suddenly she smiles—the first smile I see, not a kind smile, but oh, so beautiful. She smiles her strange smile, at once brittle and hard, and lays the necklace against the parrots on my gown. In the shadows of the mirror it glints stark and red, like a gash I got on my knee when I was four and fell, running, on a piece of glass.

"A friend gave it to me," the mermaid says in a defiant voice, as if challenging someone. "A long time ago."

We are silent then, both of us looking at me. Out of the corner of my eye, I can see the lady in the oval painting purse her lips and turn away with disapproval, but I continue to stare at my reflection, and after a while I too begin to seem different, as if the silvery, dangerous, shimmering sea were rising within my being. Around us the evening deepens, the lamp by the bed glows brilliant and distant, and slowly the room is transformed into an immense jewelry box, the blue velvet of the night enveloping us tightly, and the mermaid's deceiving eyes are emeralds now, and the congealed drop at the bottom of her glass a ruby, and on the dresser, just between the tray of portly perfume bottles and the clock that always shows the wrong time, there rests a treasure bright and dark, an unfamiliar, thrilling treasure filled to the brim with stories I do not yet understand, stories of guilty gifts, impoverished dancers, ruined churches, wars and revolutions, the grown-up, momentous things of pain and beauty and time.

From behind the door a sound bursts out, mechanical and persistent, like the tap-tap-tap of a woodpecker, and I swing around, startled, then realize what it is. When I turn back, the mermaid is gone, just like that, and my mother is fastening her old gray robe around her waist. "Your father is working, we must be quiet," she says in a near whisper as she leans over me and fumbles with the clasp of the necklace under my hair. Stupidly I watch while she neatens up the earrings and bracelets in their plush compartments, closes the lid with care, slides the box back into the drawer. "And it's time for you to go to bed."

I want to tell her about the mermaid, to ask her a question, but something stops me—whether the flat intonation of her strangely loosened voice, or else the memory of the secret, gem-like place where things seemed at once more wondrous and more frightening than in real life. I walk to the door in silence. From the threshold I glance back at the room, and it is as always, warm and cozy and small, full of pillows and blankets and smiling ladies in oval frames, on both sides of the oval mirror. I am comforted to think that the sinister treasure is once again only a wooden box of pretty trinkets under the woolen stockings in the dresser, comforted to see my mother moving her tender, steady hands over the covers of the bed, smoothing them in a gesture I have seen hundreds of times.

I prefer things this way, I tell myself. Really, I do.

"Go to sleep, my love," says my mother, looking up briefly, not meeting my eyes. "Your father will be wanting his tea now."

As I walk into the chill of the hallway, I think: But maybe I don't.

3. Father's Study

The Ideal City

IT IS JUST AFTER DINNER ON THURSDAY, TIME FOR
our weekly Culture Hour. My father and I are seated at his desk,
he in his old armchair of cherry-colored leather, cracked along
the middle, I by his side, kneeling on a stool I have lugged in from
the kitchen.

On the radio, turned down low, a concerto is playing.

"Vivaldi, *La Follia*," my father says after listening for a moment.
"Appropriate in view of today's subject."

He reaches for the stack of books beside his typewriter and
selects a volume on Italian Renaissance painting, which he opens
to a marked page; like so many books in his study, it is bristling
with slivers of green, blue, and pink paper. My father makes the
bookmarks himself by neatly cutting multicolored index cards
into narrow strips, perfectly straight, though he never uses a ruler
(he has an uncanny ability to draw straight lines), then jots down
a heading or a quotation along the strip in his meticulous, mi-

nuscule hand. The colors are not chosen by accident, either; they follow some complicated scheme of his, whose principles always escape me. As he pulls the volume closer and carefully sets the blue bookmark down on his immaculate desk, next to the framed photograph of my mother, I tilt my head sideways until I can read the words written along it: "Ideal city."

"This evening," says my father, "we will talk about the Renaissance concept of the 'ideal city.' The concept itself did not originate in the Renaissance. The first man to study it in depth was the Greek philosopher Plato—you remember, we discussed him last month. Now Plato, in his *Republic*—"

For the first minute or two, I do nothing but luxuriate in the smell of the study. It is my favorite smell in the world, a noble smell that I like to imagine as deep, quiet, burgundy-hued, though in fact it is not one smell but a mixture of smells, all equally marvelous: the sharp smell of shiny art volumes, a bit like wet autumn leaves; the softer, more complex smell of thick treatises on history and philosophy whose desiccated leather spines crowd the shelves and between whose pages reside entire flocks of shy dust sprites that come out to play at dusk—I used to watch them for hours when I was younger—the metallic, oily, inky smell of my father's mechanical typewriter, which, even when given a rare hour of rest, seems to radiate the heat of its passionate staccatos; the sweet ghostly smell of my father's aromatic tobacco, which a friend brought from somewhere far away and which he smokes only on special occasions; I know he keeps the dwindling pouch in the middle drawer of his desk, just above the drawer with a fascinating wealth of compartmentalized pens, erasers, and paper clips, just below the drawer that is always locked . . .

My thoughts return from their wanderings, and I study the book opened before me. There is one large reproduction on the page to the left, and three smaller ones on the page to the right, with thin rivulets of text snaking between them. They are views of various cities—or perhaps it is all one city, for, while the painted vistas are different, all four are united by a certain sameness, a kind of stiff geometrical precision, beautiful and cold. The skies are flat, distant, and pale, devoid of clouds and winds; there are no curving streets, no cozy nooks, only vast, many-arched, many-columned expanses of architectural perfection in the full glare of brilliant noonday, with not a shadow, not a blade of grass, not a flower to be seen anywhere, the ground itself an intricate pattern of pastel-tinted marble diamonds and ovals in majestic perspective. The orderly chessboards of empty spaces, the magnificent heights of deserted staircases, the sleek façades all seem unsettling, even vaguely threatening, as if something roaring and monstrous is just poised to erupt into the sunlit silence from somewhere below the horizon.

I wait until my father finishes his explanation.

"So, if this city is so ideal," I say, "then where are all the people?"

My father thoughtfully chews on his beard, then puts on his reading glasses, and makes a careful inspection of the paintings.

"There are some people here," he says at last, pointing.

"No, those are statues. Or if they aren't, they are the size of ants and have no faces, so they don't count. There is a dot moving here, which looks like a girl my age wearing pajamas, but at this distance I can't tell for sure—it may just be a smudge."

"Well," my father says, "perhaps all the people are inside. They are sitting around drinking wine—moderate quantities of well-diluted wine, mind you—and discussing philosophy or creating masterpieces or whatnot. This is a perfect city, after all, so they are content wherever they are, indoors or outdoors, see?"

I look again; but the evenly spaced windows are dark and dead, and the doorways gape blindly. A while back I discovered a delightful secret—some paintings possess a deeper layer of life below their still surface: if I concentrate, then glance away quickly, I can often catch things moving out of the corner of my eye, women powdering their noses above the stiff lacy collars, cherubs tickling each other, cardinals relaxing their glum faces to yawn or sneeze.

I am certain that there is no hidden life lurking here.

"There aren't any people," I say stubbornly. "There aren't even any cats or dogs. And look, there are no doors anywhere, just these open passageways. People wouldn't live in houses that have no doors."

"Ah, but that's where you are wrong," he says, smiling. "If you listened to me with more attention, you would see that everyone in the ideal city is kind and honest, and there is no need for locks and chains." He takes off his glasses, pulls out a folded square of suede always ready in his pocket, and begins to wipe the thick lenses, thoroughly, with deliberation, as he does everything, before putting the glasses back in their velveteen case. "But perhaps you are right and there are no people there," he adds, no longer smiling. "Perhaps that is really the point. Ideals are all very fine until you start applying them to real life, you see. Just let people into your perfect city, just wait until they make themselves comfortable, and before you know it, well—"

Vivaldi has just stopped playing, and beyond the crackling of the radio void, I can suddenly hear the ticking of the clock on the desk. My father rubs the bridge of his nose in a gesture I know so well, then glances toward the window; I see an odd, stark look cross his face, a look of not quite anger, not quite grief. In the spare darkness of the early-spring night, the enormous construction site across the road is abbreviated to mere grayish hints of fences and sketchy gallows of cranes in the sky, but I know it is there all the same, as it has been throughout the ten years of my life. The rising edifice itself is only a shapeless bulk blotting out the stars. None of us has any idea what it will be when it is completed. "Temple of the People," my father used to say when I was four or five and pestered him with endless queries.

My father pulls the curtains closed before turning back to me.

"Never mind," he says briskly, "I'm not afraid to admit a mistake. Perhaps this was not the most fruitful subject for tonight's discussion. Since you seem to miss people and dogs so much, how about some Fra Angelico? Here, let me show you."

Once more he leafs through the Renaissance volume. This time the bookmark is pink, and so, I see, are the predominant colors of these new paintings, in which roses bloom, ladies blush, and saints are ruddy with health, all against a background of pink cliffs, red roofs, and churches aglow with sunrises. I am charmed. My father has already begun to speak when, against our custom, I plunge into his steady stream of dates and names with a breathless, out-of-turn question.

"Papa, are houses in Italy really so pink?"

"I suppose it is possible," he says. "I'm glad you like these. But to continue, in 1436, Fra Angelico moved to Florence, to the new friary of San Marco, and there——"

And there are tiny yellow flowers in the swaying meadows and tiny blue flowers on the hems of the girls' dresses, and tiny monsters bare their pointy little teeth in the soft swell of harbors, and bells ring, and birds chirp, and everyone, everyone, has a golden halo. A few chubby monks have clumsily dropped a slab of stone onto a writhing blue imp and now stand around with guilty downcast eyes, debating how best to rescue him. A mother sits encumbered by a fat baby in her lap, and as her gaze follows the flights of some great white birds soaring toward the sun on rainbow-colored wings, her sad face brightens with the desire to leave the baby behind and fly away with them. These paintings are like fairy tales, and while the stories do not all have happy endings—I notice a number of heads freshly detached from their bodies, floating in puddles of what looks like my mother's strawberry preserves—they make me giddy with the premonition that somewhere, somewhere out there, a place so vivid, so alive, really exists.

"Haven't you been to Italy?" I interrupt again, too excited to listen.

My father coughs shortly.

"No," he says.

I tear my eyes away from the book. "You haven't been to Italy?"

"No."

"But you've been to Greece."

"No, not to Greece either," he says.

"To France, then? And England?"

"No."

"But—to Egypt? China? India?"

Silent now, he shakes his head. I stare past him, at the lacquered spines of the art volumes lined up in their neat alphabetical rows on the shelves, as I struggle to find the right words for the enormity of my disappointment.

"But . . . but you've *told* me about all these places. I thought . . . Haven't you ever wanted to go there?"

"Well now, you see," he begins, then clears his throat, and again says, "Well, you see," and falls silent. The telephone rings in the hallway. We listen to the rush of my mother's slippers slapping toward the sound, the lilt of her muffled voice. In the next moment the door of the study is cracked open.

My mother does not come in.

"Sorry to interrupt, it's Orlov," she says from the corridor. She is cupping her hand over the receiver, the cord stretched as far as it will go. "He wants to discuss tomorrow's seminar, but I've told him you're busy and will call him back in—what shall I say, half an hour?"

"No need, I'll take it, we are finished," my father answers, as he closes the book and rises from his armchair. "We must do better on our choice of subject next week. Perhaps Andrei Rublev?" He speaks the last words already past the threshold, picking up the telephone. "Yes, hello?"

Stunned, I look at the clock on his desk. There are still twenty minutes left of the Culture Hour. He has never done this before. All at once I am certain it's because I interrupted him so much, and I feel chastened.

4. Kitchen

Immortality

I FALL ASLEEP TO BURSTS OF LAUGHTER BEHIND the wall to my right and wake up, hours later, with the laughter, louder and looser, behind the wall to my left; the guests have moved from the study to the kitchen. I lie dozing for a few minutes, half traversing an arched bridge between the misty shores of some dream, half listening to the hubbub of blurred voices. The loudest of them, which I recognize as Orlov's, appears to be propounding something, while two or three others burble up in the background whenever Orlov pauses for breath. The women, though, are still in the study: when I roll over in bed and press my ear to the wall, I hear a snippet of my mother's exclamation, a saxophone wail from the record player turned down low.

The men must have gone to the kitchen to refill their glasses.

The dream bridge recedes farther into the fog as I realize I am terribly thirsty; this evening my mother let me stay up with the

guests until well past my bedtime, snacking on pickled mushrooms and cheese with garlic. My thirst makes me more and
more awake, until, giving up on sleep altogether, I toss off the
blanket, lower my feet to the floor, and wait without turning on
the light, hoping that the men will leave the kitchen at last.

It must be very late, for the street is quiet, and the ceiling,
undisturbed by the flares of passing headlights, lies indistinct in a
pool of shadow. On nights when I cannot sleep I stare at it for
what seems like hours, populating it with the geometry of imaginary constellations, with meandering trajectories of grotesque
creatures born in the deeper pockets of darkness and fleshed out
by dribbles of streetlamp illumination. But I am too thirsty to
imagine anything at present, and the voices continue to crisscross
one another in the kitchen, until my throat feels so dry it is painful to swallow. After another minute I hunt down my slippers,
nudge open my door, and walk into the corridor.

The kitchen is flooded with light. I see the men's backs—
my father's, Orlov's, Borodinsky's, two or three others'; they are
crowded around Orlov, looking over his shoulder as he speaks. I
am about to march over the threshold, making straight for the
teakettle, when Orlov's weighty tone, with none of his usual
clowning, makes me pause. He has begun to declaim a poem, as
he often does at my parents' gatherings, but it is not one of his
own humorous ditties with glib little rhymes—this poem has a
measure so solemn, so stark, that after a moment's listening I feel
with absolute certainty: These words are not meant for my ears.
No one has noticed me yet, so I take a stealthy step back, slip into
the unlit bathroom, push my father's robe out of the way, and

stand straining my hearing, one eye glued to the crack in the door, my heart beating wildly as if I am in the presence of something vastly more important than myself.

The kitchen is now so hushed that I can hear Orlov's voice with clarity, as I would if he were whispering in my ear, though he is reading quietly, under his breath—he seems almost embarrassed to be saying the words aloud.

> *"That was when the ones who smiled*
> *Were the dead, glad to be at rest.*
> *And like a useless appendage, Leningrad*
> *Swung from its prisons . . ."*

He shuffles the pages. "And this," he says.

> *"Magdalene thrashed and wept,*
> *The favored disciple turned to stone,*
> *But no one dared to cast a glance*
> *To where his mother in silence stood . . ."*

His voice trails off, and then everyone else is silent too. From the corner into which I am wedged, I cannot catch a glimpse of anyone's face—I see only the indistinct bobbing of gray and brown jackets, a patch on the elbow of my father's old sweater, a flash of light on a typescript page in Orlov's hand, and, on the wall behind them, directly in my field of vision, our old cuckoo clock, my late grandmother's long-ago present. It is almost two in the morning. I will be in trouble if I am discovered.

Borodinsky speaks, so loudly that I start.

"This will never be published," he announces, "and no wonder."

"Oh, I don't know about 'never,'" says Orlov.

"Not in your lifetime, at any rate," insists Borodinsky.

"I fear I must disagree," my father says. An argument commences, or perhaps only a discussion; my father's friends often sound belligerent and cheerful at the same time, and I am not always able to tell the difference between the two. Soon they are shouting—about the times changing or not changing, the new Party leader, some underground art show someone attended in someone's basement, some newspaper article someone is waving about. My father attempts to stride back and forth as he talks, but our kitchen is too small for striding, and he is forced to stand with the others in an agitated clump, all of them crammed together, interrupting one another now, arms jerking, shoulders shrugging. I find it hard to listen. I feel that the words read by Orlov only minutes before have left an emptiness behind them, a dark, chilled hush as after the passage of something powerful, something immense—like the profound stillness after the tolling of a deep bell, like the blackness pooling behind your eyelids after you have gazed straight at the sun—and it needs to be acknowledged by everyone, yet is ignored. It occurs to me that they sound somehow relieved, as though glad to have dispelled the kitchen silence with such boisterous promptness, glad to be debating matters that must be important but seem oddly trivial to me.

I am again aware of my thirst. I wait, my face pressed into my father's robe; it has preserved faint memories of his tobacco. At two o'clock, darkness yawns in the lacquered façade of our kitchen clock and the cuckoo stumbles out to take two stiff bows, one left, one right; it lost its voice years ago, but I can hear the wooden creaking of its aged joints. Through the crack in the door hinges I see my father's elbow grow busy as he resumes topping off the guests' glasses; then they abandon the kitchen and stomp, still arguing, into the corridor. I watch six or seven pairs of well-worn shoes stampede past me, hoping that no one decides to barge into the bathroom. A moment later the study door swings open, Orlov's wife laughs shrilly, a heedless saxophone trill leaps into the breach, the door closes.

I tiptoe out.

The brightly lit kitchen is deserted, and there, on the table, among the jumble of my mother's gold-trimmed floral cups, on top of my father's newspapers, lies a forgotten sheaf of typescript pages. My heart painful in my chest, as if my rib cage has suddenly grown too tight for it, I push the cups and the newspapers aside, gather up the pages, and sit down. The type is blurry, in places almost illegible; this must be the fifth, if not the sixth, carbon copy, and the letters seem precarious and thus doubly precious, as though in imminent danger of dissolving under my very eyes into blots of thinning ink on the brittle surface of rice paper.

"Anna Akhmatova, *Requiem*," is written at the top, and, just below:

No, not under the vault of alien skies,
And not under the shelter of alien wings—
I was with my people then,
There, where my people, unfortunately, were . . .

I read.

A chair creaks, a cough sounds. Blearily, I look up.

A man is sitting across from me at the table.

"I've been watching you for the past ten minutes," he says. "You have quite the ability to tune things out. This too may be of use to you—if, that is, you tune out the right things."

The dazzling, terrifying, cleansing revelation of the poems releases me slowly.

I frown at the man before me. He is not someone I recognize, though I know my parents' friends well. His face is handsome— the word "chiseled," at which I snickered a year or two ago, during my brief Dumas obsession, makes gratifying sense at last—but he is not young, the age of my parents if not older, and the slight hints of heaviness in his jowls, of droopiness in his eyelids, of thinness in the blond hair that he wears too long, make his beauty seem disturbingly marred, unnatural somehow. Like a statue of a god with his nose lopped off, I think—or perhaps with his chin grown double, the marble gone weak and flaccid. All at once I realize I am staring, and I feel flustered.

"You were not here earlier," I mumble.

"No, I just dropped in for a moment," he replies, smiling. It is not a warm smile. "So, reading banned poetry in the kitchen in the wee hours of the morning, are we? You're a poet yourself, are you not?"

"No," I say curtly. He is studying me, his light eyes piercing. I am not in the habit of being rude to adults. I look down at the pages before me. "That is . . . I suppose I rhyme things once in a while. When I can't sleep. Nothing like this."

"Well, no, of course not," he agrees, leaning back in his chair. "This kind of thing—it comes much later, and not to everyone." Idly he picks up a page from the table.

"I have so many things to do today:
I must murder the rest of my memory,
I must turn my soul to stone,
I must learn to live again."

He recites the lines without once consulting the page before letting it fall back onto the stack. "This weightiness, it has to be earned, and the price is high. Not everyone, you know, is willing to pay the price of immortality."

I should be in bed, not lingering in the kitchen in my night-gown, memorizing dangerous poetry and talking to strangers, but I speak without thinking, before I can excuse myself and leave. "I thought this hasn't been published. How can it be immortal if no one can read it?"

"Perceptive but wrong, my dear child. It's like that tree falling in the forest when no one is around. Rest assured, there are powers that see and hear everything happening in this world. And in any case, aren't you reading it right now? Manuscripts do not burn, as another immortal once said—though you are probably too young to have read him just yet. How old are you, anyway?"

The jazz music of my parents' party is coming from somewhere very far away.

"Thirteen." I lick my dry lips. I realize that I never did get that cup of water. Battalions of smeared glasses have been abandoned in careless disorder near the sink, and from where I sit, an arm's length away—everything in our kitchen is only an arm's length away—I can smell the half-honeyed, half-acrid scent of unfinished wine. "The age of Juliet," I nearly add, but say instead, "I'll turn fourteen this summer."

"Oh, you have some time. Not too much time, mind you," he says airily as he glances at the clock on the wall, and as if on cue the cuckoo creaks, bowing on its perch; it is three in the morning. "Time, you know, is the ultimate limitation placed on man, and you need to be supremely aware of your limitations if you desire to become a poet. Of all the different kinds of art, you see, poetry is the one most attuned to man's condition, and therefore the most noble and the most demanding of them all. Just as men struggle to transcend the inherent limits of geography, history, and biology to find the meaning of life, so poets strive to transcend the inherent limits of language, meter, and structure to find beauty and truth. And just as life wouldn't have meaning without death, so poetry wouldn't have its sublime power outside the prison of its form." He nods at the manuscript before me: "Which makes it even more powerful when you combine the limitations of language with the repressions of history. But the opposite is true as well. Poetry diminishes in times of plenty, loses its urgency and hunger, grows flabby. People of each age get just the poetry they deserve."

As he continues to talk, I begin to feel dizzy with the sense of utter strangeness and, at the same time, a kind of novel, intoxicating freedom. The kitchen has ceased to be the familiar place where I eat rushed breakfasts on school mornings while my mother waters her windowsill herbs and my father fumes at the day's headlines. In this new place, at this unearthly, in-between hour, the chilled, crisp sweetness of an April night enters through the cracked window like some barely audible promise, and souls of banished words are resurrected in guilt-ridden whispers, in paling print, in a stranger's languid, knowing drawl, to hang in the air, dark and light and eternal, mixing with the heady smell of spring, swelling my chest with some immense, nameless longing.

The man with the handsome face of a ruined god is watching me closely.

"Do you want to be immortal?" he asks.

"What?"

"It's a simple question and a simple matter. Do you want to be immortal?"

I want to say: I don't know what you mean. I open my mouth. "Yes."

He smiles again—a real, warm smile this time, though somehow cruel in spite of its warmth. All at once I think: If I lean forward ever so slightly, his breath will brush my face. I feel my skin growing hot. I do not lean forward.

The man stands, his movements fluid with loose, predatory grace. I am shocked to see bare feet protruding from the frayed cuffs of his pants.

"Well, time for a rude awakening," he says. "I could take a dramatic leap off the windowsill, but something tells me you are not easily impressed with clichés, so let me make a more subtle exit. Time waits for no man, *memento mori*, and all that."

The clock creaks on the wall, and as I look up, I see the cuckoo taking its three bows, one left, one right, one straight, which seems impossible, since it was three o'clock some ten minutes ago, unless the hands have started going backward, and then the cuckoo calls out "Cuckoo! Cuckoo! Cuckoo!" in the hoarse voice of my earliest childhood memories, and the man with the face of a thwarted angel jauntily sidesteps the bird and disappears inside the clock, which is when I know that I am asleep, just seconds before I know that I am awake because my father is shaking me.

"And what is the meaning of this?" my father asks with severity.

My head has fallen on the *Requiem* typescript. I can hear Orlov roaring with laughter in the doorway.

5. Dacha Bedroom

Nineteenth-Century Porcelain, or The Meaning of Life

MY FINGERS ARE STILL SOOTY FROM THE BONFIRE, and as I pick up my cup, I watch them leave faint smudges on the trellised flowers. We use simple cups at the dacha as a rule, thick and earth-colored, which remain rattling in the cupboard after we return to the city; but this morning my mother packed her best porcelain into starched nests of napkins, to be brought to the country along with cold chicken cuts and her famed apple pie.

I notice Olga studying the cups as well.

"Pretty," she says. "Are they old?"

I nod. "Nineteenth-century. Mama collects them."

"It suits you, you know. Ballet dancers, gypsy ancestors, family jewels, old porcelain. You'll be reading by candlelight next."

I laugh. "Are you saying I'm anachronistic?"

"I was thinking romantic. But I suppose it comes to much the same thing."

"I see what you mean. A seventeen-year-old maiden sitting on the balcony at dusk, drinking tea made with water drawn from the village well."

"With a full moon rising," she says.

"With a nightingale singing in the bushes," I rejoin.

"With facilities in the yard," she says.

"Oh, now you've gone and ruined it! That's hardly romantic."

"But true," she says, laughing also.

"Which is my point precisely. Truth can't be very romantic."

"Well, in any case. Nice cups. Sorry about the fingerprints."

For a while I sip the tea in silent contentment. I can feel the dacha's peaceful darkness behind my back. After driving here in the morning, laden with provisions, my parents have gone back to the city, to return three days hence; this lull of solitude is my graduation present of sorts, a foretaste of adulthood, a short spell of freedom between two anxiety-ridden stretches of last-minute cramming: the high school exams ended last week, the university entrance exams will commence next month. The June evening is blue and clear, the roofs at the end of our unpaved street stand out with crisp precision against the pale breadth of fields merging with the pale depth of the sky, and the world feels marvelously light, and I feel marvelously light too, as if I might take off at any instant, sail away in the small boat of the balcony into that luminous distance, the sweet smells of grasses and clover, the exhilarating expanse of the never-ending horizon—and splash through the slight chill in the air as through the waters of some cool, delightful stream, and catch the bright yellow moon like a leaping fish in my hand . . . But the balcony is moored to the rickety house by tenacious tendrils of ivy, my mother's precious porcelain cup feels dangerously fragile in my fingers, and Olga is talking again.

"You know, I almost wish we hadn't burned the old history notebooks. Chemistry is one thing, but all those transcriptions of Marx's *Capital*, all those triumphs of the five-year plans—twenty years from now no one will believe it without the physical evidence."

I can still smell the fire in the air. I planned it for a long time, for months, at first merely groaning in the school corridors between classes, thinking how good it would be to forget everything meaningless once and for all, wipe it all away, burn it to ashes—until slowly my futile frustration gave way to a secret purpose. This morning I stuffed my bag full to bursting with years' worth of accumulated assignments, tests, compositions, a decade of dead knowledge, and later sat by the fire pit behind the house for nearly two hours. Olga joined me halfway through the destruction, and we took turns mockingly declaiming this or that sentence, crumpling this or that equation into a ball, laughing with theatrical abandon as we fed the flames. I had waited for the day to condense into evening, so the fire would blaze with fierceness against the sky. I had also waited for my parents to leave. I had not told them. My mother would have worried that a stray spark might burn down the house. My father would have disapproved on general principles: he believed in the preservation of history, personal or otherwise.

"No regrets on my part," I say now, addressing my father's reproachful voice in my head. "I avenged myself for all the time killed."

"Still, they might have come in useful someday," Olga interjects thoughtfully. "I don't know, maybe I'll write a book about it when I'm old—say, when I'm forty. My childhood in the dark Soviet times. Torments of an artistic soul in the period of oppression. That sort of thing." She giggles. "Or not. At the very least I could have shown those horrors to my offspring: See, children, don't complain, your life could have been so much worse!"

"Thinking rather ahead, are you not?"

"Well, children are a given, I guess. Or don't you want them?"

After a decade of sharing dreams, fears, and long, bedbound stretches of illness, we frequently borrow each other's quirks of speech and our facial expressions likewise often mirror each other's, but Olga's eyes appear more focused than mine, and there is more resolve, more ambitious drive, in her face, in the thin lips that she purses with firmness. She always knows just what she wants before I am even aware of the choices. I do not know whether or not I want children; the notion seems irrelevant to me, and I have not given it much consideration. What I do not want, I think with sudden ferocity, is a small life—a life of mundane concerns, of fulfilled expectations, of commonplaces and banalities, of children's sore throats, of grandmother's apple pies, of fussy nineteenth-century porcelain—a life within four walls. I set down my cup, carefully but quickly; the streaks of soot, I notice, have dimmed the gilt a little.

"I would like to go to other places," I say with a vehemence that startles me. "New places. Strange places. Not to have a house anywhere but just travel from place to place, smell it, taste it, describe it, remember it all, then move on . . ."

"I want to go to America," Olga announces. "I could work there when I get my journalism degree. Do you ever wonder where you'll be at forty?"

I understand that one is expected to muse upon one's future on this momentous threshold of adulthood, but all the same, this predictable question makes me feel vaguely depressed, as if casting into instant doubt the smoky, bright, liberating hour by the fire, robbing it of color and life, flattening it into some artificial rite of passage indulged in solely for the sake of future reminiscing: *Ah yes, I too was young once, I too was full of rebellion and revelry, I laughed free and wild by the fire, I dreamed of glory on a moonlit summer night . . .* For as I sit on my beloved dacha balcony, watching the translucent June light tiptoe deeper into shadows, listening to the whistle of a faraway train, breathing in the aroma of lindens, I catch myself cataloguing the world around me, coining it into pocket-size verbal snapshots (the "soft dusk"—the "melancholy train"—the "dizzying smells"), to be retrieved at a convenient future date as a prepackaged nostalgia exhibit, or worse, as well-worn currency for some insipid poem.

All at once I am chilled by the gap widening precipitously between the present moment and my experience of it. Has life somehow, without my noticing, become its own paling reflection in a self-conscious mirror, its own stilted paraphrase on a dry page? It may be only an inevitable symptom of maturity, this politely disappointing sense of distance, this perception of the world at second hand, through words alone—but if so, I do not wish to grow up.

Forcefully I stand up, brush the crumbs off my dress.

"Time to bring out the telescope," I say. "It's grown dark enough."

The telescope is a small handheld model my father gave me on my fourteenth birthday; it remains my most treasured possession. I unscrew its plastic cap, gently rub the lens with a square of cloth, and lift it to my eye. The black fringe of leaves and the indistinct celestial shimmer beyond slide across my vision in a swift blur. As I lean over the balcony railing, training the telescope on this or that quadrant of the sky, Olga rattles off the names of stars and constellations.

"Vega, Deneb, Altair," she pronounces as she sketches the Summer Triangle with deft movements of her wrist, one, two, three. "But to be honest, I don't like looking at the sky, it makes me feel small. I imagine myself as a tiny dot in a sprawling landscape of a monstrous country on a spinning globe floating like a minuscule speck in a freezing ocean of stars . . . Brrr!"

She guides the telescope down, lower, lower, until it is level with the road; then she laughs. "Hey, look, they're having a party over on that terrace. You know, this thing is more powerful than I thought. See your boy pouring wine into three, no, four glasses?"

I attempt to shift the telescope away. "He is *not* my boy."

"Fine, your neighbor, then, if you prefer, Alesha, Serezha, whatever his name is, I thought you liked him."

"It's Tolya, as you well know. And I don't like him, I hardly know him. We just went for a walk one time last summer, that's all."

I do my best to appear nonchalant, but, as so often, I am plunged into remembering that August darkness striped with denser shadows of lampposts, and the heaps of wild roses hanging over the fences on both sides of the village dirt road, their sun-warmed smells drifting across our path like shy sweet ghosts, and our steps, in perfect, effortless harmony, and our awkward absence of words, for what one talked about with older boys—or any boys— I had no idea. As we turned into our street, his hand found mine, and its feel was big, dry, and nice, not in the least like those sweaty adolescent hands I imagined when overhearing the popular girls whisper to one another in the school hallways. But already we were approaching my gate, and there, in the cone of scanty light, under the soundless whirlwind of frantic moths, the stocky shadow of my father paced the road, three steps to the left, three steps to the right, waiting for me, though it was not yet ten o'clock, though I had never been late before. Anatoly's hand let go of mine, and the next day the summer ended without warning, for my mother had fallen ill and we had to leave for the city; and I did not know Anatoly's phone number or, indeed, his last name.

"I know!" Olga announces brightly. "Let's go over there."

I am shocked by the idea. "No, no, we shouldn't. We aren't invited."

"That doesn't matter, they'll be glad to have us, you'll see."

"No, no, I'd rather stay here. But—you can go if you want to."

And as I say it, I already feel a chill of dawning excitement at the thought that she is about to talk me into doing something so wild, so unexpected.

"Really? You wouldn't mind?" She sets the telescope down at once and begins to hunt for the powder compact borrowed from my mother, then, coming upon it, inspects her lips for stray crumbs. "I'll be back soon, I promise. You're sure you don't mind?"

Snapping the compact shut, she glances back at me.

"I don't mind," I say after the briefest of moments. "I'm . . . tired anyway."

As her steps fade away into nothing on the wooden stairs, the night reverts to its transparent silence; and so sharp, so bitter, is the taste of solitude in my mouth that I find myself wishing for the comforting warmth of my receding childhood, for my parents' habitual presence. Only after a time do I realize that being alone here and now, on this dizzying edge of the unknown, is to me a happiness deeper, a happiness more pure, than any companionship could ever be. I clear out the saucers, rub the fingerprints off the smudged cup, then, telescope in hand, return to the balcony. The night embraces me, cool and endless, and above me the stars are tiny holes in the darkness through which the light of eternity is pouring out. I can almost sense primordial stardust flowing through my veins. People are forever telling me that stars make them feel small, and I always nod noncommittally and wonder at the stuffy confinement of their minds.

Stars make me feel vast.

I think of the day at the dacha, three summers ago, when my father gave me the telescope. "We'll try it right after nightfall," he told me, "though the best time to look at the stars is at three in the morning."

"So let's do it at three in the morning," I said.

"But how will you wake up?" he asked, smiling. "We have no alarm here."

"If I wake up, do you promise not to send me back to bed? Will you teach me the constellations?"

"All right," he said with a shrug; for of course he did not foresee the need to ever keep his promise.

That night, when I opened my eyes, my room lay quiet and gray, shifting with odd predawn shadows, creaking with mysterious half-sounds. Sitting up in bed, I groped for the light switch. The clock above the armchair read a few minutes to three. As I crept downstairs, pressing the gleaming new telescope to my pajama-clad chest, I felt thrilled by the unfamiliar sense of being awake while all the world slept. The front door was unlocked. My father was out on the veranda, staring into the garden, waiting for me—or so I thought until he turned, and I saw the look of surprise on his face.

"Ha!" he exclaimed, squinting at his watch. "*L'exactitude est la politesse des rois.* I must say, I'm impressed. Well, come here, come here!"

For the next hour we stood side by side, gazing upward until our necks ached. When the night grew chilly, he draped his old woolen cardigan over my shoulders. He spoke of ships rounding the Cape of Good Hope, and Andromeda chained to a cliff, and Babylonian stargazers. He quoted early Mayakovsky:

Listen!
If they light up the stars,
Does it mean someone must need it?
Does it mean someone wants them to exist,
Does it mean someone calls these little bits of spit "pearls" . . .

He taught me dozens of sonorous foreign names, which I repeated after him, enchanted. "Do you know, Shakespeare writes somewhere of the futility of astronomical knowledge," he said at one point. "How does it go, let me see . . ." He riffled briefly through the index cards of his prodigious memory; he knew entire volumes of poetry by heart. "Ah, yes!

> *"These earthly godfathers of heaven's lights,*
> *That give a name to every fixed star,*
> *Have no more profit of their shining nights*
> *Than those that walk and wot not what they are . . ."*

His English was strongly accented but clear. "Magnificent, no? *'Their shining nights . . .'"* He paused to let the aural afterimage of the words linger in the air. It was so quiet that I imagined I heard a slumbering wagtail ruffling feathers in my favorite apple tree and some nocturnal creature splashing through the forest pond beyond our fence—and involuntarily I strained to catch the sound of the stars circling above in their slow, majestic, infinite river, though I did not know what they should sound like. A remote tinkling of melodious crystals? An unearthly choir of angels? A maddeningly beautiful, maddeningly indistinct poem mumbled into his beard by the unknown, unknowable God? A dry clicking, as of many precise mechanical instruments? A frozen wind howling out of one icy abyss into another?

My father went on: "Personally, as a philosopher of gnosis, I can't quite agree with the Bard's sentiment. Our constant desire for deeper, ever more exact knowledge, our urge to find the right names for all the things around us and thus attempt to make the mystery of life accessible somehow—these are prerequisites to being fully human, a part of what makes us know ourselves."

I had already entered my moody adolescence, the age at which big, *bloated* words (as I once termed them in a fit of self-mockery)—"soul," "God," "truth," "beauty"—had gotten hold of me with all the urgency of life-and-death questions demanding immediate answers. Ordinarily I would be too embarrassed to speak of these matters to anyone, of course, but that night seemed to belong to a separate, deeper place—a still, hidden pool on whose bottom weightier truths and fuller perceptions had come to settle.

"Papa, do you believe there is any meaning to life?" I blurted out.

"I do not believe," he said sternly. "I know. The meaning of life—the meaning of a single, individual human life, since I assume that is what you are asking—consists of figuring out the one thing you are great at and then pushing mankind's mastery of that one thing as far as you are able, be it an inch or a mile. If you are a carpenter, be a carpenter with every ounce of your being and invent a new type of saw. If you are an archaeologist, find the tomb of Alexander the Great. If you are Alexander the Great, conquer the world. And never do anything by half."

His face, I noticed, was being released by the darkness; the sky was growing pale in the east. He too must have realized it at the same instant, for he stopped talking, and looked at his watch, and snorted into his beard.

"Four-thirty already! Off to bed with you, little sunshine. Oh, and—" His expression had turned somewhat sheepish. "It's not absolutely necessary for your mother to hear about this, don't you agree?"

Later I wondered: If he had not been expecting me that night, what *was* he doing on our veranda at three in the morning?

But mainly, I wondered about the meaning of my life.

For a while I stand on the balcony looking at the stars. A white fleet of corpulent angels passes above the village roofs in a mathematically precise formation; a bat cuts across the light of the closest streetlamp in the jagged movement of a knife slitting a throat. I go inside, hunt down a pen, a blank sheet of paper, and a sturdy volume to prop it on (Hegel's lectures, as it turns out; books that gravitate to our dacha shelves tend to be of a thick, dry, sadly neglected bent). Returning to my armchair, I curl up in its plush nest and scribble without turning on the lamp—a useful skill I have perfected over countless school nights of pretending to be asleep. My soul feels swollen with my private certainty, immense with my private joy. For this, I know at last, is why I am here: to experience deeply, my senses a heartbeat away from exploding, then take everything I am feeling—the insignificance of being human, the enormity of being human, the intoxication of being young, the ache of being alone, the dizzy thrill of witnessing the steady rotation of the universe, the cozy warmth of a small wooden house teetering on the edge of a vast Russian forest, of an untamed Russian night— yes, take everything I am seeing and hearing and smelling, every dusty book by a forgotten writer on a shelf, every furtive mouse scurrying under the floorboards, every sneeze of the *domovoi*, our old brownie, sifting through my childhood clothes in the cluttered attic, every nocturnal flower unfurling in the grass, every sound, every color, every fleeting impression—and use the best words I have to convey it all, to pin it all down, to snatch one single moment from the oblivious flow of impersonal time and make it bright, make it personal, make it forever.

And as I sit in the dark, Hegel hurting my knee with his somber heft, and wrestle with words in some relentless, sleepless delirium, I see that my earlier fear of a secondhand reality muffled and diluted by words was misplaced—for it is through the power of words alone that the world can be truly captured, truly understood. Not just any words, to be sure: words can be alive or they can be dead, and dead words will dull the sharpest feeling, will turn the rarest vision into a vulgarity. I do not yet know what makes some words live and others die, but I believe I can already sense the difference between the two. And so I write, struggling to stretch the language until it bursts the stale confinement of the rhymed "nights" and "lights" and becomes something else, weighty yet plain, stark yet beautiful; and later, when I imagine the creak of the gate, the stealthy rustling of steps, the hushed, treacherous giggling on our garden bench, and two shadows bending close together, and the soft wetness of a first kiss, I gather my new sense of desolation—for I like him, I do, of course I do, I always have— and cram it raw into my half-formed poem, which I can already feel opening sonorously in the dark, unfolding its many petals of sounds, its many layers of meaning—until I wake with a start and find the room caught in a net of shifting starlight, a nightingale trilling in the forest, and my enigmatic acquaintance perched on the arm of the chair, holding my scribbles before his eyes, tapping his bare foot against the floor in rhythm with my lines.

I draw in my breath and stay very still. He has visited me a handful of times since the fateful night of Akhmatova's *Requiem*, but I have not gotten used to his presence. A full minute passes. It must be very late. On the cot across the room, Olga is breathing tranquilly in her sleep. He releases the page, and it drifts to the floor.

He looks down at me then, smiling his slow, cruel smile.

Light-headed with the exhausting labor of creation, I feel brave enough to ask.

"Do you like it?"

He shrugs. "Heavily influenced by Tyutchev. Also, it's not finished."

"Yes, but—do you like it?"

He is the only one who ever reads my poems; I never mention them to anyone else. My poetry is a secret of which my mysterious night visitor is also a part.

"Oh, I suppose it shows promise. But you know what they say: The road to hell is paved with good intentions—and, I should add, with early promise." He unwinds himself from the chair with his usual careless, feline grace. "So easy to end up trapped inside a nineteenth-century porcelain cup, my dear," he says. "Especially for a woman, trite as that may sound." He leans toward me—close, closer still—and the smile on his handsome, ruined face melts into a leer. Flushed, I look down. The nightingale's song swells clear and ebullient in the sudden silence. My heart is pounding. I am seventeen years old, I am a poet, and I have never been kissed.

I expect—I do not know myself what I expect.

When I look up, only a puddle of starlight trembles on the floor.

6. My Bedroom

The Proof of God's Existence

"NEEDLESS TO SAY," LEV PROCLAIMS TO THE ceiling, "for most of our illustrious history the so-called profession of journalism was nothing but an embarrassing joke—red banners this, grain harvests that. Comrade Vasily, kindly pass the champagne. Nowadays, though, we have a sacred role to perform, no less than that of an artist."

Lev rolls over and, leaning on his elbow, takes a swig from the bottle, then hands it over to Nina, who is sitting cross-legged on the carpet next to him, peeling an orange.

"Well, that's going rather far," she says. "I like having an inflated sense of self-importance as much as anyone, but journalism just isn't art . . . Hey, now my orange tastes bitter! And anyway, it's lukewarm and disgusting."

"Give it back, then. And I'm not saying it's art, either—but you must agree, today's artists can't claim to speak the truth to the extent we journalists do."

"And historians," Anna, Lev's older sister, mumbles. "Don't forget the historians." She hiccups. Alone of us all, she is attending the history department.

"Sure, historians are responsible for exposing the truth of the past, but journalists deal in current truths—so much more vital as far as the people are concerned." Lev is sitting up now, his thin, sharp-chinned face flushed with excitement. "Just as an example, when I wrote about the polluted vegetables sold at our market—"

A communal moan escapes from everyone in the room, even Sergei and Irochka unglue their lips long enough to exchange snorts, while Nina weakly pelts Lev with orange peels.

"Yes, yes, we know all about your sacred mission of bringing hygiene to the masses." Vasily hangs off the bed to intercept the bottle, then leans back and throws his free arm around my shoulders. Only now I notice that the record has stopped playing. Wriggling out from under Vasily's proprietary arm, I stand up to cross the room and move the needle back to the beginning. Okudzhava's quiet, wise voice starts up anew, singing of doors forever unlocked to welcome a stranger on a wintry night, and valiant cardboard soldiers who step into the fire, reciting a noble catechism of friendship that burns steady amidst the dangers of betrayals big and small:

> And when the hour arrives to divide the spoils,
> Free bread handouts will not seduce us,
> And paradise will open—but not for us,
> Yet all of us will be remembered by Ophelia . . .

Anna hiccups again. Sergei yawns and rises from the single chair in the room, Irochka entwined tipsily around him. "Well, people, I have a deadline tomorrow. What time is it, anyway?"

It is close to eleven o'clock. Weightless snowflakes are blowing this way and that outside the window. Two by two, my friends take their leave—Lev with his sister; Sergei with the giggling Irochka; Olga, who has dropped in without my noticing, with yet another boy whose name I will not bother to commit to memory unless I see him again. Indiscriminately I hand out damp hats and scarves in the hallway's dimness, certain that a good half of them are ending up with the wrong person, to be sorted out in the grimy light of the lecture hall the next morning, as together we plunge into yet another heady day of epigrams scribbled in the margins of our notebooks, cigarettes bummed in the girls' bathroom, half-hearted kisses in the shadow of the kindly bronze Lomonosov, crumbs of momentous truths unearthed, devoured, and discarded between seminars in the yellow corridors of the eighteenth-century mansion in the threadbare heart of the ancient city.

When I lock the door behind the last of them and step back into the room, Vasily is sprawled on my bed, cradling the nearly empty bottle.

"Finally," he says. "Come here."

My parents have gone to a premiere at the Bolshoi and will not return before midnight. Stalling for time, I move about the room, straightening things—the rug's corner flipped up at a rakish angle, the wet mark of the bottle's bottom on a bookshelf, a volume of Annensky left spine-up on the windowsill. Even without turning, I can sense him breathing in expectation, grinning at my neck. As I needlessly rearrange my few trinkets (a shell from the Black Sea, a polished shard of amber from the Baltics, a statuette of Don Quixote someone gave my father years ago), I take comfort in thinking how familiar everything is here, how simple, monastic even, and how self-sufficient—the window, the bed, the desk, the chair, the hundreds upon hundreds of books, none of which ever gets dusty.

When the silence grows audible at last, I hasten to break it.

"Isn't it strange to think that of my seventeen and a half years, I've probably spent at least seven years reading and doing homework at this desk? And another six asleep in this bed? That's more than three-quarters of my entire life!"

Conscious of babbling, I stop. And yet, as I would add if I felt able to discuss such matters with him, the room never seems like a confinement, for when my door is closed and I am alone here, I am—as nowhere else—absolutely free. I have fallen into the small private habit of imagining it as a room full of windows—different, of course, from the sole window facing that eternal eyesore of a construction site, still far from completion, its gigantic piles of cement and rusty machinery now often abandoned for months at a time. No, these are other windows—windows opening into other places, other moods, other realities, which I struggle to translate into words as I pick up my pen every night. I glance toward the book I have just wedged into its place on the shelf of my special favorites. Annensky succeeded where I have failed so far; his poem has lived for so long in my mind, on the tip of my tongue, in the back of my dreams, that I sometimes wonder whether he merely captured, with angel-like precision, that elusive, vast, vertiginous feeling that so often fills my entire being—or whether his poem has itself given birth to that feeling, has gifted me with the joyful sensation of some invisible, endlessly rich, mysterious life just a heartbeat, just a perfect word, away.

Do you not imagine sometimes,
When dusk wanders through the house,
That here, alongside us, lies another plane,
Where we lead entirely different lives?

There a shadow has merged with a shadow so softly,
There a moment will come at times
When with the unseen rays of our eyes
We seem to enter each other.

And we fear to frighten the moment away
With a gesture, or to intrude upon it with a word,
As though someone has leaned in so close,
Making us hear distant things.

But as soon as the candle is brought in,
The brittle world retreats without a fight . . .

For this is what I have come to believe in all the years spent hidden away in my bedroom, with its only window darkened by winter as often as not: that the place I live in does not matter; nor do the daily tasks I perform; nor even the people with whom I spend my time—all these lie on the surface, fortunate or unfortunate accidents of birth and transitory vagaries of choice, which should not in any profound way affect my true essence, my only real life— my self-contained life as a poet—unfolding with its own powerful, inexorable logic, quite apart from political upheavals or career decisions or oppressive boys, in that other, perfect world whose remote starlit music and fresh springtime breezes I catch now and then through my invisible, tantalizingly cracked windows . . .

"Homework and sleep, eh? Time to broaden the spectrum of activities, I think."

I have forgotten Vasily's presence so thoroughly by now that his voice makes me start. He pats the bed next to him. "Come here."

When my narrow bed is made—as it is without fail every morning—it can pass for a couch, which somewhat alleviates the awkwardness of the two of us sitting side by side on its shaggy yellow spread. I accept the bottle from him, take a hurried sip; warm champagne makes the inside of my mouth taste muffled and sour. He pulls me toward him for the inevitable kiss. I like his irreverent clowning at seminars and the clever pieces on new rock bands that he writes for the student newspaper, but I do not like his kisses. I suspect I do not like kisses in general—perhaps my blood is stirred by poetry alone—but I have no grounds for comparison. His tongue is rubbery, thick, and insistent. After an anxious lapse of several seconds, which I count in my mind (one-two-three-four-five—is this enough?), I open my eyes and find his one visible eye likewise open, slanted at an odd angle, staring into mine, almost white in the light of the overhead lamp.

Freeing myself, I glance at the clock on my desk.

"My parents may come back any minute," I announce with barely hidden relief.

He too checks the clock, and sighs, and, drawing me toward him, speaks into my hair. "This is hard on both of us, I know, but we just have to hold out a bit longer. In March my father will get his new posting, I'll have the apartment all to myself. Do you understand?" His voice has become a whisper, and when I try to lift my head and look at him, he presses me back into his shoulder. "Wait. Listen. We should talk about the future. My parents approve of you, and yours approve of me. It's not too early. I'll be nineteen this summer. I have excellent prospects. My father——"

He continues to whisper, his breath hot and moist in my hair. I sit propped up against him, stiff with sudden horror. It occurs to me that even though my daily, superficial existence may have little to do with the deep well of my poetry, any trivial repetitive actions, just by virtue of steady accretion, may with time translate into something amounting to an actual change. If I spend days and weeks and months attending a random higher-education program for the simple reason that Olga applied her inflexible will to the task of becoming a journalist while I had little interest in puzzling over possible professions and let her make up my mind for me, one morning I will likely find myself bent over a typewriter in some newspaper cubicle; and if I spend days and weeks and months kissing a random boy for the simple reason that the acquisition of such an experience seems a prerequisite for being a proper university student, one day I may find myself married to the son of a prominent diplomat, living in a cavernous apartment on Gorky Street with a zebra skin crucified on the wall above our conjugal bed. In a moment of pure panic I see my future flash before my eyes, just as one's past reputedly does in the moment of dying—— and my future is a succession of increasingly suffocating rooms.

When I can breathe once again, I become aware of a new quality of silence, tense, bordering on hostile, as I fail to reply, and fail to reply, and fail to reply . . .

"There is something I want to show you," I say in desperation.

I slip off the bed, run over to the desk, and jerk open its drawer. The letter is lying amidst dried-up corpses of pens and half-spent erasers, still in its jaggedly ripped envelope that bears a foreign postmark. I pull out the single sheet of paper and hand it to him. Expressionless, he reads it while I stand before him, waiting.

When he looks up at me, his eyes are narrowed.

"When did you get this?"

"Last week."

"Why didn't you tell me you were applying?"

"I didn't tell anyone. I—I wanted to wait until I heard back."

That is true; nor do I have the slightest intention of going— although I do not tell him that, not yet, because I am hoping to soften my impending refusal to consider what I fear was a marriage proposal by speaking vaguely of future possibilities and broadening horizons. I climb back onto the bed and attempt to nestle into his shoulder, as before, but he shakes me off, stands up, drops into the chair across from me. The empty champagne bottle, caught by his abrupt movement, rolls over the bedspread and falls onto the rug with a dull thud.

"So why *did* you apply?"

"Oh, I don't know. Just to see what's out there, I guess."

And that is true also; I am not entirely sure of my reasons. Perhaps I applied because—because I had taken my secret gifts for granted for so long that I had come to doubt them and wanted to set myself a test that would have some validity in the eyes of the outside world; or because a small part of me questioned my ability to upend my life, to move to a distant spot on the map; or because Olga, who did everything I myself considered doing, and did it better, talked of attending Harvard in the fall.

"Don't you have everything you want here? What do your parents say?"

Every question comes at me like a stab. I have never seen him like this. He sits in the chair, rocking slightly, his fingers twirling my acceptance letter, his gray eyes pale with anger, sliding past me. There is something raw, something dangerous, in his ordinarily ironic snub-nosed face. He looks like a scorned lion, and I am startled by a faint twinge of regret at the thought that I may never touch his lips again.

"My parents think it's a great opportunity. But Vasily, I haven't yet decided—"

"This is stupid," he spits out. "I never thought of you as stupid before. You would have a much better life here. You're somebody here. Your family is important, my family is very important. You and I, we can accomplish anything we want. Over there, you'll be nothing, a pathetic little immigrant, an empty space. A zero."

I too am beginning to feel angry, but I force myself not to abandon my mollifying tone. "Look, I'm not talking of *moving* overseas, it's just a four-year college. It would mean seeing a bit of the world, no more than that. Don't you ever want to have some new experiences?"

"You can have plenty of new experiences here," he says, and a tight, ugly smile twists his face. "In fact, I can arrange for something new right now."

I no longer find the hardness in his eyes enticing.

Things are shifting inside me.

"I think," I say slowly, "I think I will do it."

He holds up my letter with the tips of his fingers as if it were something contagious, and pretends to study it, rocking the chair faster and faster. "Never heard of this place. Some dreary provincial hole, I gather. Didn't peg you for the type who'd want to live in an Uncle Tom's cabin among beggars, niggers, and Jews."

For one instant I am speechless. In the next, I receive, for the first time ever, the indisputable waking proof that there is a God who watches over us—a benevolent God with impeccable timing and a twinkle in his ageless eye. My childhood chair breaks apart under Vasily in a spectacular explosion of cracks. As the seat falls in, he falls in also, his arms and legs now crammed into the wooden frame, sticking straight up. And even though I already know that in the next few months, before I leave for a college deep in the American South, there will be many unpleasant encounters—lips thinned, eyes averted—in the university hallways, awkward silences among our mutual friends, gatherings and memories ruined, for the next few minutes—three full minutes, no less, until he manages to extricate himself at last—for the next three minutes, as I watch him flail and strain and turn purple, I am certain that someone is up there, gently holding my life in the palm of his hand—and all is right with the world.

Part Two
Past Perfect

College Campus

7. Library Cubicle

The Grateful Dead

"HEY, YOU'RE THAT SOVIET GIRL, AREN'T YOU?"

I raised my eyes from the page. A bear of a boy in a rainbow-colored shirt was leaning on the corner of my desk, setting my towers of books to a dangerous wobble.

"I prefer 'Russian,'" I said.

"Sure," he said. "Russian. So, how do you like it here?"

"I like it very much," I said. "It's quiet. And it stays open all night."

"Oh," he said. "No, I didn't mean . . ." He seemed vague, amiable, good-looking in a bland, healthy, entirely forgettable way. "I meant, how do you like America . . . You know, what do you like most about it?"

I smiled politely.

"The library," I said. "It's quiet. And it stays open all night."

He had something written on his shirt. For a moment I puzzled over the meaning of the words, then grew impatient, and glanced at my book.

"Well, anyway, you're studying. Sorry to have disturbed you," he said.

I turned the page, heard his steps retreating into the silence of the stacks.

In the past few months I had been asked many things—whether it was true that Soviet children marched to school in formation and were one and all atheists, and did I know Tatiana in Leningrad, and how did I like hamburgers, fraternity parties, and freedom of speech—and while I set much stock by good manners, I did not feel the need to answer every question in the obliging spirit of upstanding national representation. That was Olga's concern. Upon arriving in the States, she had found herself an unwitting celebrity of sorts—something to do with her timing, her being the first-ever Soviet student in the country, or maybe the first in an undergraduate program, or perhaps just the first on the East Coast—some statistical fluke, in short, which nevertheless meant that she would spend her entire fall giving interviews and visiting local schools, posing for photographers, assuring everyone that she adored freedom of speech, complaining in private that she had had by far more freedom in Russia and that the burden of being the "face of the country" was dulling her complexion.

I suspected that she was enjoying herself.

My own entry into my small southern college had passed unnoticed by comparison—a few lines in a student publication, mild curiosity from my fellow freshmen; enough to be recognized now and then and asked about hamburgers, not enough to feel that I stood for anything larger—anything other—than merely myself. For that I was grateful. It was all very well for an aspiring journalist like Olga to inhabit a political essay. As for me, I had never given much thought to the current affairs of the world.

I wanted to live in a timeless poem.

I returned to my collection of Silver Age verse but soon found my concentration flagging. I was tired, of course—it was past midnight, and I had subsisted on very little sleep for a long time—but also, I felt oddly bothered by the encounter with the boy. Had I been unnecessarily short? Rereading the same two lines over and over, I thought of the look that had settled on his face, apologetic and offended at once. When, a wasted half-hour later, I heard footsteps approaching through the stacks, I was relieved at the impending interruption. I would be friendlier when I saw him next.

But when the bookshelves parted to reveal the nearing shadow, it was not the boy in the rainbow shirt—it was the secret visitor of my Russian adolescence, strolling nonchalantly down the aisle, coming to a stop before my desk.

He was not smiling, nor was I pleased to behold him.

The last time I had seen him—well over a year before—we had quarreled. For weeks I had been studying ancient Greek tragedy till the wee hours, my mind gloriously full of heroes, oracles, and monsters. He stormed into my bedroom one night just before sunrise, wrapped in some absurd billowing sheet. I felt disturbed and elated—I was certain he would kiss me at last—but instead he pontificated about Aeschylus, quoted reams of Pindar at me, and ended by pronouncing himself the god Apollo, here to inspire me. I was appalled at how pompous he had become of late, and told him so. He threw his laurel wreath to the ground and slammed the door behind him, his only conventional exit in my memory. "Pompous *and* unimaginative!" I shouted in his wake.

Frowning, I considered him now.

"Asleep in a library cubicle, how embarrassing," I muttered. "Am I drooling, I wonder. Even snoring, perhaps? Did I collapse with my face in the book, and will the print of some poem transfer to my cheek? I hope that boy doesn't pass by again."

"You've been thinking about irrelevant matters too much," he said, and, unceremoniously sweeping the corner of my desk free of books, settled on top of it, swinging his leg. He sported a neat new haircut and was dressed in a dapper suit of spotless white linen; yet in spite of his jaunty appearance, he looked somehow diminished—smaller in the way childhood rooms seem smaller to an adult returning home after half a lifetime's absence.

"At the risk of being smacked by this Goliath of an English–Russian dictionary, I will brave the question. How *do* you like America?"

His voice was dry, but I saw that there would be no mention of our last encounter, and was glad, and tried to thank him by giving an honest answer.

"I like it very much," I said after a moment's thought. "I like the sense of anonymity. Living here is like—like being just a story among other stories, so I have time to read my own story without peeking ahead or skipping any words, if you know what I mean. And I can access an entirely new range of experiences and feelings, and these feelings are larger somehow, as if I can now see myself and the world simultaneously from two separate vantage points instead of one—a bit like gaining entry to a new dimension . . . But you know, I wasn't being glib earlier—I mean with that boy—I really do love the library the most. I more or less live in this cubicle. They let you stay all night, did you know? Actually, it wasn't until I spent my first night here, back in September, that I realized what I'd been missing. Have you ever been to the library in Moscow? You fill out a form, then take your place at one of these communal tables in a gigantic marble room that makes you feel dwarfed, and wait until the book you've requested is produced from some unseen depths of the building. When your turn comes, you are summoned to a tiny window and the book is slid over to you on a tray. Of course, they have everything there, but you always have to know exactly what you want beforehand—there are no surprising discoveries, you see, no sense of exploration, no *browsing*. Oh, one day I'll write an Ode to Browsing—it's such a delightfully American concept! It's what I do here: I walk the aisles, alone, at night, and when something catches my eye—anything new, anything exciting, anything unpredictable—I grab an armload of books, as many as I can carry back to my desk, then stay up until morning reading about Mayan glyphs, or Arctic expeditions, or the art of stained-glass windows in medieval France, or underwater archaeology in Egypt, anything and everything, but always poetry, poetry first and last—" I glanced over at him, and stopped abruptly. "Am I boring you?"

"You *are* being unusually loquacious tonight, my dear," he said, staring off beyond me, into the white electric glare of the shelves. "Personally, I dislike libraries. They smell of death and oblivion. True poetry isn't meant to be stashed away in pitiful little volumes catalogued on moldy index cards, then buried in the commu-nal grave of the Dewey Decimal System, to be exhumed once every few years by some pimply graduate student scratching out a tedious paper that no one will ever read. True poetry is meant to be recited—or better yet, sung—thundered to the sky—danced to—made love to—celebrated . . . It should pulsate in your ears and your heart, but all I can hear in these repositories of dust is the clamoring of the forgotten dead on their neatly catalogued shelves, begging each visitor to resurrect them, to bring them into the light, if only for a few pale moments, grateful even for such sorry scraps of attention—"

Suddenly I laughed. "The grateful dead!"

"What's that, my dear?"

"Oh . . . nothing."

A petulant look crossed his face.

"There it is again—you are thinking about boys too much. You must be careful."

I felt his presence to be an acute disappointment. He belonged to my Russian childhood, to the otherworldly realm of fairy tales, secrets, and revelations that—even at my eighteen years of age— was so quickly receding into the distance of both time and space that I could already see myself believing someday that half of it had been real, or perhaps half believing that all of it had been real. Here, under the even, artificial light of humming lamps, in my brand-new, rational life of class schedules, advisor meetings, and black coffee, I no longer felt the need to be gentle with my persis-tent dreams.

"You sound like my mother," I said.

"Hardly. I don't care about your getting hurt. As Catullus proved early on, wretchedness is rather good for poetry. Very few, in fact, are capable of writing well while happy in love—or indeed content with life in general. It takes a special kind of greatness to write about happiness, and, just between us, Horace himself smacks too much of a self-satisfied philistine. One might even argue that the poet's primary function is to make the misery of the human condition more bearable by converting raw pain into the orderly music of verse . . . But no matter. I mean something else altogether."

Nimbly he leapt off the desk and stood looking down at me.

"In the beginning was the Word, remember? Now, generally speaking, I'm not fond of those simpletons, but old John did know a thing or two. Listen. *In the beginning was the Word, and the Word was with God, and the Word was God.*" His voice rose, gaining in strength, cutting through the hush of the well-lit windowless night, multiplying in echoes, until a chorus of mighty voices seemed to be booming from everywhere around me. *"The same was in the beginning with God. All things were made by him; and without him was not any thing made that was made. In him was life; and the life was the light of men. And the light shineth in darkness; and the darkness comprehended it not."*

He fell silent, and for some moments the silence continued to widen like circles upon waters closing over a crashing boulder.

"Walk with me, my dear," he then said mildly.

I rose, obeying the unspooling of the dream, and together we made our way into the harshly illuminated stacks, straight and orderly as hospital corridors. He walked a step or two ahead, not glancing back at me, talking all the while.

"Everyone is born as a light, a naked spirit, a pure longing to know the world. Some lights are dimmer, and some brighter; the brightest ones have the godlike capacity not only to know the world but to create it anew, time and time again. The light shines at its purest in your childhood, but as you move farther into life, it begins to fade. It doesn't diminish, exactly, but it becomes harder to reach: every year you live through calcifies around your soul like a new ring on a tree trunk until the divine word can barely make itself heard under the buildup of earthly flesh. None of this is anything new, of course—just read some Gnostics while you go about your browsing."

As we walked, the stacks became darker, the static humming of lamps more remote. Here and there deeper patches of twilight lay on the shelves, the book spines growing less distinct, melting into one another, escaping the alphabet's confines.

"Unfortunately for you, my dear, a woman's flesh tends to be . . . oh, shall we say, more insistent than a man's—and thus her choices may be harder. For every human being, no matter how brilliant, has only a predetermined capacity for creation, and a child, you see, is no less a creation than a book, albeit of an entirely different order and often less lasting. Well, naturally, that depends on the book and on the child . . . Back in the days of Queen Elizabeth, I used to visit her namesake, one Elizabeth Heywood. You've never heard of her, of course, but who is to say that today you wouldn't speak of her in the same breath with Shakespeare had she not chosen to birth, raise, and bury a child for nearly every one of his great tragedies? On the other hand, one of those children was John Donne—so one never knows how this sort of thing will turn out. There are different kinds of immortality, after all. Choosing the spirit or choosing the flesh is ever a private matter."

We should have reached the far end of the stacks long ago, but the shelves went on stretching before us into what was now a murkiness of densely shifting shadows.

I found myself slowing my steps.

"Walk with me," he threw over his shoulder. "Now, one of the things I find so boring about this modern age of yours is all the nonsense about women being discriminated against throughout history, beaten down by the male hierarchy, forced to do house-work while their men achieve greatness. Never believe it. The Muses were all women, if you recall; Orpheus was the odd one out. But the Muses were virgins. Well, not in the technical sense of the word—I had to divert myself somehow between all the lyre-strumming bits, and now and then they did stray into some transient unions of their own. But they were never devoted wives and never committed mothers, and all their time, all their passion, was dedicated solely to their art."

It had become so dark I could not see the shelves at all. I fol-lowed his voice blindly. Gravel or perhaps seashells crunched under my feet, and I stifled a cry when the flinty wing of some swift nocturnal creature brushed my cheek.

"Now, as always, you have a choice. You can spend your days baking cookies for your offspring, or—as ever through the ages— you can become a madwoman, a nomad, a warrior, a saint. But if you do decide to follow the way of the few, you must remember this: Whenever you come to a fork in the road, always choose the harder path, otherwise the path of least resistance will be chosen for you. Here, turn around."

He stopped with such abruptness that my face was pressed into his jacket in the instant before I felt his arms grasp my shoulders and swing me about. I could see nothing at first—it was so black I thought for a moment that I had forgotten to open my eyes—but I had a sure sense that we were in the library no longer: the darkness, though impenetrable, breathed of vastness, and the ceiling with its dead electric lamps had long given way to the cosmic circling of infinity. Then slowly, out of the void, a steady light emerged, and another, and another, until lights were floating all around me—numerous but not endless, a thousand sparks, two thousand perhaps, setting the emptiness aglow as they drew their fiery trajectories across the night, until the night itself was relieved of its oppressive blackness and other, paler lights shimmered in a faint haze of lesser constellations beyond.

"There," he whispered. His breath was in my hair; his right hand, slipping off my shoulder, was pointing into the luminous depths. "The lights of the earth—both men and women, of course, but look at the women: in the eyes of the masses, nothing but a gathering of perversions and monstrosities, of recluses and harlots. Sappho over there—my Tenth Muse, they called her, a heartache of mine—just a handful of her lines survive today and, oh, if only you knew what beauty has been lost . . . Curious, is it not, that so many of them shared Sappho's tastes and predilections—Tsvetaeva, Colette, Virginia Woolf, Djuna Barnes, Gertrude Stein, numerous others . . . And here are the nuns, the mystics, the philosophers, the odd and the solitary and the sickly ones, the ones who never married—Teresa of Ávila, Hypatia, Jane Austen, Emily Dickinson . . . And don't forget all the wild ones as well as the quiet ones who gently and unswervingly eschewed convention—the two Georges, Sand and Eliot, come to mind. And most of the married ones were childless, and of the ones who did have children, so many became what the world would brand 'unnatural mothers'—take Akhmatova and Colette, who sent their children away to be raised by relatives, or Tsvetaeva, who let her daughter starve to death in an orphanage. Heartless? Most certainly, by any human standards—but they lived and died by other, higher standards, the divine standards of art."

His right hand was still pointing as he talked, but his left had begun to stroke my neck, ever so lightly. Waves of glowing flame swirled about me, through me, and I was aware that there was no ground under my feet. I felt queasy, and wanted to wake up.

"Alternatively . . ." I said, and my voice was hoarse—these were the first words I had spoken since we had abandoned the safety of my cubicle. "Alternatively, one could just marry an understanding man of means and hire a nanny."

As soon as I spoke, his hand on my neck grew heavy and inert, as though made of marble, and the swirling lights guttered as in a gust of wind, and went out. Blackness crashed upon me, suffocating and enormous, but I had no time to feel frightened before the electric lamps whirred to an abrupt glare. Blinded, I shut my eyes. When I opened them, I expected him to be gone, but he was still there, looking down upon me as I sat at my desk—and I was shocked to see his face, for it was not as before, not handsome and hard and leering, but tranquil and beautiful, filled with a gentle radiance of autumn sunlight and, also, an odd kind of sadness.

Unable to sustain his gaze, I lowered my eyes to the floor.

"You aren't barefoot tonight," I mumbled, to hide my confusion.

"There was a notice on the library door," he said flatly. "'Shoes and shirts required.' And don't start thinking about that boy's shirt again, or one day you may find yourself laundering it."

I laughed, knowing full well that this time I was truly alone, and raised my eyes again, to discover that two or three books had fallen off my desk onto the floor; I must have pushed them with my elbow while dozing, and the crash had woken me up. I hunted in my overflowing bag for a compact mirror to check my face for any signs of drool, just in case anyone wandered by, and marveled at the unsought wealth of ideas that had sprung up in my mind fully formed, out of nowhere, while I had slept. The Cycle of Memory, I would call these new poems. There would be one about a blind girl who lived in the library and summoned ghosts of her favorite poets to life every night; and another about a compendium of immortality carelessly updated by an angel who kept drifting off to sleep in the softness of his cloud and forgetting to jot down a name or two; and yet another about a peasant in some desert discovering the missing manuscript of all of Sappho's masterpieces—this one would weave in and out of Sappho's lines, real and imagined, as the *fellah* would stumble and mumble over them before tearing the papyrus into strips to bind his aching feet—oh, and maybe one about a woman creating a marvelous, perfect poem about each child she had refused to have, though on second thought, no, I knew nothing about children . . . So, then, how about a Muse of Apollo—I would make her Clio, the Muse of History—who fell in love and renounced being a Muse for a spell, causing entire civilizations to be obliterated in human memory while her love affair went on—and more, and more, and more . . .

I felt awake and young and exhilaratingly happy.

8. Boyfriend's Bedroom

The First English Poem, Written at the Age of Nineteen

"AND WHILE THE RATS WERE HAVING SEX IN THEIR cage," the girl shouted over the noise, "this guy next to me actually stood up to see better. Can you imagine? And Professor Roberts noticed him and said, in front of everyone—" The music took off anew, a galloping folk tune this time, and a cluster of boys across the room roared and linked their arms and stomped about, vigorously throwing their legs up in the air, so the end of her sentence was drowned out. I watched her eyes widen with excitement in the eyeholes of her feathered mask. She leaned closer. ". . . so intense, you know!"

"I'm supposed to take it next semester," I shouted back, "but I'm not sure—"

"Ah, here you are!" Lisa cried, elbowing her way through the dancers. "What are you still doing with your old drink? I brought you a new one."

I squinted into the plastic cup she was holding out.

"It's green," I said.

"Yes," she agreed happily. "So finish the pink one already. They have something blue too. Embrace the rainbow."

"I'm going to take a shower," the girl in the mask announced unexpectedly and wandered off, walking on tiptoe, her long black hair slapping against her back.

I looked after her.

"Does she live here?" I asked.

"No. This is Hamlet's place. She wants to be his girlfriend, I suspect. Who doesn't, though? But he is trouble. And if you're not going to drink that, pass it over."

The folksy hurly-burly had given way to an Oriental whine, and a boy in an ankle-length caftan spread his arms wide and twirled about the room, keening loudly.

"Lisa, who *are* all these people? And what's with the music?"

"It's eclectic," she said, unperturbed, and gave her cup an energetic shake; a few ice cubes leapt out and somersaulted in the air before plunking back with a green splash. "And I told you already, they're in my theater class. You really should leave your library cubicle more often."

For a while we watched the crowd, most of them dressed in black, the rest decked out in some outlandish garb, a few wearing masks. The lights were turned down low, but what little could be seen of the apartment—a flea-market couch, beige wall-to-wall carpeting, shelves made of crates—created a contrast I found unpleasant, as if all present here were trapped in a simple, one-dimensional story and were striving frantically, almost shrilly, to clown their way out in order to inhabit a more interesting one.

Someone thrust a potted geranium at me in passing.

"Enjoy," he said with a beatific smile.

Feline whiskers, I saw, were scrawled across his cheeks with an orange marker.

I set the pot on a nearby crate and poured my untouched pink drink into it.

"Lisa, I'm going back to the dorm," I said. "I'm bored. And I'm not dressed for this anyway."

"One day, you know," my roommate sang out, "one day you'll look back at your youth and regret all the things you haven't done. Talk of years wasted! Here you are, almost twenty years old, and have you ever been drunk? No. Have you ever had a proper boyfriend? No. Have you ever even——"

Quickly I interrupted, "It's too loud, I can't hear anything, I'll see you later."

I wound my way toward the doorway, swerving widely so as not to step on a python that slumbered in a woven basket in the middle of the floor, skirting some commotion; people were beginning to drag the furniture against the walls. Past the living room, the kitchen was deserted; a wet trail of bare footprints glistened across the entire length of its white linoleum floor. I followed the footprints into the hallway, in time to see a bare-legged girl, her face hidden by a soaked tangle of long, dark hair, her shoulders heaving with sobs, being draped in an oversize trench coat and gently pushed across the threshold by a tall, thin man.

The man closed the apartment door behind her and turned, and saw me.

Embarrassed to have witnessed something private and unpleasant, I squeezed past him with my face averted. In the hallway mirror, my awkward double in blue jeans and a checkered button-down shirt, her hair pulled back in an unfashionable ponytail, her face bare of any feminine artifice save a careless swipe of gloss across her lips, prodded the lock.

"Leaving already?" his voice asked softly at my back.

"I have a paper due on Monday."

"That's a pity. You are easily the most fascinating person here."

I looked up at him for the first time. He stood watching me, leaning with casual elegance against the wall, dressed in a cardigan of gray cashmere, his face pale and vivid and arresting in its fierce intelligence, a gray cat draped around his shoulders. Behind him, framed by the two doorways, I could see the dim rectangle of the party room, now freed of its couch and armchairs; just then, a conga line of slender girls was undulating across it, crowned by a gigantic papier-mâché dragon's head.

My mousy reflection nudged me with her shoulder.

"I seriously doubt it," I said, and resumed tugging at the lock.

He glanced back into the room.

"Oh, you mean them?" he said. "No, no, they try too hard to be original. All they really do is create a background against which true originality stands out . . . But I see you're anxious to go. I won't detain you, of course, but won't you take just a sip of this very fine whiskey for the road, so I'm not left feeling that my hospitality was wholly lacking?"

He held up his drink in a squat crystal tumbler. I heard the ice clink invitingly against the glass, and thought: No plastic cups for this one. He was looking at me over the rim, one eyebrow lifted. The cat was looking at me too. Their eyes were alike, light and cold and amused. I renewed my assault on the door.

"Thank you, but I don't drink whiskey."

Oh, what the hell was wrong with this thing, did it turn right or left—

The man spoke unhurriedly.

"Is this a principle of yours, or do you simply not care for the taste?"

"I've never tried it."

"Then forgive me the obvious question: How do you know you don't like it? Personally, I'm an ardent follower of the immortal lessons of Dr. Seuss."

"Who?"

"Dr. Seuss. *Green Eggs and Ham*. You know. *Try them, try them, and you may?*"

"I don't have the slightest idea what you're talking about," I said, abandoning the lock to look at the man once again. I was intrigued by my sudden realization that he was only a year or two older than I, and yet I did not see him as a boy, the way I summarily perceived—and dismissed—all the boys in my dormitory or my classes.

"Oh, no. I thought I'd detected an accent. You must be one of those unfortunates who didn't imbibe Dr. Seuss's classics with their mother's milk. This simply can't go on, it must be remedied this instant. Please follow me."

He had spoken without smiling, then, before I could object, turned and walked off, not pausing to check whether I followed. I did, after a moment's hesitation. We threaded our way through the confusion of the noisy living room, to a door shut at the end of a corridor. "My humble abode," he said with a half-bow, opening the door, sweeping me inside, closing the door behind me.

The music and the stomping grew remote. I tried not to wonder about the soft click of the lock, and then forgot to wonder about it, distracted by the room in which I found myself.

It did not appear to belong to the apartment we had just crossed. It was spare and refined, furnished in uniformly muted gray tones—a soft sea-gray rug, velvety mossy-gray curtains, a thick gray throw on the bed, a slim floor lamp with a mushroom-gray shade. In spite of my profound obliviousness of, not to say distaste for, all things interior decorating, I discerned that everything here bore a mark of distinctive taste. There were architectural engravings in black and white frames on the walls, bookshelves of leather-bound volumes, and on the ceiling, for some unfathomable reason, an enormous mirror. It made me uncomfortable, this room. I felt as if I myself had strayed into someone else's story, and I was not sure that I liked the style.

"I can only stay for a few minutes," I announced sternly, just in case he had misinterpreted my presence.

"Yes, your paper on Monday, I remember." He topped off his glass from a cluster of bottles on a silver tray, reached for a book, sat cross-legged on the floor, his movements leisurely yet precise. "Not to worry, it's very short. I'll read it to you, it's best when read aloud."

As I settled across from him on the carpet, the gray cat flowed off his shoulders and pooled into my lap.

"Dorian likes you," he said. "It's a great compliment, he doesn't like just anyone, I assure you. Did you know that a group of domestic cats is called a pounce, and a group of wild cats a destruction? Have a sip in the meantime . . . Now, the happy creature here is Sam-I-am, but we never get to learn the name of the grumpy one. It used to bother me quite a bit when I was a child . . . What do you think, by the way?"

"Interesting. Tastes like smoke, wood, and acute angles. I can't say I'm fond of it."

"Well, and now you know. Here, try this, this is sweeter, a coffee liqueur."

"I don't really drink," I explained.

"Oh, but this isn't drinking. This is sampling. Purely educational in spirit."

And so I sat on the floor in the soft gray twilight of the strange room with the cat warming my thighs, listening to the light-eyed man read about eggs and ham, and thing one and thing two, and the clocks full of tocks, and the shoes full of feet, all the while sipping from an array of plump multicolored glasses that kept appearing before me out of nowhere—this one a golden-smooth honey of almonds, that one a sharp jolt of a plunge into a cold lake at sunrise, the last a dusty mouthful of vintage lace and genteel regrets.

He laughed at that.

"I knew it," he said with satisfaction, and touched his glass to mine. His fingers were very long and thin, an aristocrat's fingers. "I would recognize a fellow poet anywhere. Something about the way you hold the words in your mouth a fraction of a second longer, as if tasting them. Read me some of your poems."

"No," I said, though I felt secretly pleased. "I don't read my poems at parties. Words are not to be bandied about like cheap coins."

"But parties are precisely where one's poems should be read.

Where then *would* you read them? Poetry seminars? Libraries? I must say I'm shocked. Next you will tell me your poems do not rhyme."

"Sometimes they do. Not always. And I don't read them anywhere."

"But this is heresy!" he cried. "Poems demand to be read, otherwise they are no better than solitary trees falling in the woods." (Didn't someone say something much like this to me before? I could not remember, but an odd feeling of recognition started inside me, and I felt myself growing flushed with an unfamiliar thrill.) "And of course they should always rhyme properly. Their very power derives from that anguished tension between the poet's flights of fancy and the fetters of the form within which he labors. 'The best words in their best order,' as Coleridge noted, 'order' being the crucial idea here. Rhyme imposes order on dreaming, and the greatest poets rise to true greatness by transcending that order from within, by exploding preset boundaries and clichés with beauty and passion."

He spoke with all the fervor of conviction, but the colorless eyes in his narrow, agile face were bright with mockery, and I could not tell whether he was being earnest or making fun of me. Someone had begun to knock on the door.

"Read me some of your poems," he repeated.

"No. They are all in Russian anyway." I was beginning to feel rather giddy, but pleasantly so. The light was very dim now, though I had not noticed him turning it down. "Shouldn't you see what they want?"

"No, just ignore them and they'll give up after a while. Why don't I read you one of mine, then, to break the ice? Though I warn you, it has nothing on Dr. Seuss."

The knocking on the door became a pounding and a rattling, gray Dorian purred in my lap, and his low voice wove in and out in a rhythm that would soothe for a line or two, then jar with an unexpectedly jagged, urgent word, and I knew it was brilliant, absolutely brilliant. Then the pounding went away and I thought I heard the distant slamming of a door. It occurred to me that much time had passed since I had entered the muted gray room—an hour perhaps, perhaps two—and now the music had stopped, the party seemed over, we were alone. He had finished reciting and was looking at me, as ever with that gently mocking smile on his lips; and though I wanted to praise it, I found that I could not recollect a single word of it, for it had been just like the pungent smoke drifting from the cigarette in his hand—melting wisps of mist refusing to shape into anything tangible.

"But wait a moment," I said, realizing something. "There was no rhyme!"

"All rules exist to be broken," he said, and shifted closer to me across the carpet, so I took a drag on his odd hand-rolled cigarette, and coughed, and talked. I talked because I was suddenly nervous, but also, mainly, because all at once I no longer wished to be a solitary tree falling in the forest. So I told him about rhymes not being the only way of ordering poetry, and of my grand ambition to catalogue the entire human experience in poetic cycles, of which I had already completed a few: The Cycle of Exhaustion (a modern take on Tsvetaeva's Insomnia poems), The Cycle of Home, The Cycle of Memory, The Cycle of . . .

"The Cycle of Love?" he suggested, studying me with his penetrating pale eyes.

"No, no," I said, moving away a little, "nothing so banal"—and I might have felt uneasy again, but I was genuinely curious to find out what he thought of various things. Take, for example, Proust's haunting melody that had floated in the universe until discovered and set down by a composer—or, similarly, Michelangelo's claim that he merely rescued the already existing statues from the marble blocks in which they had been trapped—did he think that this Platonic idea could likewise be applied to poetry? Was there perhaps a treasury of perfectly resonant, universal phrases somewhere out there, waiting for their Shakespeare or Pushkin to set them into harmonious words, and if so, how would one circumvent the problem of language, languages being particular and divisive? True, the most profound, most basic poetry crossed linguistic barriers with no effort—"To be or not to be" was just as powerful in Russian, though, to be fair, I could not vouch for Finnish or Chinese—but what about more nuanced sentiments? Or was that precisely what distinguished the monolithic universality of truth from the intricate embroidery of beauty: its meaning transcended its expression?

He splashed a bit of something into my glass and said that, speaking of Shakespeare, he himself dabbled in the theater now and then, as a matter of fact he had played Hamlet in a modest production last year, had I seen it perhaps, ah, a pity. Anyway, he had been working on an amusing little theory of his own, inspired by the Bard's "All the world's a stage," namely, that the playwrights of genius had touched humanity so deeply because each of them had been able to distill the essence of a wholly unique worldview into their plays, and even centuries later, all of us mere mortals unconsciously molded our own lives into would-be plays penned by this or that giant, our very natures reshaped by someone's words and plots. Some cheated and schemed through a Molière farce, others longed for a better existence in the dreary monotony of Chekhov's uneventful drama, still others attempted to love in tragic Shakespearean terms, and the less one said about the hapless crowds stumbling through Ionesco's and Beckett's worlds, the better.

"And you, you definitely belong in Oscar Wilde," I said, laughing.

"I will take it as a reference to my taste and wit only, not to any extracurricular activities," he said, "as I hope to have a chance of proving to you shortly."

I opened my mouth to form some clever reply, and could think of nothing, and then he was kissing me, and his kisses were not at all like the rubber kisses of my Moscow youth. And even as I was falling into some dark, hot, dizzying swirl, a small, clear-minded part of me stated coldly: This is rather predictable, a bit of a cliché in fact, for I believe I am being seduced, which is obviously what happens often in this soft, warm, gray room with low beige lights and the mirror on the ceiling and the cat with those unnatural white eyes slinking off to stare at us from the top of the dresser. But later, when the clear part of my mind had long fallen silent, another, deeper voice continued to speak—because it was all interesting, and frightening, and intoxicating, and I felt myself changing, becoming someone new, yet staying myself, always myself in some still, secret place reached only by words, a kernel of me at the very heart of this whirlwind, this chaos, and the voice continued to speak, imposing order on the chaos, and somewhere in that small, secret place, quite apart from the world, I found myself writing a poem, my first poem in English, a poem with proper rhymes.

Met.
"Nyet."
Bet.
Duet.
Pet.
Wet.
Not yet.
Beset.
Let.
Sweat.
Regret?
Not yet.
Cigarette.

9. My Dorm Room

The Sacrifice

THE TELEPHONE SHRILLED IN THE HUSH OF MY dorm room, jolting me out of cramped armchair sleep; I had dozed off while waiting. I let it ring another time before lifting the receiver, willing my heart to slow from a gallop to a canter, then said "Allo" with all the brightness I could muster. Lisa's voice burst into my ear mid-laugh. She was just calling to tell me she would be spending the night at Sam's, but oh, the funniest thing had happened to her this morning in the cafeteria, could I imagine—

"Lisa," I interrupted, "you know I can't tie up the line right now."

"Oops, it's Sunday, I forgot." She hung up before she had finished speaking.

Carefully putting the receiver down on its cradle, I sank back into the armchair, checked the clock. It had been an hour already. Sometimes they were able to get through right away, but it often took two or three hours, longer on occasion. Too anxious to read,

I thought of smoking a joint, then decided against it: I wanted my head to be clear. Music drifted through the half-open window—Constantine was readying for another party. The March breeze made the lowered shade rattle lightly against the pane.

I settled back for another stretch of expectant silence.

Every Sunday, as I waited by the telephone, I could picture them with that rare clarity for which I treasured these weekly vigils—my father at his typewriter, working with only half his usual absorption, ready to pick up the second line at a moment's notice, my mother perched on a stool in the corridor, dialing, hearing the hateful busy signal, dialing again, hearing the busy signal, dialing again, her lips pressed taut with concentration, willing into being the operator's curt response. Our conversations themselves were disappointing, five minutes' worth of forced cheer shouted over static; but the hours of anticipation allowed me to convince myself that my home truly existed, that my childhood had been real—that it had not all been an invention, a fairy tale I told myself whenever I felt lonely, a heartrending song of stars and destinies, dissipating in the harsh light of days and the neon glare of nights conducted with the dry precision of a foreign language.

Sitting immobile for so long had made me stiff. I stretched, yawned, closed my eyes; when I opened them an instant later, the world had shifted: the familiar earthy smell lingered in the air—perhaps I had rolled that joint after all—and the room was flooded with silence and darkness. The silence had a different quality to it, a humming thrill of unreality, and the darkness was deepest in the armchair across from mine.

"So," he said matter-of-factly, "you've decided to break it to them at last. They won't be pleased, you know. No, don't turn it on, or you may just see a dragon instead of a handsome youth."

"Aren't you getting your myths mixed up? I'm hardly Psyche, and you're too old to be Cupid." Still, I moved my hand away from the lamp. "In any case, I'm not worried, I know they'll understand. I've sent them some of my poems."

"Yes," he said. "Your On the Other Side cycle. It wouldn't have been my first choice—it's more Dionysus than Apollo, too much raw feeling, not enough thought. And that ditty about a nun sleeping with the devil, that's painfully obvious, really, and as close to pornography as is acceptable in civilized society. Well. You've practiced your arguments, I assume?"

"I'm hoping my poetry alone will be enough," I said, a bit dryly.
"But if it isn't?"

"Then I will tell them that going home is a predictable thing to do, and someone once taught me not to take the path of least resistance." I paused for the sound of acknowledgment, but the darkness lay still around me. "Fine. I will tell them that I'll be twenty-two in just a few months, but I have yet to start living. I've spent my entire existence until now sheltered under the parental roof, in library cubicles and dorm rooms, and my future is all mapped out for me as well: my old Moscow routine waiting to close in upon me, a short interlude of graduate school followed by a desk job in some dusty institute, a marriage to someone like Vasily, then children, then middle age, then death. It's like one giant board of tic-tac-toe, spanning years and years, and as life crosses off one square, I'm expected to obediently put my O down in the next logical place, knowing all the while that the game can't be won. But somewhere out there—somewhere out there are street carnivals and mountain peaks and sunlit squares, and I just want to—to get off the board for a while."

"But what exactly will you do, my dear?"

"I don't know. Does it matter? Maybe move to New York. Or New Orleans. Or San Francisco. Rent a studio. Wait tables in some smoky den. Learn how to mix mean cocktails and play the guitar. Master poker. Take up karate. Work at an art gallery or a post office. Get a job as a conductor on a train between the coasts. Or a backup dancer. Or a window washer. Anything. Everything. I've never even *been* anywhere. I want to throw myself into adventures. Plunge into the twentieth century before it runs out, so I can write about it in the fullness of experience. Because no one can discover anything new while staying within four walls of a bookworm's cell, never venturing out to taste joy or pain. Art is all about stretching the limits of being human, is it not? It can't be born of a small, predictable life."

A night breeze swept into the room, and the shade beat a fluttering rhythm against the windowpane. I peered into the shadows. "Are you still there? Hello?"

"I wish," he said, and I could hear him stifling a yawn, "I wish you hadn't fallen into the trap that has claimed so many others. An artist doesn't need to lead a life of distraction in order to create. In fact, if you are ever to prove worthy of a myth, you must devote all your time to your calling and leave the manufacturing of adventures to your future biographers. For you must remember: Limits are best stretched by going inward, not outward; pain will find you no matter how cramped the cell you hide in; and joy—joy is always only a poem away. And there are no such things as small lives, there are only small people."

I felt a sudden flare of irritation at the smooth readiness of his maxims, at his seeming inability to understand anything about real choices in a real life.

"Noble callings, divine standards, creation with a capital C . . . All you ever do is talk in absolutes and abstractions." I spoke sharply. "Don't they say God is in the details? I want—no, I need—to experience the *details*, don't you understand—the particular, gritty, wonderful details of *life* out there. The smell of dew and garbage trucks at dawn. The bracing taste of bitter coffee at the chipped counter of a roadside diner. The wild thrill of jazz spilling out of a basement window into a still, dark alley. These are the kinds of things I want to pin down in my poems. Things and feelings that will be unique to the here and now. Things and feelings that will be unique to *me* in the here and now."

All at once conscious of shouting, I stopped. The hush in the drafty room grew hollow like the inside of a tolling bell.

When he spoke, the indifference of his drawl was a punch to the stomach.

"Sometimes, my dear, I forget what a child you still are. Oh well. Take care, while out browsing, that you don't get lost in the stacks. I will be leaving you now."

He sounded remote, as if already walking away to some other place, growing more distant with every word. The memories of my last days with Hamlet overtook me with unexpected violence, as they had not for months—that shrugging gesture of his, that condescending half-smile, the pale, bored eyes sliding past me obliquely . . .

I felt desolate once again, and bright with anger.

"So go, then!" I hissed into the orphaned darkness. "Go! I'm sick of your speeches, and I'm sick of you! Time I outgrew this juvenile little fantasy once and for all—"

I nearly screamed when his whisper brushed past my ear, so close I could feel the grazing of his hot, dry lips against my temple.

"If you make me a proper sacrifice, I may answer a prayer or two. Just this once."

The unnatural blindness pressed on my eyelids. My throat was tight.

"What, you want me to slaughter a goat for you?"

The telephone shrilled in the hush of the room, jolting me out of cramped armchair sleep; I must have dozed off while waiting. I let it ring another time, to steady my voice before answering, but it turned out to be only my roommate Lisa, calling to tell me that she would be staying at Sam's tonight, but oh, did she have a story for me—

"Lisa, you know I can't talk right now," I interrupted. "It's Sunday."

"Oops, sorry, I forgot!" She hung up.

Upbeat music was pulsating through the half-open window; Constantine was having another party. I turned on the lamp— night had sneaked past me somehow—and sank back into my armchair, feeling disoriented and upset. An obscure dark presence loomed at the back of my mind, as if something terrible had happened or was about to happen, yet I could not give it a name;

I just felt the impending threat of its misery in my bones. I sat still for a minute, then shook my head to dissipate the lingering sogginess of sleep, and, picking up the sheaf of pages by the telephone, read the top one.

> The pale angel whispered, "Hallelujah!"
> But the angel was missing his left wing
> And could fly in loopy circles only,
> Lopsided, tilting as if tipsy to one side.

Would it prove sufficient to make my parents understand the full force of my determination to devote myself to this—this solitary quest of capturing the formlessness of living in a net of language? I leafed through the pages, plucking a line here, a couplet there, sounding them out in my mind, trying to see them as my parents would, as would a stranger; but the lines refused to coalesce with any cohesion into verses, or verses into poems. The more I read, the more I sensed, with growing horror, that the meaning I heard ringing so clearly within my being had not broken through the husks of dried words—that life was absent from the littering of adolescent sentiments and empty phrases.

The telephone rang.

"Moscow for you," barked the operator's voice—and then they were there.

Allo, allo, how are you, we are well, I am well, all is well! All three of us shouted, then stopped at the same time, waiting for someone to start speaking, but no one said anything for a couple of seconds, long enough for me to imagine the thick cable line stretching in the silt of the ocean floor between the continents, overgrown with mollusks, strewn with skeletons of ships, shadows of primordial monsters slithering in the green murk above.

"So . . . have you read the poems I sent you?"

"Yes, we have, yes." Again they were speaking at once. My mother was laughing a little, as she did when embarrassed, saying that she hoped they were not altogether autobiographical, and something about drugs, while my father mumbled indistinctly behind her laughter. My mother stopped laughing, my father cleared his throat. Another monster floated through the murky ocean waters.

"Well, anyway, composing poetry is part of youth—who doesn't have a few sonnets hidden in a drawer somewhere?" my father said with finality. "So, have you given more thought to graduate schools? Moscow University has several programs—"

"About that," I said. I could feel my face burning with shame. "I thought I'd stay here for a bit longer. Another year or two."

I heard my father's careful breathing, the muffled clutter of my mother dropping something, her receiver perhaps. I waited for the fumbling to subside.

"Ah, so," my mother said at last. She sounded very far away now. "Will you be applying to graduate schools in America, then?"

This would not be the moment to mention that the unfailingly perfect Olga was considering Yale Law School. "No, I just . . . I thought I'd get a job for a bit."

"What kind of a job?"

"Maybe I'll work at a post office or something. I thought—"

"But this isn't serious," my mother said in an injured tone.

My father said nothing.

"I mean, just for a short while. While I research graduate schools."

"Well," my mother said. "Why don't you sleep on it, and we'll discuss all the options next week. There isn't that much time, you're graduating in two months. This isn't a practice run, you know, this is the only life you get."

My father still said nothing.

When the line went dead, I looked at the room where I had spent four years' worth of nights, minus two or three dozen library vigils and one short spring of romps with Hamlet. I looked everything over with care—I wanted to be certain. I moved my eyes over the two side-by-side desks, the schoolgirls' bunk beds, Lisa's posters of Klee and Kandinsky on the walls, my modest cluster of mementoes pinned in a corner, a bald spot in the middle where a Cat in the Hat postcard used to be. No, indeed, nothing real could have come of this—a diligent girl playing at being a poet in a public sandbox. My mind made up, I gathered all the pages from the floor, and, stepping over to my desk, proceeded to empty its drawers of more pages, handwritten originals all, some in Russian, some in English.

I felt quite calm.

There was a lighter in my pocket, white letters on red spelling "Siberia"; some friend of Constantine's had brought it from one of Amsterdam's coffee shops; I had borrowed it weeks before and forgotten to return it. It would not work right away, and the ball of my thumb grew sore with repeated attempts before I managed to cajole a small blue light into wavering being. The sink in the corner was too shallow to hold all the paper at once. A fireplace would have made for a much more poetic scene—and one should always do these sorts of things with style, I thought with bitterness, and dropped the first handful of pages into the sink; The Cycle of Solitude it was, I noticed. I was all done with cycles anyway. The top page blossomed into glowing life, as if the words had burst into flame on their own accord, from the sheer force of some inner fervor. I could not help reading them then, stark black against dazzling gold, quivering with transient beauty, in the moments before they disintegrated into dampened ash and disappeared down the drain half stopped up with clumps of Lisa's long blond hair.

In the darkness of an autumn night
I imagine golden beehives of a fireplace
Where the embers' honey slowly ripens
And a cat is snoring by the flames.
And I am, once more, my own grandmother,
I am knitting an eternal scarf,
And my life is pasted in an album
In a row of brown old-fashioned photos.
As I knit the scarf, for my granddaughter,
In the resonance of solemn hours—
It could not be me
Who is awakened
By my own moan,
By the remembrance
Of your lips.

The page below lay revealed, writhing in turn, new lines flaring up with brief farewell heat. Not wanting to see any more, I dumped the rest of the papers in at once, and their dead white weight poured into the small grimy sink like cement. Nothing happened for a full minute; then smoke began to curl lazily at the edges. From the mirror above the sink, I was observed by an unfamiliar girl with a determined dash for a mouth, her gaze not bitter but lit up with a ferocious joy. I found myself hiccuping with sobs that sounded like laughter, or else laughter that sounded like sobs. There you go, Apollo, a nice little sacrifice for you—the sum of my entire existence to this day, all erased, so I can start anew, so I can create something real, something alive. There, there, can you smell the sweet rot of toy words, of dead words, rising like cloying incense to your heaven? And if I believed in you, and if I could pray, what would I ask in return? To be granted the strength to persevere, first and foremost—not to swerve from my path, not to lose my desire to capture the world bit by bit, word by word, until, in the fullness of time, my small words would number so many they would become a door opened into life as I had known it—opened to anyone who would accept my invitation to walk through. And maybe, lowering my voice to an embarrassed whisper, I would ask to meet someone new—someone I could love fully and forever, my soul mate, my missing half, if I believed in such things. And oh, I would ask you to punish the man who humiliated me so easily, in passing—you would likely find this request the most pleasing of all, for are not the gods ever thirsty for vengeance? But one should be wary of wishes fulfilled and prayers miscarried . . . And as the pages smoked and flared and crumbled away, I wondered at the savage-eyed girl in the mirror, then forgot all about her, thinking of a poem I would start as soon as this tedious rigmarole was over. God's Book of Complaints and Suggestions, I would call it; it would be a polyphony of prayers, curses, and regrets, layered and contradictory as life, bits of it tragic, bits of it funny, bits of it violent, bits of it—

The fire alarm blew up above my head.

Without thinking, I turned on the water, and the room vanished in a hissing cloud of acrid steam. The alarm screamed and screamed. My door was flung open, someone ran in, and, coughing, I watched him pull up the armchair, climb to the ceiling, and unscrew something with manly efficiency.

The noise stopped.

"That's better," he said, stepping down. "Lucky I was passing by. What on earth were you doing?"

"Destroying compromising materials," I said.

"I understand," he said. "Dirty photographs." His tone was weighty with mock seriousness, and his eyes alight with laughter in his face.

"I wish," I said. "My life is nowhere near that interesting."

"Burning down the dorm seems interesting enough to me," he said. "I'm on my way to a party."

"Constantine's?"

He nodded.

"Watch out for the ouzo, it's deadly."

He pushed the armchair back to the wall.

"You should air out the room properly. Need help cleaning up?"

I turned and considered the sink, choked with soggy gray paper.

A charred, half-drowned shred was plastered against the enamel, a few lines still legible.

You can escape this maze if you grow old in it first.
The windows here are transparent walls,
Your fingers stick with the blood of childhood games,
And Ariadne's thread is a ball of chewed gum . . .

I became aware of his standing next to me, looking at the corpse of the poem, and flushed, and smeared it quickly into wet soot, and hid my blackened hands behind my back.

It had just occurred to me that I remembered every last word of my vanished poems by heart.

"I'm fine," I said. "Thanks."

Our eyes met. His face had the broad, clean planes of a Michelangelo nude, and his hair was the boyish, curly mop of a Raphael angel. His eyes were no longer laughing.

"Well, I'll be going, then," he said.

"Yes," I said. "Thanks."

Still he stood there.

Rental Studio

10. Studio room

11. Bathroom

10. Studio Room

Conversation in the Dark at the Age of Twenty-two

HAPPINESS THIS DEEP IS WORDLESS.

11. Bathroom

A Poem Written at the Age of Twenty-three

I SAT ON THE MATTRESS, MY SWEATER WRAPPED tightly around me, my arms wrapped around my knees. I felt chilled to the bone. Adam freed a shirt from its hanger, tossed it into the open suitcase, and threw the hanger onto a growing pile; plastic hit plastic with a dry, loud clap. He would not look at me. Through the basement's two small street-level windows I watched the rain battering dark winter puddles. A woman's shoes rapped past, sharp and reptilian. I made another effort to speak, though my words felt like ghostly wisps of real words, passing right through him, helpless to change anything.

"Please understand. I followed you up here because of your school, and now you want me to follow you across the ocean because of your job, and I just . . ."

Another hanger smashed into the pile with an angry clatter.

"Please. I don't want to leave you. Maybe later . . . when you get back . . ."

He looked at me at last. His eyes were dark and flat.

"We were going to spend our lives together." I could see the jaws clenching in his face. "Now, at the very last minute, I find out that you went behind my back to extend the lease on this dump, and you tell me you won't be coming."

"Please. Please listen . . . I just . . ."

"No," he said, turning away. "I will finish packing and go. I will stay somewhere else tonight. I don't know where. A hotel. I will go to the airport directly from there." I tried to interrupt. "No," he said again, and the force of it was like a hand clamped over my mouth. "I don't want to say things I'll regret later. I'll call you from the hotel. If you change your mind, pack and join me. Otherwise—otherwise we'll work out the details later, and I wish you well."

Stunned, I listened to the skeletal clacking of the hangers for another minute, then stood up and, without looking at him, walked into the bathroom and shut the door behind me; there was nowhere else to hide from each other in our cramped closet of a place, and, like a frightened child, I needed to close my eyes so I would become invisible to the horrible monster stalking me through the basement. But the monster got me here just as well. He had already taken his toothbrush and his razor, but in the corner of the bathtub a giant gladiolus leaned against the moldy tiles, its wilting petals stuck out like red tongues from its many maws, mocking me, mocking me.

("By the time it dies," Adam had said when he had brought it home a week before, "you and I will be strolling along the Seine."

"But we don't have a vase large enough," I had protested. "Come to think of it, we don't have any vases at all."

"So let's put it in the bathtub. It'll make for some interesting showers."

"Do you know, I haven't seen one of these in years," I had said. "I remember carrying a bouquet of gladioli on my very first day of school. I was seven, and the flowers were taller than me, and—You're not listening."

"I am," he had said, but I could see that he was thinking about his music again, so I had stopped talking and he had not noticed.)

Crumpling onto the floor by the radiator, I pressed my forehead to the wall, tried to drown out the unbearable clash of the hangers. After a while the noise stopped, all was quiet for some time; then the rip of the suitcase zipper gashed my hearing, and his steps crossed the room—it took only four of his strides to reach the door from the bed.

The front door opened and closed.

Frozen with disbelief, I listened for the turning of the key. But the door flew open instead, his steps tumbled back in, and he burst into the bathroom and kneeled beside me, cupping my face between his hands in just that way he had, and his eyes were no longer dead, and as always, as ever with him, I was overtaken by the warm rush, and everything within me fell into its proper place.

"I can't leave like this. Tell me. Do you no longer love me?"

"I love you more than I ever thought possible. More than you'll ever know."

"Then why are you doing this?"

"Do you remember the first night we spent together, I asked you whether you would prefer to be happy in this life or immortal after your death, and you said immortal, and I said I was the same, and we marveled at the serendipity of having found each other? Except I fell in love with you, and when I'm with you now, I just want to be happy. That is, I *am* happy, deliriously, astonishingly happy, but I'm also terrified of losing that happiness, and wondering whether you're happy enough with me, and trying to make you happy, and worrying whether I'm really as happy as I seem to be or whether I'm just fooling myself into believing I'm happy because I don't want to admit that I'm also a little sad and a little lost, and with all that fretting about happiness, as well as being so exhausted from all the odd jobs I've taken to help pay your bills, I barely have the energy for my poetry anymore—but for you, for you it still is all about your music. And what bothers me most is not the knowledge that I need you so much, that I love you more than you love me—although that's pretty hard to take—but the fact that—"

"Oh, but you don't! You can't possibly love me more than I love you. All I want is your happiness, I don't care about my job, I'll call them and tell them I don't want it—"

"Oh no, you can't do that, it's your future, our future, I will come with you, of course I will, all I ever wanted was to hear you say that—"

And our lips drew close together, and all was righted in the world, and in another heartbeat I did hear that key turning in the lock—he must have paused on the landing before the closed door for a long moment, perhaps likewise imagining me running after him, throwing myself into his arms, reading who knew what stilted script of unlikely, corny phrases. His steps thundered up the stairs. The springs of the outside door wheezed.

He was gone.

I did not know how much time had passed before I became aware of the deep, all-pervasive cold—at least an hour, probably longer. I was shivering. The radiator was lukewarm under my stiffened fingers, and my legs had gone numb on the icy floor. I felt that I could not move, that my body did not belong to me, and for one mad instant I was possessed by an absolute certainty that somehow, without my noticing, I had died, and was now condemned to spend a meager afterlife trapped in the grimy hell of a narrow, dim bathroom, remembering in an agony of perfect regret the light I had chosen to walk out of, the love I had chosen to lose.

I forced myself to rise and strip. Stepping into the shower, I pushed the gladiolus down into the tub and turned the water on full-blast, as hot as it would go, until it felt scalding, until the steaming stream ran red with the blood of the flower. I began to scrub myself, scrub myself hard, so hard it burned, and at last tears came, big wracking sobs, and still I kept scrubbing, scrubbing the memory of his touch off my skin, the memory of slow kisses in the dark small room, dancing naked to Bach and Django, the threadbare carpeting coarse under our bare soles, our souls always bared, breakfasts in bed at two in the afternoon, feasts of grapes and vodka at two in the morning, reciting Apollinaire and Gumilev to each other—his fluent French, my native Russian, arriving at clumsy English together—candles guttering in pewter holders picked up at a sidewalk sale, conversations intense with questing after truths, the romance of youthful poverty, a three-legged rat scratching night after night at our basement window, boots stomping past, the trembling web of moonlight on the ceiling, the abandon of nights deep and hard and raw with life, the taste of crisp green apples on his lips, the perfect exclamation point of New Year firecrackers bursting on the street outside just after I said: "Yes, yes, I will."

In the room beyond, the telephone started to ring.

Leaping out of the shower, naked and wet, heart pounding, flinging open the bathroom door, steam pouring out, damp footprints on the grim gray carpet, not caring who peeked into the bare windows, tearing the receiver off the cradle, breathless from the cold—Hello, hello, are you there, is it you? Where are you, give me the address, stay there, don't go anywhere, don't go anywhere ever again, I will come right away, I love you, I will always love you, I can't live without you—

And as I stood still in the shower, the scalding water running down my back, my breasts, my thighs, the circles of telephone rings widening on the surface of deep winter silence, I watched that other girl through the bathroom door she had left wide open behind her. I watched her flying around the room, pulling on clothes, tossing clothes into her bag, throwing on her coat, running out the door, coming back to pick up the keys she had forgotten, running out again. The girl looked frantic with the relief of happiness—happier, I knew, than I was ever likely to be now—but also somehow less real, diminished. The door closed behind her, just as it had closed behind him.

In the empty room, the telephone stopped ringing.

I turned off the water, dried myself, got dressed, and bent to fish the discolored petals of the dead gladiolus out of the tub.

"When I was seven years old," I said aloud, "I carried a bouquet of flowers just like this on my first-ever day of school. We were all supposed to give flowers to our teachers, you see, and gladioli were traditional. I felt ridiculously proud. The teacher had all the new children come up to her one by one, hand over the flowers, and announce in front of everybody what they wanted to do when they grew up. All the boys wanted to be cosmonauts, all the girls wanted to be ballet dancers. When it was my turn, I said that I just wanted to live in a castle full of beautiful paintings and old books. The teacher was indignant. She hissed that it was dangerous bourgeois rot and that she would have to speak to my parents. She made an example out of me, and at recess all the other children called me names and laughed. I was so distressed that I became ill and spent the next two weeks in bed with a fever. My mother read me Charles Perrault's fairy tales, but my father read me poems. I fell in love with Blake's 'Tiger' and Gumilev's 'Giraffe.' Remember, I translated it for you—

"I see that today your gaze is especially sad,
And your arms, as they hug your knees, seem especially thin.
Listen: far, far away, at Lake Chad,
There wanders an exquisite giraffe . . .

"But ever since then I have detested gladioli."

I finished stuffing what remained of it into the trashcan, then meticulously rinsed the dark red pollen off my hands, the last traces of the murder committed. I thought about what had bothered me most, about what I could have told him—all the things about art and fulfillment and not wanting a small life consumed by happiness. The Muses may have been women, I could have complained, but they had still inspired men, had they not? I would have lied, though, about what bothered me most.

What really bothered me was that I loved him more.

I worked the smooth golden band off my finger, scraping my hand to blood in the process. I put the ring in the empty soap dish—had he taken the soap, or were we, was I, just out? I thought of the past two years of my life—gone, gone, gone just like that—and, dull with wretchedness, wanted to cry again. So I found a stray sheet of paper in the medicine cabinet, behind some bottles of aspirin and a calcified face cream, pulled a pencil stub out of my pocket—he always laughed at the habit—and, kneeling on the floor, scribbled against the side of the bathtub.

It was so cold that all my words felt frozen
and flew away, a brilliant blue cloud.
One fancy adjective sped toward a close-by chimney,
attracted—all that warmth, and noise, and smoke—
a real life, it seemed.
I watched as it went down, its tail atremble,
while we in silence sat, and then he asked
(the smell of imitation phrases musty):
"What color flowers do you like the most?"
"None," I responded, "flowers always scared me"—
and looked away.
My fingers bled again;
my hands had never any luck, it seemed.
"I do not think I'll come with you to Paris."

"Oh no? A pity."—And he sipped his coffee,
and then pulled on those leather gloves of his
that stranglers would have envied any day,
and strolled away—politely.
My night grew warmer then, and my best words
bounced back to me, my loyal, joyous pets.
They flocked into my lap, and lapped their milk,
and were at home at last—
alive and needed.
And then I knew that I had prayed for numbness—
that I had hoped to be enwrapped by winter—had wanted him
to change my mind, it seemed.

The paper was damp and curling with steam by the time I was done. I decided to call it "The End." It was not any good, I saw upon rereading, but one had to start somewhere. And as I sat on the cold bathroom floor, struggling to chisel the poem's true, muscular shape out of the awkward lump of fatty phrases and petulant sentiments, I already felt—rising slowly from within the muddy misery of loneliness—the hard, bright joy of my new-found solitude.

Part Three
The Past

Penthouse Apartment

12. Kitchen

14. Living room

15. Bedroom

A Mansion Somewhere Else

13. Guest bedroom

1 2. Kitchen

Apollo's Arrow

THE THREE LARGE WINDOWS GLOWED WITH A perfect April sunset; its colors reminded her of a tropical drink in a glossy advertisement—something cool, sweet with fruity liqueurs, crowned by a pink paper umbrella. From up here, the rows of townhouses on the street below, with their dark tile roofs and neat arrangements of potted plants on the narrow balconies, looked clean, toylike, European somehow, and she said so, more in the spirit of indiscriminately voicing her thoughts aloud than of making conversation, for with Paul she did not much think of what she said.

"Though I've never been to Europe. Well, technically Moscow is Europe, but it isn't really. *Yes, we are Scythians, yes, we are Asians with slanting, greedy eyes,* and all that."

He looked up from slicing the mushrooms. "What was that Scythian bit?"

"Oh, just some famous lines from Blok." She added after a beat, "A Russian Silver Age poet."

"Ah. Poetry. Never got into it myself. Anyway, Europe. You should really go, you know."

"Travel's not so easy for me," she said. "I have issues with documents——"

She could have added, "Nor do I have the money," for in truth she was nearly destitute. She had long before quit her day job in a department store and her night job in a restaurant, and now survived by taking on occasional translation projects; the assignments, however, paid by the page, and she had proved inconveniently slow, agonizing as she did over the most trivial word choices with all the obsessiveness of a thwarted poet. Every night she jotted down her earnings ("Proposal for installing latrines in Central Asia, 3 pages, $48") as well as her expenses ("March rent, $525; apples, $3.60; bus from the library, $1.10"; she always walked there to save the fare, but the piles of books she invariably checked out were too heavy to lug home on foot). At the end of each week, if the subtractions worked out, she would allow herself the single luxury of a cappuccino and pastry in a nearby café. She carried her poverty lightly—she believed that her upbringing had inoculated her against needing comforts or longing for possessions—but she sensed that any mention of her situation might embarrass Paul, who, after finishing business school, had landed a vague but clearly well-paid job at some management consulting firm and was now living in a furnished penthouse apartment in a finer part of the city.

Quickly she changed the subject.

"Are you sure I can't lend you a hand?"

"I would never make a guest cook. Besides, I love cooking for people. Just sit back and enjoy your Chardonnay, dinner will be ready in no time."

Swirling the wine in her glass, she watched him as he moved between the stove and the island with an agility unexpected in someone of his massive build, until at last she admitted to feeling surprised, and pleasantly so. Ever since they had run into each other on a street downtown (he had been leaving his new office; she, walking to the library), they met for coffee every few months, but this was the first time he had invited her over for dinner. She had, she realized, envisioned a grimy bachelor's den and a plate of overcooked spaghetti topped with lukewarm sauce from a can (the extent of her own culinary endeavors). In the near-ascetic bareness of her life, had she fallen victim to the trite assumption that someone at ease with numbers—just as someone at ease with words—could never be altogether at ease in the physical world? It held true in her case, to be sure, yet here was Paul the math major in a white apron embroidered with grapes, wielding a knife with efficient grace as he chopped asparagus in his immaculate kitchen, exuding a sense of serenity amidst boiling pots and hissing pans and mysterious gleaming utensils at whose purpose she would not even attempt to venture a guess.

She found his capable presence relaxing.

"I hope it won't be too rich for you," he said as he stirred more cream into the sauce. "I haven't tried this one before, it's from a new cookbook—"

"Whatever it is, the smell is making me hungry . . . And just look at all these books! I don't have any books in my kitchen. Granted, my entire kitchen is the size of a teapot—" Wineglass in hand, she rose from the table and inspected the shelves, then, pulling a book out at random, leafed through it idly.

"But these are like poetry," she exclaimed then. "Ossobuco Gremolada with Risotto Milanese! Marseille Bouillabaisse with Aïoli! Or how about this militant Duck Flan with Maltese Blood Orange Sauce and Shallot Confit? I don't think I know two-thirds of these words. Can anyone actually cook these?"

"Possibly. One never knows until one tries," he said, smiling.

"And you have two entire books of desserts! I can never pass up anything sweet, it's my one weakness . . . Here is something called Casanova's Delight. Mmm, it has kiwi sauce and Grand Marnier ice cream mousse."

He stepped closer, bumping her arm. "Oh, sorry. Let me see. This one's a little ambitious." As always, when he stood next to her, she was startled by his football player's bulk. "Still, let's brave it for our next dinner, shall we?"

"So generous of you to volunteer feeding the masses."

He resumed his place at the stove, his face reddened with the heat of cooking.

"So," he said after a short pause, "heard from any of the old crowd lately?"

"Just Lisa." She opened another book. "She married Sam, you know, as we all expected. They've just had a boy. What in the world is cardamom? . . . And Maria and Constantine split up, but I haven't spoken to either of them since."

"I keep in touch with them. Maria is in New York, trying to break into acting. Constantine went back to Greece and inherited his shipping empire. And Stacy is renting her own childhood room from her parents. They are crazy as bats, she says. And, of course, the horrible thing with John . . . Not that I liked him much, always thought he was a pretentious ass, but one shouldn't speak ill of—"

"Who?" she asked, turning a page. She was enchanted by the precisely quantified lists of exotic ingredients, the casual mentions of distant places, the pure linguistic pleasure of melodiously named concoctions—a vocabulary entirely new to her. Since Adam's departure (fourteen months, eight days, and two hours ago now), she had barely stirred from the monastic confinement of her dim basement cell, and she felt her very soul squinting, blinded by the brightness of life out in the open, so sophisticated and varied, so full of adult things she appeared to know nothing about. It occurred to her that she was not giving the senses their proper due. It might be interesting to attempt a poem for each sense, like the verbal equivalent of one of those allegorical seventeenth-century paintings with Lady Taste licking a sugared plum, Lord Sight studying stars through a telescope, Lady Smell lifting a rose to her nose, and Lord Hearing serenading the courtly gathering on a mandolin, while Lord and Lady Touch pawed each other in the discreetly darkened bushes in the background. The Hearing poem would be the easiest, no doubt, sprinkled liberally with alliteration and onomatopoeia, but the others would present a challenge, for the trick would be to convey in words alone the unique nature of—

"John. Hamlet. Didn't you date him at one point?"

"Oh," she said, closing the volume. "Yes. Briefly. Did something happen to him?"

"I thought you knew." She continued looking at him. "He—

apparently he was in some kind of accident last winter. At first they thought it was drinking or drugs, but it wasn't. He just lost control of the car. Drove into a tree. A branch pierced his lungs . . . Sorry, that was gruesome, I shouldn't have—"

She set her glass of wine on the table, lowered herself into the chair.

"Apollo's arrow," she said quietly.

"What was that?"

"Nothing." She stared out the window. Streetlamps were beginning to glow in the green twilight. *Do you not imagine sometimes, when dusk wanders through the house, that here, alongside us, lies another plane, where we lead entirely different lives . . .* She felt cold, so cold. "Paul. Do you ever feel that there is more to life than we can see, near us but just out of reach?"

"You mean like ghosts? Or . . . angels or something?"

"No, nothing so obvious. Just . . . I never tried putting it into words before, but . . . When I was younger, I sometimes felt that, just below the surface of ordinary things, there was another, secret layer of—well, not magic exactly, but forces of the universe ran deeper there, or things were brighter and had their true names, or . . . or something like that. And if you were special enough to see into that other, hidden place through the veneer of here and now, a little of its light would be yours to keep. Sort of like wishes being granted if you found the secret words with which to ask. Except sometimes you forgot it wasn't just a child's game, sometimes you wished for things that weren't . . ."

She stopped, inarticulate with guilt, confused by the remnants of a half-remembered dream. The silence between them swelled with the gauze of curtains blown into the kitchen on the breath of a sudden light breeze. In the street below, a blushing rain of petals fluttered down to the sidewalks.

"I'm not sure I follow. Everyone is special in some way. And—forgive me for being blunt—but I don't believe in mystical mumbo-jumbo. Here is here. Now is now. Do unto others as you would have them do unto you. End of story." He sounded almost hostile. After a pause, he added, his tone softening, "I'm sorry about John."

"It was a long time ago," she said, not looking at him. "I don't really know what I'm saying. You just took me by surprise. It's . . . very sad. I don't want to talk about it anymore."

"Of course. Here." He splashed more wine into her glass. "Dinner will be ready in fifteen minutes."

They talked of other things then, professors whose classes they had both attended, his job, his parents, her recent translation contract, but she was not listening to what he told her, or paying attention to what she told him, speaking mechanically, for a dark, superstitious voice muttered with increasing insistence inside her. All gifts have their price, whispered the voice. If you are indeed one of the chosen of the universe, and not just a poor deluded sap with an inflated sense of self-worth, what you ought to feel is not flattered but frightened half to death. And she knew that she was indeed frightened, deeply, irrationally frightened—frightened to leave this well-lit, solid, modern place with its polished expanses of stainless steel and its smells of good living, frightened to creep back to her underground, out-of-time life, the damp, the dark, the stillness, the solitude, the three-legged rat whom she had named Long John Silver in a reckless moment of despair, the feet always passing by her blind, naked windows, the growing gaps of silence in her telephone conversations with her parents, the unwritten poems whose ghosts haunted her nightly, the written poems she no longer mentioned to anyone at all, the memories of her lost love shooting through the dreary fabric of her days like threads of brightly colored silk, which turned brittle and hard and drew blood if she ran them through her fingers. Hers was a small and lonely life, a rigorous servitude in preparation for a bigger life, as she tried to see it; yet now, just beneath the thinning fabric of her existence, she sensed an invisible roiling of vast, terrifying, dangerous things—things that would play with you if you pleased them, things that would kill you if you proved a disappointment.

And night after night she was alone with them.

"Voilà," Paul announced, stepping away from the stove and sweeping his hand in a theatrical gesture. "Sea bass in champagne sauce. Wait, don't get up, I'll serve us. Or we could move to the living room if you prefer—"

"No, please, let's stay here, I love the view. Do you know what I find so likable about you? You're so sensible."

"Sensible, huh. Not a very sexy quality when you're trying to impress a girl."

"Are you trying to impress a girl?" she asked, startled out of her thoughts. "I somehow thought you were . . . aren't you with someone?"

"There was Tiffany, yes, but that's over now." He carried the plates to the table. "As a matter of fact," he said, and sat down, but instantly stood up again to retrieve the bottle of wine from the counter and refill her glass; his was scarcely touched. "Cheers. So.

I was thinking, you know. Maybe, you and I—do you think we could—ever—"

"Oh," she said, putting her fork down on the table. "Paul. I'm not good at romance, it always ends badly, they stop talking to me, or I stop talking to them . . ." Or they die, screamed a panicking voice inside her. "I just really like having you as a friend. I have very few friends, and . . . and I'm counting on tasting that Casanova's Delight someday—" She attempted a laugh, inwardly wincing at the dessert's unfortunate name, hoping that he would make some joke in return. He was silent, and for an instant she imagined that his face bore the same look of mixed apology and hurt that she remembered having glimpsed on it six years before, in the library stacks, when he had sported longer hair and a Grateful Dead shirt. Stricken, she went on rambling. "Or . . . it doesn't have to be you cooking, I can cook something for you too, though I should warn you I'm not a very good cook, in fact I'm dreadful, my rice always comes out lumpy, and I wouldn't want you to see my place either, it's a bit . . ."

"Hey," he said, briefly covering her hand with his. "It's all right. I'm not asking you to marry me, you know. It was just a thought. Since we are both single at present. Not a big deal." He speared some asparagus onto her plate, at ease again, a friendly giant who could whip up a three-course gourmet meal as readily as do your taxes. "Let's not mention it ever again. Shall we dig in?"

She picked her fork back up, took a bite.

"It's delicious." She felt obscurely but deeply ashamed.

"Just wait till you taste the crepes. Grandma taught me. My mom's mom. A waif of a woman, but boy, she was like a force of

nature in the kitchen. She had such a beautiful name, too—
Cecilia. I don't think there are many Cecilias nowadays, I guess
it's too old-fashioned or something. She died two years ago."

"Tell me about her," she asked.

While he talked, she looked out the window. It was dark now,
and her reflection floated in the glass, pale and stark-eyed, dis-
torted by slashes of shadow into a semblance of some mad medieval
hermit. Beyond it, confetti of stars dotted the skies, while below,
townhouse windows shone with the warm, tranquil glow of domesticity, trees rustled gently, and pavements gleamed white and
soft with drifting blossoms. She remembered reading somewhere
that people on mountaintops—people who enjoyed great, sweeping views—were supposed to live longer. Perhaps, she thought, if
you lived in a place like this, you would get to live longer too, and
you would then be more willing to forgive yourself any mistakes,
any spiteful wishes, any wrong turns along the way.

You would have more time to fix everything.

13. Guest Bedroom

The Silk-Covered Buttons

THE CHRISTMAS GATHERING WAS STILL IN FULL swing in the living room, a cluster of uncles discussing the recent election over libations, a circle of cousins inspecting old photograph albums, two or three toddlers playing with crumpled gift wrapping in the shadow of the imposing tree, when she excused herself and slipped away. The noise of the party receded quickly, became a jolly hum diffused in the succession of high-ceilinged rooms. As she crossed a sudden strip of silence, she was conscious of the blunt clatter of her heels (bought used, just for the occasion, at her neighborhood thrift shop) against the hardwood floors.

In the foyer, at the foot of the staircase, stood the second, smaller tree. When they had pulled up the driveway the night before, it had shone through the glass-paneled front door like a many-splintered, Cubist image of Christmas, each diamond-shaped pane bearing a burst of white light within a nest of dark green fir, all dusted with the snow of glass frosting. "Your parents have a glass front door?" she had cried.

Paul had laughed, but she had been too astonished to join in his laughter.

She had not known that houses like this really existed.

The foyer was deserted now save for a little boy in a plum-colored velvet suit, the son of one of Paul's many cousins, whom she had not yet learned to distinguish. His head tilted back, he stood staring up at the tree. She was about to slip past with a vague smile when the boy turned to her.

"Our tree has lollipops on it, you can pull them off and eat them," he said. "This tree is all grown up. Can you keep a secret? I have to whisper."

She nodded and crouched before him. Children made her nervous. He poked at a lower branch where a pinkish angel circled slowly, its brittle wings sparkling with illusory sugar, then breathed in her ear: "Angels taste dusty."

"Oh, but these angels are not for eating," she said. "Every night, when everyone in the house goes to sleep, they leave their trees and fly to the bedrooms of little boys and girls to wish them sweet dreams and sing beautiful songs and—"

"You talk funny," said the boy. "I'm hungry. I want my mom."

She watched him waddle off, when a creak sounded above her, and, glancing up, she saw Paul on the landing, leaning over the curve of the staircase. Feeling embarrassed, as if caught in a small lie, she rose and went up to meet him. He pulled her into a bear hug, and for one instant they tottered a bit precariously at the top of the steps.

"Everyone loves you," he sang into her hair.

Extricating herself, she inspected him in some surprise. He stood towering above her, chuckling and swaying, his shirttails untucked, his auburn hair plastered over his moistened forehead, his eyes glazed with elation that was ever so slightly unfocused. He looked very young, a bit blurry at the edges, perhaps, but just as wholesome as ever.

"Never thought I'd see the day," she said. "You're tipsy!"

"I'm celebrating," he said. "You are so beautiful tonight. You should always wear diamonds. Everyone loves you. Uncle Curtis said you look like a porcelain doll."

His inebriation had an unmistakable quality of relief to it, of exhaling after the stiffness of tense expectation. She knew, of course, that his family had been nervous about meeting her, but it had not occurred to her until now that he had been nervous as well. Her smile wavered, as she struggled to ignore a minute pin-prick of disappointment.

The grandfather clock began to chime in the polished depths of the house. When the faint jingle of crystals in the chandelier overhead died in the wake of the tenth boom, she said, "I think I'll turn in, I'm tired. I thanked your parents already. Everyone has been so kind. Come kiss me good night later if you think it's all right."

Paul was staying in his childhood room; she had been given the guest suite.

Once behind the closed door, she kicked off her shoes, sank down on the velvet vanity bench, and looked at the blue and silver room poised in the vanity's mirror. The mirror room was flaw-less. The glossy silk duvet had not a wrinkle on it; the light blue curtains fell to the dark blue of the rug in beautifully sculpted curves; elegant flocks of lamps, vases, and clocks lined up in stately symmetry on antique tables and nightstands. It took her only one moment of contemplating the perfection to realize that things were not as she had left them. Seized by a childish suspicion, she turned around and stared at the room itself. As one would expect, the original was no different from its reflection, and therefore the silent dark-skinned woman with a feather duster whom she had encountered gliding on slippered feet in the upstairs hallway must have remade the bed she herself had made, rather haphazardly, that morning, as well as pulled the curtains closed and removed the chaos of lipsticks, tissues, and clothes she had strewn on dressers and flung among pillows while getting ready for the party some hours before.

She faced the mirror again.

The girl in the mirror, she saw, looked somehow different too, made subtly foreign by the sparkling of dainty teardrops in her ears and a brighter flash on her finger. She lowered her eyes. On the vanity's surface, a half-dozen elaborately framed black-and-white photographs of unsmiling brides with wasplike waists stood sentry around an engraved toiletry set much like one she had once admired in the window of a fancy antique shop, with a price tag that had made her laugh. Picking up the heavy brush, she tried to read the initials but could decipher only the first, M, the other two letters choked past the point of recognition by the virulent proliferation of Victorian scrolls. She ran the brush through the tangle of her hair, once, twice, then set it back down; objects here were clearly not meant to stray too far from their allotted places. Next to the toiletry set, a round silver tray bore a precise arrangement of perfume bottles, some severely geometrical, others plump, still others twisted in flirtatious spirals, all crowded by their saffron, topaz, honey doubles in the mirror. She chose one at random, dabbed a bit in the hollow of her neck, and looked up.

"Charmed," she said, aloud, to the mirror girl.

The mirror girl smiled back most graciously. She looked perfectly at home in her perfect Cinderella bedroom, if one paid no heed to the somewhat wild, startled look in her Scythian eyes and the pair of scuffed black pumps with soiled insoles, sprawled with all the indecency of peasant abandon in the middle of the lovely blue carpet.

The scent was sweet with vanilla, and a trifle stale—an older woman's smell. She took a cotton ball from a gilded crystal bowl and started rubbing at her neck, thinking of a poem she could write—each verse an enigmatic vignette reflected in the same mirror, a massive Renaissance mirror that would start out in some palace in Florence or Siena five centuries before and end up in an American suburb in the present day and age—when there sounded a delicate tap on the door.

"Come in," she called out, leaping to shove her unseemly shoes to the wall.

"I hope I'm not disturbing," Paul's mother said, flowing across the threshold in her queenly, straight-backed manner. "Paul told me you were going to sleep soon."

"Thank you again, Mrs. Caldwell, the party was delightful."

"Please." It sounded like a sentence of its own on Mrs.

Caldwell's lips. "Call me Emma. I wanted to give you this." Carefully she lowered a large white box onto the bed and lifted the lid. "It was my mother's, and then mine. It's been in storage, but I had it cleaned just before you came up. It's only a thought, you don't have to use it if you don't like it, perhaps you'd rather choose your own, or maybe you have something in your family already—"

Over Mrs. Caldwell's shoulder, she watched the creamy foam of vintage lace spill out of the box.

"No, there is nothing like this in my family," she said quietly.

"You can see it full-length here." Mrs. Caldwell pointed to one of the pictures on the vanity. When she moved, the sculpture of her gleaming blond hair did not move with her. "That's my mother on her wedding day, she is nineteen here . . . Oh, which one? Ah, that was my grandmother, this toiletry set belonged to her, a present from my great-grandfather on her sixteenth birthday . . . No, no, you're most welcome. I'll leave it with you, unless you'd like to try it on tonight. But you're probably too tired . . . Are you sure? I'll be right outside then, just call when you're ready."

When Mrs. Caldwell exited the room, she hurried to strip, anxious not to make her future mother-in-law wait in the hallway. Underneath her prim black sheath, she wore a racy red bra, the tiniest of thongs, and stockings with a garter belt; earlier in the day, she had nursed a halfhearted plan of paying Paul a tiptoeing visit at two in the morning. Now the appearance of a gartered tart amidst the bedroom's blue-and-silver refinement made her avert her eyes from the mirror with something nearing shame.

She looked again at the photographs on the vanity, at the solemn young bride in her luminous sepia fog. This must be Paul's grand-

mother Cecilia, dead these three years, she thought—and felt
suddenly, deeply touched. In the hazy warmth of her expanding
emotion the palatial room itself appeared transformed: not a daunting museum exhibit with constellations of fussy trifles, where one
was not allowed to indulge in the mess of living, but a cherished
collection of family memories stored, preserved, and amplified in
heirlooms made priceless with meaning. She touched the brush
again, overwhelmed by a surge of affection (a poet's affection, she
said to herself) for all the old things that carried echoes of former
lives. Her own family was rich in stories, of course, but theirs were
mostly tales of dramatic upheavals and forbidden romance—wars,
revolutions, secret trysts with gypsies and dukes—with only a few
chance treasures and hardly any photographs surviving to provide
illustration or offer proof; she had never even seen the faces of her
great-grandparents. To her, family past was a misty realm of con-
jecture and imagination. The idea of mundane, practical objects—
combs, vases, dresses—perpetuating the quiet remembrance of a
different kind of life, the tranquil, linear progression of several generations' worth of marriages, children, traditions, took her completely by surprise.

All at once she longed to become a part of someone's tangible
history.

The dress, when unfolded, proved long and narrow, with
sleeves of intricate lace and a row of incredibly small silk-covered
buttons all along the back, from the neck to well below the
waist—no less than a hundred, she thought. Imagine some seam-
stress's skillful hands encasing them in silk one by one, what infinite patience! She was glad, for the sake of her gratitude, to find

the gown so graceful and simple, but the buttons—oh, she just fell in love with the buttons.

She stepped into the dress, instantly nervous—what if it did not fit? The neckline was modest but wide, and the straps of her red bra hung out slovenly on both sides. She shrugged the bra off, then fumbled for the buttons at her back.

"How is it going in there?" asked Mrs. Caldwell's voice from behind the door.

"It's beautiful, Mrs. Caldwell, I just need a few seconds," she replied.

The buttons were tiny and sleek and slipped out from under her fingers. After a minute of panting contortions, it became clear that not only could she not reach any of the buttons in the middle—she could not manage any of the buttons she could reach. Abandoning her acrobatics, she wiggled out of the sleeves, twisted the bodice around, and, ignoring the cold air on her naked skin and the sensation of her nipples turning into raisins, hastily traveled along the row of buttons, doing them up. Finished at last, she breathed a sigh of relief, twisted the dress back into place, and found—naturally—that she could no longer squeeze her way back into it. She felt like Alice before the locked door to the Wonderland garden, with the key forever out of her reach. Cursing her stupidity under her breath, she set about undoing the buttons, which grew agile like water bugs and kept skidding away from her increasingly frantic fingers. She counted them this time: there were forty-eight, and she hated each and every one of them.

"Is everything all right, dear?" asked Mrs. Caldwell from the hallway. "Do you need help?"

"No, no, I'm fine, I'm really done, just one moment——"

It now occurred to her that she should indeed ask Paul for help; but he would not hear her shouts across the mansion, nor could she very well send Mrs. Caldwell on an errand to get him, and it would hardly do to go wandering in search of him while falling out of his grandmother's nuptial gown. Yanking it all the way down, she stood half naked in her red wisp of a thong and bordello stockings, surveying the room, wondering where the maid had put the sweater and jeans she had worn earlier, the dress piled at her feet——and it was precisely then that Mrs. Caldwell chose to propel herself inside, saying, "Perhaps I could . . . ah, ah, so sorry!"

The door slammed with a loud bang, and Mrs. Caldwell was now gasping apologies in the hallway.

"No, no, please——" As she lunged to grab her bra off the floor, she got entangled in the gown's silk folds and made an awkward step. There was the terrible sound of something ripping, something popping, which she hoped to all the gods was not audible outside the room. "I——I'm just having some trouble with the buttons. Please, do come in."

By the time Mrs. Caldwell edged into the room, she had struggled anew into the imprisonment of the dress, and, her back gaping open, stood in silent mortification, crimson-faced, not meeting the mirrored eyes of Mrs. Caldwell, who for the next minute, the longest minute of her life, strained to button the buttons.

In the end, it proved much too tight.

"You couldn't be any skinnier, my dear," Mrs. Caldwell repeated for the third time, smiling kindly if somewhat grimly. "People were just frailer in the old days, I think, not as healthy as today . . .

We could take it to my tailor, perhaps, see what could be done . . ." There sounded another ominous creak of a seam about to split. "Oh, but we wouldn't want to tear it. Well, we'll think of something. Vera Wang makes lovely gowns."

Later that night, when Paul stopped by for his—conjugally chaste—good-night kiss, she chose not to tell him of her sartorial misadventure. Later still, already in her nightshirt, she walked along the perimeter of the bed, liberating the impossibly starched, taut sheets, when she stepped on something hard and cool with her bare foot. A tiny silk button the color of spilled milk lay on the carpet. She bent to retrieve it, held it for a moment on her palm, then pushed it deep between the mattresses. She realized, of course, that Mrs. Caldwell could not have failed to notice the damage, but all the same, she did not want anyone stumbling upon the fresh evidence of her crime.

If I sleep soundly tonight, she thought as she climbed into the bed, it should put to rest my mother's theory of royal blood in our veins. Though I rather suspect I've flunked my princess test already. Ah, that was awful, just awful . . . Well, but I can learn, I can attend princess evening courses, I'm sure if I iron enough curtains, I will get good grades . . . No, I must be asleep, this makes no sense—or does it? She giggled aloud, indeed surprising herself out of a shallow dream, then waded back in, smiling a little into her starched, lacy, color-coordinated pillow.

14. Living Room

Gestures of Kindness

"DO YOU WANT ANY HELP WITH THE REST?" her mother asked without moving from the armchair.

"No, thanks. It's embedded in my muscle memory by now."

As her mother turned back to the window, she chose the largest parcel from the remaining pile, ripped off the schoolgirl bows and elaborate cherub-print wrapping, and from beneath it produced a hefty cardboard box, which she proceeded to carve open with a knife and from which she then extracted, like a magician from a hat, never-ending swirls of thick packing paper followed by another box, smaller but still substantial, filled with careful wisps of lavender tissue inside which she could already feel something solid, something metal.

She fumbled for a purchase, pulled, and screamed.

"Please, please keep your voice down," her mother said in an exasperated undertone.

She glanced at the closed door to the bedroom. "Sorry, I keep forgetting," she whispered. "But shouldn't we wake him up already? It's almost time to eat."

"Did I hear a scream?" Paul popped his head in from the kitchen. "What is it now?"

"Bookends. Or maybe doorstops." She held out a pair of weighty birds, one in each hand, grasping them by their long tails like hammers. "Unless they are weapons of marital discord. Or idols for the altar of Hera?" She consulted a floral card twined around one of the sturdy necks. "Why would your great-aunt Hazel send us two iron peacocks?"

"Pewter pheasants," he said patiently. "They are centerpieces. For the dining table."

"Ah," she said. "You mean, like those glass grapes."

"Yes."

"And the porcelain rabbits."

"Yes."

"And the fake apples."

"Honey, we don't have to use any of it. Just put everything back in the boxes and stick them in the closet. I told you we should have had the registry. People have their own ideas of decorating."

"Yes," she said. "I see that now, but why——"

"Your parents' farewell dinner is about to burn," he said, ducking back into the kitchen.

She set the pheasants down on the overflowing table, next to the jeweled candle extinguisher, the ivory saltshaker shaped like the Taj Mahal, and the set of four fantastically ornate picture frames whose kaleidoscopic lumps of flowers, insects, leaves, and fir cones symbolized the four seasons, and regarded everything with a sinking feeling.

"The butterfly plates are pretty," she said doubtfully. "Perhaps you can take them back with you, Tanya might like them. Mama? Mama, are you listening?"

Her mother was still sitting in the armchair by the window, gazing out at the darkening autumnal street, her empty hands folded in her lap.

"Mama?"

"I'm sorry, I was thinking about home. What did you say?"

"Do you want to take any of these things back to Russia with you?"

They were speaking in hushed voices, to avoid waking her father.

"No, the suitcase is already packed. And you can certainly use them yourself. Give this room some personality. It looks like a hotel."

Paul's apartment had come fully furnished, its style contemporary and sparse, and while she had made tentative incursions into the bedroom (library books on the nightstand and pajamas shed on the bed) and the kitchen (half-drunk cups of tea in the sink and apple cores on the counter), the main room, whose glass dining table they never used and whose white leather sofa seemed too immaculate to sit on, retained the untouched sleek quality of a photograph in an interior design magazine.

"But these are all so . . . so unnecessary," she said, and sighed, surveying the jumble of opened and unopened boxes. "All this stuff."

She understood, of course, that underneath their patina of time and museum veneration, an ancient Egyptian spoon in the shape of a girl was still only a spoon and a Greek amphora in all its laconic glory of heroes and beasts only a vessel for oil; yet she sensed that somewhere in the amorphously defined sphere of applied arts, a thin but clear line was drawn between art and domesticity, between beauty and material ostentation—and once the line was crossed, clutter took over. She wondered how all these trifles would appear to someone far in the future. Would her distant descendants be puzzled as to the purpose of the pheasants and the grapes, would they invent their own, wildly inaccurate, explanations that would be accepted as archaeological verities by people who no longer ate at tables and thus required no centerpieces? In fact, it might be interesting to do a series of short poems, each one describing a simple common object in terms both precise and dense with its inherent mystery, with its material randomness. The titles would offer the only clues to the subjects—lines like "A child's face floating upside down in its silver convexity" under the succinct heading "Cereal Spoon"—

Her mother had come up to the table behind her.

"You aren't doing this right," she said, sighing in turn. Though she was nearing sixty, her face was still beautiful, but now it often looked opaque, like a mediocre portrait of itself, missing the light that had flared in the original with dazzling, if infrequent, intensity. "Wedding presents aren't *stuff*. They are wishes, gestures of kindness. All these people are aware of your existence, they've spared a thought for you, and that thought is now part of your home. It comforts me to think about it. About you not being alone. You seemed so lost before Paul. This is the first time I'm leaving you here with my heart at rest."

Her own heart seized with a familiar, worn-out ache.

"I wish you didn't have to leave at all," she said.

"Please, we've talked about it enough, I think." Her mother turned to glance at the closed bedroom door. "Our life is there, you know that."

There seemed to be nothing to say after that. For a silent minute, they listened to the practiced clatter of pots in the kitchen. The place was rich with smells of roasted potatoes, caramelized onions, rosemary, sugar, cream—a nearing feast.

"Shouldn't we wake Papa up?" she said at last. "He asked us to. It's past seven."

"No, let him sleep until dinner, our flight is so early tomorrow . . . Here, why don't I give you a hand with these."

Together they sliced the remaining boxes open, unearthed more crystal, silver, and porcelain, some of it beautiful, some of it ugly, none of it matching. At the bottom of the pile she discovered a flat white parcel barely larger than a pack of cards, three burgundy-colored stamps with Notre Dame in the upper right corner. She stared at the words "Mrs. Paul Caldwell" written in a shockingly familiar handwriting. There was no return address. "Well, that appears to be everything," her mother said, and busied herself with gathering up the torn cardboard and crumpled paper. She held on to the parcel's mystery for one moment longer, not touching it, listening to the whoosh of blood in her ears, then ripped the wrapping off.

Inside she found a small, prim card of thick cream-colored

paper, typed this time, which contained only a terse "Congratulations" in its precise center, and a kit of magnetic poetry— "Original Edition"—the kind one stuck on one's refrigerator.

There was nothing else.

"So, what are your plans, then?" her mother said, her tone insistent, as if this was not the first time she had asked the question.

"Plans?" she echoed flatly. Through the clear plastic of the lid she could see the rectangles of several words—"scream," "how," "you"—and an orphaned "ly."

"Yes, plans. Have you two given any thought to children?"

She flushed with an indeterminate feeling—anger mixed with startling bitterness, and something else underneath, something very different. Jerking open the nearest drawer, she shoved the box with the insidious little words deep, deep into the sideboard's prosperous recesses agleam with an earlier crop of useless treasures, and swung around to face her mother.

I don't ever intend to have children, she wanted to say, fiercely. I will not live a life of platitudes, I will not sink into the plush swamp of a comfortable marriage. I will always walk the harder path. Mine will be a life free of the commonplace and drudgery, full of travel and thought, unstinted in feeling and experience— an artist's life, do you hear me? But there was a look disturbingly like supplication in her mother's eyes, so instead she said, her voice taut with suppressed emotion, "Mama, I'm twenty-six years old. We got back from our honeymoon three days ago. There is plenty of time for that later."

Paul appeared on the kitchen threshold.

"Almost ready," he announced. "Maybe you should wake the

professor. And we should eat properly this time, at the dining table, don't you think? Although . . . uh . . ."

He looked at the absurdly cluttered table.

"It's all right," she said, picking up the pheasants. Anger still had not loosened its hold on her throat, and she would not look at either Paul or her mother. "It won't take too long to clear this off." Paul nodded and vanished into the aromatic cloud that hung over the kitchen. "Mama, why don't you go and wake him up while I pack everything away—"

"Let's use it," her mother said.

"What?"

"All these things. The dessert china. The tea set. The champagne flutes. The deer and the peacocks. Let's use them."

"Pheasants," she corrected mechanically. "Why would we do that?"

"Did I ever tell you about my collection of old postcards? They were my grandmother's. My father gave them to me after her death. I was eight or nine. My grandmother had kept them stored in a striped pink-and-white hatbox, and there were theater programs and dried flowers in there as well."

As she talked, she began to push the many-colored glasses of sundry shapes and sizes and the plates, no three alike, into incongruously mismatched islands amidst the cornucopia of gilded fruit, arranging them on embroidered placemats and silver chargers.

"When I opened the hatbox for the first time and saw what was inside, I was enchanted. There were postcards of castles and moonlit lakes and girls in elegant dresses. The pictures themselves were black-and-white, but the girls' lips, cheeks, and parasols were rouged red by hand. I had never seen anything like it, and it just took my breath away. But I was a secret hoarder. I didn't want to squander my enjoyment on just any ordinary day, so I didn't allow myself to look at anything properly, I just piled it all back into the hatbox, shut the lid, and hid it under my bed. For weeks afterward I went about, pretending nothing was there, all swollen with my secret. And every single day I was just dying to get the box out and pore over my treasure, to look at the beautiful girls, but I didn't let myself. I thought I had plenty of time, so I would choose a perfect moment, make it a special occasion. My birthday, perhaps, or maybe New Year's."

She watched her mother in silence, without stopping her, without helping her. A chill was starting to creep up her spine. Her mother's face had hardened into an unfamiliar expression of grim determination, and her movements as she darted about the table, sorting, shifting, rearranging, grew faster and faster.

"Then one day, when I was at school, my father's new wife cleaned my room. She found a pile of old junk under the bed, and she threw it all out. So you see, I didn't have any time, as it turned out. When you put something off to do later, it just doesn't get done, not in the same way. Because there never is any time, there never is any later . . . There, all finished. Where do you keep your matches? I want to light these now."

She stared from her mother to the table, groaning under its mad glittering, gleaming, sparkling weight, and back to her mother.

Her heart was beating slow and hard.

"Mama," she said. "Has something happened?"

"Five minutes!" Paul trumpeted from the kitchen.

"We really should wake him up now," her mother said.

Together they looked at the closed door of the bedroom. The candle flames bent left, bent right in an invisible breeze. The certainty of an imminent disaster hollowed out her insides. She said, "Something is wrong."

"Yes." Her mother stood still, her hands hanging loose by her sides, as though depleted all at once of her frenzied energy. "Don't tell him I told you, not yet, I want tonight to be . . . to be like before. I promised him I wouldn't tell you at all, and I didn't, not before the wedding anyway, I didn't want to ruin it for you. But it's time now, I think. Papa is sick. Really sick. It's cancer, and not the kind they can . . . That is, they don't know how long . . . Well. All I wanted to tell you is, if you want Papa to see your children, you should start having them now."

"And dinner is served!" Paul announced, carrying in a steaming tureen. "Wow, look at all that, it's like the cave of Ali Baba! . . . Hey, shouldn't you wake your dad now?"

"I'm awake, I've been awake," her father said, entering the room. "I've just been resting a little."

She heard him shuffling as he walked, but that was only because of Paul's slippers, of course: they were much too big for him, weren't they, and his own had been packed away already. She could not bring herself to look into his face at first. When she did, she saw what had escaped her in the fuss of the preceding days. He seemed much older than his sixty-eight years, and his skin had a grayish cast, and his eyelids were shadowed by exhaustion, and his mouth was thin and hard. Sorrow washed over her because she knew that she would never again be able to recall his face from before, the way it had been, that he was somehow already lost to her—and then he noticed the outrageous, clashing abundance of the table and laughed, laughed in just that contagious way in which he used to laugh when she was a child, slapping his knee with his hand, his face starting into life with a myriad of wrinkles, his eyes dark with a disarming, childish mirth; and she went all quiet inside.

The four of them sat in the festive light of a dozen candles, amidst the pewter Thanksgiving pheasants and the bronze Christmas deer and the porcelain Easter rabbits and the glass grapes, and lifted mismatched champagne flutes in a toast to the new couple's happiness. The bubbles fizzed on her tongue, tasting of innocence and loss.

"Please, may you pass salt," said her mother to Paul, exhausting her English.

"Don't offend now, but this Taj Mahal thing? Is ugly," said her father, laughing again.

Why, she thought, why hadn't they told her before the wedding? She would not have gone through with it but would have returned home instead, would have added no more days to the careless tally of years she had already missed in her father's life. But it was too late now, and there was only one way left to hold at bay the numbing grief that was spreading through her like a slow, viscous spill.

Gods, my gods, sometimes the harder path is the opposite of what it seems.

15. Bedroom

Conversation in the Dark at the Age of Twenty-seven

"ARE YOU ASLEEP?"

"No. Well, maybe. I guess I am. Is something wrong?"

"I just can't sleep. I've been lying here thinking."

"About?"

"Not anything in particular. Just things. Did I ever tell you about this seminar I went to in my first month in America?"

"Yes. Possibly. No."

"I don't remember now what the subject was, but it was one of those workshops where everyone sat in a circle, and the professor had us write down our 'strengths,' what we were really good at, you know, on a piece of paper, and then we went around the circle, and everyone read what they'd written. It's the usual stuff, right, everyone has done it dozens of time, in interviews, and class discussions, and church meetings, everyone here always talks about their strongest points, their weakest points, and the answers are all a given—'I'm creative,' 'I excel at multitasking,' 'I'm good with languages,' 'I'm a great team player.' Except that I had never done it before, so I had no ready pat formulas in my head. I remember sitting there for the first minute, absolutely mortified, not having any idea what to say. Then I thought about it, I mean really thought about it, and wrote this long, earnest paragraph. I wrote that I believed I could sometimes sense the essence of things—houses, books, faces, moments in time—that I sometimes caught a whiff of their innermost souls, their unique smells, and that what I was hoping to do with my life was to render these impressions in words so vivid, so precise, that others could feel them too. Then the five minutes were up, and we started going around the circle, and all the long-haired boys said they were creative and all the foreign-exchange girls said they were good with languages. By the time my turn came—it was toward the end—I had caught on perfectly, so I too said I was good with languages. I remember feeling so relieved that I had not been the first one to give my answer . . . But I wonder now . . . It's like life, you know: the more you learn what is expected of you, the more you fall into these patterns, these grooves, these ruts, the less unique your experiences become, the less unique you become yourself. If you didn't know, for example, that people got married at a certain age and had children at a certain age and retired at a certain age, would you know to do any of those things, or would you do something else, something entirely different? Because it can't all be pure biology. I mean, I know you pride yourself on believing only the things you can see, and I love that about you, it's so reassuring, but—but don't you have this sense sometimes that our life is essentially just the tip of the iceberg, and if you stop clinging to your puny bit of ice in fear or out of habit and just dive into the water, you will discover this luminous mass going down, deep down, and meet creatures you can't even imagine, and have thoughts and feelings no one has ever had before . . . That is really why I came here in the first place, and why I stayed here, you know. I mean, I told you I stayed because of that relationship I was in at the time, and that was part of it, I suppose, but mainly, I knew what was expected of me in Russia, and I thought that here I would be able to escape it, escape having a predictable life . . . Well, that, and the language, of course. Because languages are like that too, you know? When you are first learning a language, you are swimming in this glorious sea of possibilities—you feel that you are free to take all these little specks of meaning floating around you and combine them into the most fantastical, gorgeous, dreamlike structures that will be yours and no one else's, amazing castles, cathedrals, entire cities of words rising out of chaos. But then you start learning the rules, the grammar, what goes with what, and then, worst of all, all these common expressions and mass-issued turns of phrase start impressing themselves onto your brain, so that when you say 'time,' you think 'valuable' and 'waste of' and 'waits for no man,' and when you say 'love,' you think 'star-crossed' and 'blind,' and when you say 'death,' you think 'kiss of' and 'bored to' and 'dead as a doornail'—and before you know it, your words have become these prayer beads strung together and worn-out through countless repetitions, and what original meaning there was is completely obscured . . . Perhaps the longer you use the language, the more in danger you are of becoming gray and trite and shallow, I thought, but if you learn a new language, you can start all over again. And I feel, I really do feel that there are these great big truths out there, or no, not truths, exactly, just these pure slabs of . . . of meaning, of feeling, these monumental things we contend with as humans—you know, love, death, beauty, God—and I thought, if I come to them clean and childlike and with my mind free of preconceptions, or else if I come to them using two roads at once, both the front door of my native language and the servant entrance of my adopted language—or is it the other way around, do you think?—in any case, maybe then I will actually stand a chance of stumbling upon some vast reservoir of poetry just waiting out there in the universe . . . Because I write poetry, you know. Whenever you see me scribbling and I tell you these are just thank-you notes or grocery lists, they aren't really. Well, you've probably figured it out for yourself by now, but I wanted to tell you anyway. I wanted to tell you for a long time, but I was being . . . superstitious about it. I guess I felt I needed to keep my poems secret from everyone until I was ready to share them with the whole world. And I'm still not ready to do that, but I've been thinking about something my mother said right after our wedding, and, well . . . I just wanted to tell you. Because I feel happy, you know, happy about us, and the baby, of course, but I'm also scared about the baby, and so sad about Papa, and sometimes— and please don't be upset now—but sometimes I feel a little lonely, too, so I just thought, if I told you . . . Hello? Hello? Oh, gods, I'm talking to myself again, aren't I? Paul? Are you asleep?"

"What? No. Well, yes, I'm afraid I was. But I heard you saying something about a seminar and that you were good at languages . . . Oh, and did you say you wanted to name our son Mustard, or did I dream that?"

"Yes, actually, Mustard is an old family name on my father's side, so I think it would be nice . . . Ah, you should hear your silence right now. You dreamed that."

"Phew, I was worried for a moment there. I think I can stay awake now. Sort of. Do you want to try saying it again? Whatever it was you were saying?"

"It was nothing, really. Just go back to sleep."

"You should get some sleep too while you can. Only three more weeks now."

The First House

16. Covered veranda

17. Kitchen

20. Bedroom

19. Living room

18. Nursery

16. Covered Veranda

The Swing

WHEN THE SCREEN DOOR BANGED BEHIND THEM
and they entered the covered veranda, her initial impression was
of something narrow, gloomy, and tired.

It had appeared different the night before, when they had driven
along the street for the first time, the baby asleep in the backseat.
The sign "For Sale" had flashed in their headlights, and beyond it,
they saw three arches aglow in the dark. The house itself was barely
visible behind the trees, just a low bulky shape against the paler
blackness of the sky, but the lights on the veranda made it seem
cozy and warm. "Slow down, slow down!" she cried, but they had
already passed. He turned around, and they crept along the street
for the second time. It looked even more welcoming then, that yellow light glowing through November drizzle.

At the end of the block they realized that another car had been
forced to a crawl behind them for an entire minute.

"They didn't honk, imagine that," Paul had said. "Looks like a nice neighborhood. Probably kid-friendly. Honey, I have a good feeling about this one."

"Yes," she had said; but what she had liked most about the invisible house with the shining arches was its ambiguous promise, the darkness concealing it. It did not belong to any neighborhood at all, was not pinned down to an address somewhere in the monotonous suburbs of a busy American city, but instead was all shadows and light, and one could just as easily imagine it perched on the side of a lush Caribbean mountain, frangipani trees blooming, ice clinking in the jewel-colored cocktails of a festive crowd on a terrace suspended above the immense mystery of the moonlit sea—or maybe squatting in the deep slumber of a somber medieval village in Portugal or France, all the villagers long asleep, only a solitary poet rocking back and forth on the lit-up porch, his verses slowly adopting the creaking rhythm of the rocker—or even poised as the last human habitation on the edge of a great Siberian forest, yes, a mossy little house out of some old fairy tale, where evening after evening a small, soft-spoken family gathered in the snug seclusion of light to drink tea from chipped cups and talk about birds and stars and books—a house under a timeless spell where everyone was together, and no one was ill, and everyone was happy . . .

"What we could do," Paul had said, "is put a swing on that porch."

"If we bought the house," she had said.

"If we bought the house."

Now they stood on the damp, starkly lit veranda, and the

realtor woman jingled the keys again—it seemed to be a nervous habit of hers, almost a tic—and said, "It's not heated, but you can think of it as a sunroom really, it would be perfect for breakfasts in warm weather." The enthusiastic lilt in her voice did not match her eyes, which had a dull, bulging look to them, like thick bottle glass. She waved toward the shadowy corner, where three low wicker chairs with enormous pink peonies on the cushions crouched around a lopsided wicker table. "Now, the furniture doesn't come with it, of course, it's just to give you an idea, but do try it out, try it out!"

"No, that's all right, thank you," Paul said, ready, she saw, to proceed into the house; but her arms were aching from trying to restrain the squirming, sniffling bundle of blankets, so she walked over to the table and sat down. The cushions proved unpleasantly soft, and as she sank into them, further weighted down by the baby, a faint but visible cloud of dust billowed around her—either the house was not shown very often, or no one before her had ever followed the realtor's invitation to sit down.

The baby stopped whimpering and began to wail.

"He is adorable!" the realtor woman shouted, to make herself heard over the cries. "What's his name?"

She was struggling to quiet him, so it was Paul who replied: "Eugene."

"A beautiful name!" exclaimed the woman. "So uncommon."

"It's her father's name," Paul said, his voice reserved. "Shall we see the rest of the house, then?"

"Yes, yes, of course, let me just find the right key . . . Do look at the doorbell chimes on your way in, they are a very nice feature, and of course fully functional, everything in the house is fully functional, here, I'll show you, such a distinctive sound—"

The inner door moaned on reluctantly yielding hinges. As the woman wedged it open, talking all the while, a long, mournful note that put her in mind of a departing train escaped onto the veranda, and a pale slash of autumnal light cut through the low-ceilinged murkiness beyond. She caught a whiff of stale, unused air. She had been excited by the thought of seeing the place, had felt important and capably adult in her role as a prospective buyer; she had even worn her teardrop diamond earrings and her new black shoes, whether to impress the realtor or to enter her potential house in a fashion befitting a young woman eager to take the next step in the upward progression of her life.

Now she found she did not want to go in.

"Please go ahead without me," she called. "I'll stay out here a bit longer, get the baby to sleep."

The two of them paused on the threshold, looking down at her, the realtor woman smiling glassily and jingling the keys, Paul's expression bemused. Then they vanished inside; Paul, she noticed, ducked his head as a precaution.

The door crept closed behind them.

The baby was still crying, though with less desperation now. She wound the blankets tighter around him—the veranda was chilly, with a deep, dungeonlike chill—and stared outside. The street lay empty in both directions; the trees that lined it were bare of leaves; on the other side, identical one-story houses with darkened verandas sat in the puddles of graying lawns under graying skies. She could see no signs of life. Perhaps everyone had gone to church—wasn't that what people did on Sunday mornings, especially in kid-friendly places where neighbors did not honk at neighbors?

"Bun-ga-low," she said under her breath, trying out the new word. It sounded strange, almost barbaric, to her ears, and for one disorienting moment, the unremarkable suburban vista looked as foreign to her eyes as a row of grass-thatched African huts with monkeys hopping from roof to roof; it was certainly just as far removed from the vague expectations of her childhood. All at once, an overwhelming sensation of randomness struck her— why this house, why this street, why this city? (Why this country, continued a dangerously soft voice inside her, why—but she managed to hush it up before it asked anything else.) And when one stopped to think about it, how odd, how unnatural, how daunting it was to go about choosing a *house*. She had never pondered the desirable number of bathrooms or the virtues of gas stoves before. She had never owned—had never wanted to own—anything that would not fit in a small suitcase. Now the notion of waking up one day the owner of a mind-bogglingly complex conglomeration of pipes, wires, masonry, and carpentry loomed over her in a vast shadow, almost as ambiguous, thrilling, inevitable, and terrifying as motherhood itself.

Anxiously she inspected the baby's face—she could not bring herself to call him Eugene yet. He had grown silent at last and was gazing past her with his pensive blueberry eyes. She pulled the blankets closer to his reddened nose, then looked again at the poisonous pink peonies on the dusty cushions. Something much like panic was starting to stir inside her. She reminded herself to breathe—the peonies did not come with the house, she would be free to get different cushions or have no cushions at all, just as she pleased. But the imminent prospect of all that empty space to furnish only made her breathing quicken. For a house was not like a student dorm room or a rented apartment: in time it became a reflection of one's being, a monolith under whose foundation one buried one's roots, a tinted lens through which one viewed the world. It set the mood, the timbre, the pitch of one's entire life, and for a poet, the pitch of her life would, as likely as not, vibrate through the pitch of her work. Would Byron have ever become Byron if he had resided in an elderly lady's fussy seaside flat with flowery chintz curtains and a pug for a pet? Could Pushkin have sung the Russian countryside with such fluid simplicity if his abode had been a brooding moorland ruin full of echoes, ghosts, and massive oak cupboards? Could Shakespeare have penned his immortal tragedies if he had chosen to live in a suburban bungalow with peonies on the cushions? At sixteen, she would have replied with a resounding "Yes," but at twenty-seven, she was no longer certain. (And wouldn't it be fun, said a voice that never was completely silenced inside her, to compose an "architectural" poem, each verse set in a dwelling, each written in the style most suited to the dwelling itself, from a Poe-inspired wail of woe and loss describing a dilapidated gothic mansion to a cheerful couplet akin to a Mother Goose rhyme sketching a cottage in a sunlit meadow? She brushed the irrelevant thought away.) And if it were indeed true that deciding on the kind of place you would inhabit meant deciding on the kind of atmosphere that would seep into your very blood and, by osmosis, the kind of poet you were bound to become, did she feel confident enough in her real estate acumen and her decorating skills not to fail her art?

Blankly she considered the dingy tiles of the veranda, the wet black trees across the road, the bleak symmetry of the lawns— and at last panic caught up with her and overtook her.

The baby had fallen asleep.

What if she just stood up right now, and walked away?

The door issued a moan, and the realtor woman stepped out.

"Your husband wanted me to check on you," she said, jingling the keys. "He's inspecting the closets. Ah, Eugene is resting nicely. He feels at home here, I see."

She looked at the realtor mutely.

"Eugene is such a lovely name." The woman dropped into the chair next to hers, raising another, thicker cloud of dust. "So distinctive. Personally, I've always been interested in his namesake Eugene of Savoy, the famous Hapsburg general, you know. But of course, there is a bit of a family connection there: my father is a direct descendant of the Hapsburgs, you know, and—"

The door moaned. Paul emerged, remembering to duck his head.

"It's great," he announced with gusto. "We'll take it."

The realtor, flustered, tried to clamber out of the chair.

"I'm joking," he said. The woman giggled warily, and sank back down. "I'm going to whisk my wife away on a tour now, if you don't mind."

"Go ahead, go ahead. I'll stay here, give you some privacy."

Paul held the inner door open. She rose, staggering a little under the baby's bulk.

Just before going inside, she stopped.

"Paul," she said, and smiled up at him to make it almost resemble a joke. "Do we even need a house?"

He laughed a short belly laugh, appreciative of her sense of humor.

"If we buy it, we'll put the swing right here," he said, pointing, and gently prodded her over the threshold.

17. Kitchen

The Only Poem Written in Her Twenty-eighth Year

BY NOW, THE RITUAL HAD BECOME SO FAMILIAR that she kept the overhead lamp off, going through the motions in an automatic haze. At four in the morning, the kitchen looked as if underwater, the cabinets and counters lost in shadows, her progress illuminated by a succession of feeble bluish lights: the subterranean glare of the refrigerator as she squinted into its poorly stocked depths in search of the bottle, the dim oven glow flooding the pans as she pushed them aside to reach the smallest pot, the purple flickering of gas turned down low as she put the pot on the stove.

As she waited for the milk to warm up, she leaned against the counter, swaying slightly. She was never fully awake these days (these weeks, these months), her reality blurring at the edges. She was never fully asleep either, her dreams only a baby's whimper deep. She recalled The Cycle of Exhaustion she had written at nineteen—nearly a decade before—and choked on a sob of a laugh. The college all-nighters had possessed a bold hussar quality, a youthful devil-may-care flair, and their feel had been hard, light, and vivid in her triumphant, springing step. This sleeplessness was a wet, heavy weight, relentless and inescapable, creeping into her bones, turning the world gray, the urge to weep ever close to the surface. It filled her with an absolute despair—and, at the same time, a kind of sweet relief: it was good to give up worrying about achievements for a spell and let the weakness of her body take over—good to surrender to the inevitability of her temporary escape from destiny.

She was going to do this only once, after all.

Pale moonlight slanted through the narrow window; she could see a thin dusting of snow on the ground. She stirred the milk in the pot. Her feet were cold on the tiles. In the bedroom across the hall, her husband snored in a steady, energetic rhythm, and the baby—almost six months old now—made a meowing noise, a precursor to a bout of crying. On an impulse so vague it felt like the prompting of a dream rather than a conscious action, she bent to pull out the bottom drawer near the stove, sifted through a pile of partially unopened mail—advertisements, telephone bills, takeout menus—that nowadays seemed to drift through the house in unabated flocks, sprouting colonies in chance nooks and crannies. Underneath the envelopes lay a flat box scarcely larger than a pack of playing cards. She took it out. Plastic still clung around it, so she sliced through it with a knife, and lifted the lid.

Tiny bugs of words leapt out and ran all over the counter. She trapped them with both palms, scooped them up in handfuls, pinned their slippery, wiggly little bodies to the door of the fridge, then played with them sleepily, sliding them about, almost at random, in the quivering of the gas flame, in the blue glimmer of the winter moon, until the words began to draw together into lines and she saw that she was making a poem of sorts, except it was like composing on the other side of the looking glass, composing backward—not the usual hum solidifying into sounds, the misty glow of meaning slowly growing more defined, until it sharpened into disparate words, but instead, timid sense trying to sneak its way into the cracks between the silly words already there.

Also, she could barely read the letters in the dark.

Feeling comforted somehow, she stood pushing the half-invisible magnets to the left, to the right, stirring the milk, nodding off now and then, until it seemed like some memory from long before, the familiar excitement in her fingertips, the baby whimpering, the kitchen floating underwater, the cold in her feet, the baby crying, the swell and fall of the snores, the baby wailing . . . Waking with a start, she abandoned whatever dream she had been pursuing, rushed to test the temperature of the milk with her little finger, quickly poured it into the bottle, and hurried out to feed him; but at seven that morning, when she entered the kitchen with the baby sniveling in her arms, she discovered Paul standing before the fridge, a half-emptied glass of orange juice in his hand, his head tilted. The poem she did not remember writing snaked in wobbly, uneven lines through a widely dispersed cloud of unused adjectives and verbs.

"When did we get this?" he said, motioning with his chin. "My sophomore roommate had one of these. I didn't know you wrote poetry, ha-ha!" He declaimed in a loud, exaggerated manner, grandly waving his free hand in the air:

"My cook is a drunk and my eggs are bitter
my driver is a dreamer and we always go so fast
my friend is a player and I cry all day
I have a crush on the boy
who waters the roses
he has bare pink feet
and a lovely behind
I live in the sea—"

The poem stopped abruptly.

"I would feel threatened if we had a garden," Paul said, smiling, and finished the juice in one gulp. When he lowered the glass, there was an orange mustache above his upper lip.

"I think I was asleep," she said.

"My turn." He swept her lines aside, and as her five dozen words merged with the remaining two hundred, her small creation dissolved without a trace. Pushing the magnets off to the very edges of the door, he selected just three or four—she could not see which ones behind the broad expanse of his back—and arranged them in the middle of the empty space before stepping away. "Ta-da!"

I love my honey, read the magnets.

She moved to hug him, but the baby in her arms started to cry, so, aborting the effort, she settled him in the high chair and went to get more milk. When she slammed the fridge door closed, a bit too firmly perhaps, a couple of words were dislodged and plopped down to the floor. She glared at them, bleary-eyed, light-headed with sleeplessness, then began to flick all the magnets off one by one. An unpleasant image of roadkill being scraped off the pavement came to her out of nowhere.

"What are you doing?" he asked.

"I'm going to put them back in their box."

"Maybe you should leave them. They seem like fun."

"We have enough clutter as it is, I think," she said in a level voice.

The baby, now full, cooed happily. She looked over at him, and her heart, which had been momentarily unsettled, came to rest in its rightful place.

18. Nursery

The Mushroom Hunt

THE NURSERY WAS A CHEERFUL ROOM; SHE HAD painted it herself. The walls were lime green on one side and emerald green on the other, the ceiling light blue, and the windowpanes and baseboards azure. All across the green of the walls she had drawn yellow flowers with neat round petals, while the ceiling was peppered with plastic stars that glowed in the dark. When her parents had walked into the nursery for the first time, her mother had been volubly enchanted, but her father had seemed not to notice it at all—the only thing in the room he had noticed was Genie himself.

He sat in the armchair in the corner now, small and sullen, like a ruffled bird in winter. "Isn't it time for the boy to wake up?" he asked again.

He always called Genie "the boy," whereas her mother called him Zhenechka.

She glanced at the crib, then at the minute hand of the smiling moon on the wall.

"No," she said, "not yet."

He pursed his lips and resumed gazing outside with a vague frown, and immediately she felt guilty; next time he asked, she would have to wake Genie up. In his presence her father's face became like a stained-glass window with the sun shining through. At all other times, though, a new sour look lodged itself in his eyes, in the deep crease between his eyebrows, in the lines tugging his mouth down into his beard. Whenever she glanced up at him from folding shirts or tidying toys, a sweaty hand took hold of her heart and dragged it sideways.

"So what's beyond this street?" he asked.

"Another street just like this one," she replied.

"And beyond that?"

"Two more streets like this, and then a highway. There is a grocery store on the other side of the highway, but it takes a while to cross with a stroller."

"You must get a car," he said, sounding displeased. "It's impossible here without a car. You should learn how to drive. You never leave the house. The boy is pale."

She started to explain about taking him out on the veranda for his daily allotment of fresh air, and about not having needed a car before they had moved here, and Paul working on weekends and never having the time to teach her, and, in any case, her not wanting to practice with a child in the backseat; but halfway through her apologetic mumbling, her father made a short, annoyed sound deep in his throat, and she fell silent. He resumed looking out the window, his face closed off. All at once she wanted to abandon the trivial, fussing tasks and the insignificant small talk on which she was squandering what little was left of their time together—she wanted to sit at his feet instead, prop her chin on his knee, stare up at him, and ask him things, the way she had done when she was a little girl. Back then she had tried to pry the mysteries of the universe out of him—"Why is the sky so black?" and "Does it hurt your shadow when you step on it?" and "Why does this song always make Mama cry?"

She had just as many questions now, though the questions had changed in nature.

Mama tells me your treatments are going well, are helping you—is that true? How much longer do you really have—how much longer do we have together? Is there enough time for me to prove myself to you? Whenever I see the way you look at Genie, I thaw inside, but I am also hurt: it's like I have done my part and no longer matter as much. Are you disappointed in me, are you hoping that he will turn out to be more like you? Do you *need* someone to be like you, to preserve some echo of your life? The meaning of life as you explained it to me that one time, at the dacha, under the stars—do you still hold that to be true, and do you fear that you have not done enough, that after all the decades of unsparing work, your life has not succeeded on its own, not fully, so you want the reassurance of seeing a piece of yourself carried forth by future generations?

Are you afraid of dying?

Do you believe in the afterlife?

Do you believe in God?

Listen, Papa: I love you. I will give you more, so much more, than a grandchild. I will keep your memory alive to the outermost limits of my soul. I will write a long poem about you when I'm finally good enough as a poet to write it. That should count for something, should it not? I love you.

She went on folding Genie's tiny shirts in silence, and her father went on sitting in the armchair, staring out the window with a deepened frown, and in another few minutes Genie woke up from his afternoon nap. He always woke up happy and alert, often rolling some recently learned word around in his mouth—"cup," "fish"—like a delicious treat, tasting its novel sound with a surprised, pleased look on his small pink face (not pale, not pale at all, she took good care of him). Now, within seconds of opening his eyes, he bounced up, held on to the crib's railing, and rattled it, eager to get out, eager for whatever wondrous adventures his grandfather had prepared for him that day.

Genie was blond and blue-eyed, and looked nothing like his grandfather—or, for that matter, nothing like her either.

"Today," her father announced, beaming, as he groped for his cane, "I will teach you to hunt mushrooms. Repeat after me: *grib*. Try again. *Grib*. Now, real mushrooms grow in a forest, of course, I will take you there when you are a bit older and come to visit me at our dacha in Russia. For now, these buttons will have to do. The white ones are the best, *belye griby*, we call them, and the red ones—"

She wanted to intercede: the buttons did not seem safe, Genie was not yet two, he put things in his mouth, he could choke; but she looked at her father and stayed silent, just watched them hawk-eyed for the next ten minutes, while they traipsed all over the rug, Genie wobbling a little, her father's cane tapping as he limped up and down, both crowing with excitement when they stumbled upon yet another button; and every time, her father admonished the boy to clean the stem thoroughly of leaves and dirt before they gently lowered the button into their imaginary basket.

In the suburban American room with the painted grass, painted sky, painted flowers, she remembered the smells and the sounds of the Russian woods she had walked with her father two decades before. Once, they had brought home a baby owlet, and another time had come upon a small dead fox curled up in a snowy hollow by a fallen oak. There had been that misty autumn morning, barely past sunrise, when a moose had rushed at them out of a thicket; it had been so close she could see the moist, agitated flaring of its nostrils. A quote she read somewhere came to her mind: "A poem begins as a lump in the throat, a homesickness or a lovesickness"—or something like it. And would it also be true, she wondered, that the bigger the lump—say, if you happen to have both sicknesses at once—the better the poem?

Her mother appeared in the hallway, seemingly shrunk in Paul's kitchen apron.

"Zhenechka should have a snack now," she said, but she too paused to watch them play. Genie had just spotted a button that had rolled all the way under his crib, and was gurgling, then screaming, with laughter. Her father began to laugh too, until it looked as if he was crying.

"The main regret I have in life," her mother spoke from the

doorway, "is that your father and I didn't have another child. A child growing up alone doesn't learn to think about others as much, and if you stay in your head all the time, talking to imaginary friends and not noticing other people, it's harder for you to be happy in life later on."

Her breath went out of her; she was winded with the sense of injustice. I notice other people, she wanted to shout, but aloud she just said, "*I* am happy."

Her mother did not seem to hear her. "The best age difference between siblings," she went on evenly, "is one or two years, no more than three. Then they are friends growing up, and when the older generation . . . that is . . ." She stumbled, continued in haste, "I mean they will always have each other, no matter what." Her unspoken words hung heavy in the air of the cheerful blue-and-green nursery. "And if you had a girl, think how joyful it would make your father to spoil her . . . Come now, Zhenechka, let's have some of Nana's apple pie."

Wildly she turned to her father, hoping that he would shrug her mother's words away, that he would say something, at least. But he said nothing at all, just stood looking after the boy, the laughter leaking out of his face until only the traces of tears remained, and the hunger in his eyes made her lower her own.

That night, after everyone else in the house was asleep—her parents in the bedroom, relinquished to them for the duration of their visit, Paul stuffed into the Procrustean snugness of the living room couch, Eugene the younger in his crib, clutching his toy hedgehog that looked like a bear, or else a bear that looked like a hedgehog, a present from Eugene the elder—she lay awake on the unfolded nursery chair, listening to her son's even breathing. She knew that her mother was wrong, that this could not possibly be all there was, this measured, resigned wisdom of one generation succeeding another, this somnolent song of biological fulfillment in her blood; for her childhood premonitions of the darkly dazzling mysteries that underlay her existence, the dreamtime glimpses of magic that felt so terribly real, the light-headed hum of inspiration that still coursed through her veins now and then—all these things filled her with a sharp, if fleeting, sense of immeasurable depths beneath the thin veneer of her temporary suburban masquerade. Just a corner, just an instant, just a poem away lay an unimaginably rich world where gods walked alongside the chosen few; and if you ever won your way there, your reward was meaning conferred upon your daily labors and travails by the promise of immortality, by the clarity of secret luminescence.

In her first decade of life, she had understood, albeit dimly and without reasoning, that a certain kind of inner fire was required if you were ever to see the things no one else saw. In her second decade, she had learned that work and daring were necessary also, and in her third, she had added experience—of pain and joy both—to the list. But was she discovering, on the cusp of her fourth decade, that selfishness too was an essential part of this celestial equation? In the end, when all accounts were totaled, did you become great only by disregarding the happiness of those around you—was the mark of a true genius his perfect solitude, his absolute inability to consider anything beyond his art?

If so, she would have to postpone seeking entry into heaven, for she had other, human, equations to balance first.

So listen, you up there, she thought as she lay stretched on the uncomfortable chair in her boy's room, staring at the ceiling. If anyone is up there to hear me, and if my voice is in any way special, if I have earned my right to trickle a few words into your ear, I will make a bargain with you. I will give up my life for a while longer in exchange for my father's life. I will do my best to make him happy, I will have another child—a girl, please, if you will be so kind to note my special request—I will even give up all thought of poetry while he lives, I swear—just please make him live, make him live—

And in another, rational, adult part of herself, she knew, of course, that she was being melodramatic and laughable, that she was addressing no one—that she had no power to bargain with the gods, that there were no gods—and still she lay in the dark of the nursery, whispering fiercely. On the ceiling above her, the greenish toy stars glowed with their pale plastic light. For a while they trembled hazily, as her eyes kept spilling over with tears; then, after some time, their stored phosphorescence began to fade away; and still she stared at them, at their pale outlines, at the places where they had been, for a long sleepless stretch, mouthing promises—and unlike the magnificent stars of her childhood, these stars did make her feel small.

19. Living Room

The Call

WHEN THEY FIRST MOVED IN, THE LIVING ROOM had been her least favorite place in the house. It gave her the impression of some cramped, low-ceilinged cell, like a cabin on a nighttime ship; its windows led onto the covered veranda and stayed dim even in the brightest sunlight, and the sour smell of the previous inhabitants' feet seemed embedded in its darkened floors. She used to pass through it quickly, feeling an odd constriction in her chest, as though she were unable to take proper breaths. But as the space gradually filled with sofas, tables, and armchairs, her distaste for it just as gradually lessened, until, in their third year in the house, she found herself retreating here more and more often; the mouse-colored, well-heated room soothed her parental frustrations and domestic anxieties, made her feel grounded and calm at the end of another long day.

She had just sung Genie to sleep when she came into the living room that evening, looking forward to the ease of sofa blankets and a cup of herbal tea. A chilly draft leapt past her, ruffling the pages of the magazine in her hands—one of the windows had been cracked open, she saw, and April was trying to dance its way inside. As a rule, spring in their city lasted two or three weeks only—a cool, green breeze that swooped on light wings one clear morning, sifting drifts of petals along downtown sidewalks, turning evenings long and crisp, before departing just as lightly when the inevitable heat set in. Its flight had always saddened her in the past, but now she suddenly wished for the harsh blast of summer; the wild spring smell unsettled her, awakening an odd, teary longing for nameless, distant, unfamiliar things. She shut the window with firmness and pulled the heavy drapes closed, then, sinking into the pillows of the couch, switched on the lamp that cast a circle of seemingly solid, brown-tinted light, rearranged her belly in her lap, and, after a short hesitation, reached for the telephone.

He answered on the second ring.

"Paul Caldwell."

"I was wondering," she said, "whether you might be coming home soon."

"Honey, you remember, I told you it would be a tough month. The proposal I'm writing—" She stopped listening. "Why, are you not feeling well? Is Eugene giving you trouble?"

"No, he's just fallen asleep, and I'm fine. It's just—" It's just that my father is in some hospital in Moscow, and my mother keeps telling me it's nothing, it's only for routine observation, but I don't know, the hospital has no direct line to the patients, so I can't speak to him myself, and there is something about my mother's voice I don't like, some tightness to it. I really should go over there, you know, but I can't leave for Russia right now, I can't even leave for a café or a library, because I'm seven months pregnant, prescribed rest by my doctor, trapped in the suburbs with a toddler and no car, and my husband hardly ever comes home. Oh, and I don't like to complain, but, since you ask, I will be thirty this summer, thirty, do you hear me, Lermontov was only twenty-six when he died, and Keats even younger, and Rimbaud had written all his poems by the age of twenty, and by the time Pushkin was my age, *Eugene Onegin* had all its best chapters, and I— I've written nothing for so long—

Her bitter mood took her by surprise. She closed her eyes briefly. It's only the spring, she thought, people often feel unmoored in the spring.

"Honey, the sooner I wrap this up," he said, "the sooner I'll be home. I have some news—well, potential news, anyway. This proposal, it may turn out to be important—"

She stopped listening again. After he hung up, she frowned at the unopened home decorating magazine, then picked up the address book she kept by the telephone, flipped through the pages, punched in Lisa's number. Remote ringing went on for a while before ending in a recording; she left a message, though without much hope, and leafed through the address book to another letter, and tried a new number. Maria was running late for an audition, and Stacy had a deadline, some paper due for her graduate seminar; she did not pay much attention to their explanations. After two or three more attempts, she was out of friends to bother. There was always Olga, of course, but Olga was invariably busy, and she was loath to interrupt yet another fascinating chapter in the ongoing novel that was Olga's life: she was either packing for a trip to Venice with her boyfriend of the month or rushing to a holiday reception at her New York law firm—or to a symphony—or a museum . . . Time and time again, as she tried and failed to force her own life into a narrative of any kind, she understood how dreadfully ordinary and drab she must appear next to the brightly plumed companion of her childhood; yet after Olga's self-assured voice faded away from her mind, she would remind herself that Olga's kind of life was nothing but bubbles and baubles, transitory pleasures and illusory accomplishments, while hers was a quiet life of substance, wisdom, and reflection—a life close to the earth's immemorial springs and rich in universal human experience, which would serve as fertile soil for her future art.

All the same, she did not feel like thinking about Olga right now.

Setting the telephone down, she picked up a pencil and absently doodled in the address book, filling a page with daffodils and balloons and birds wearing hats, wondering whether Lisa might call her back after all. Abruptly the drapes at one of the windows swelled up, startling her; the brown-colored lair of the room came alive with a fresh, cool smell. She realized she had left another window open, but was too tired to stand up, so she continued moving the pencil, drawing circles and zigzags, breathing in the clean, wonderful, troubling smells of opening buds and rushing waters that wafted past her every now and then; and when she looked down at the page some time later, she discovered verses sneaking their way through the doodles.

On a round hill she sat
While the sky turned green
And the grass turned blue:
An absentminded evening
In a black bowler hat,
With a silver-headed cane,
Was walking through.
She was thinking.

Furtive odors of the world
Crawled out of wet holes,
And a frightened white bird
Would not stop screaming,
Not even when they freed
A fine pink balloon
So it cleaved to the ceiling
With its silk rope dangling
As the night swept in—
The land's toy moon.
She was thinking.

When she melted in the air,
On the damp blue hill
There lingered for an hour
A patch of trodden grass,

A bicycle wheel,
And a golden ring—
Lost, or discarded.

The baby kicked, and, uneasy, she pushed the address book away, then, reconsidering, reached for it again and tore the offending page out altogether. I'd better not meet anyone worth knowing whose name starts with G, she thought as she slipped the page into the pocket of her robe. She had always despised the notion of a poet as an inspired romantic pouring out his soul in unconscious, effortless trills; true poetry was hard work, hours and hours of mental acrobatics spent juggling sounds and walking the tightropes of meanings. This—this was not poetry at all, just scribbles and vapors, involuntary and unpremeditated like springtime birdsong.

She righted her belly, settled deeper into the halo of brown, steady light, picked up the telephone, dialed Paul's number.

"Paul Caldwell," said his voice, as always on the second ring.

"Do you ever leave your desk?" she asked (and one of these days I will really figure out what it is that he does all day long in his office, she promised herself with a familiar pinch of guilt, then, feeling wearied already, set the thought aside). "It's nine o'clock. I think I'll be going to sleep very shortly."

"I'm almost done," he said. "Another half an hour. If you stay up, I can—" A beep cut into his voice, then he resurfaced. ". . . and some ice cream . . ."

There was another beep.

"That's Lisa calling me back, I should go now," she cried. Of all her friends, Lisa alone had children, and complaining to someone who understood never failed to cheer her up. "Hello! Hello?"

The line crackled and clicked and stayed silent.

"Lisa? Is that you? Lisa? Hello?"

The silence had an odd quality to it: not the static void of a dead line but a wordless presence, it seemed to her, not quite of some-one breathing, but of someone there nonetheless, so she did not hang up for another few moments, herself silent as well now, lis-tening, listening intently, wondering at the sudden loosening of sadness coiled inside her, and the flush of warmth, of love, that seemed to surge through her entire being, listening still, until she imagined that she heard her name spoken—not aloud, but beneath the silence somehow, reaching her more as a thought—just her name, spoken once, through the silence, across the silence, in a familiar voice that sounded infinitely kind and had a smile in it.

"Papa?" she said uncertainly.

The telephone burst into irritated chirps in her hand; it must have been off the hook all along. She glanced at the clock, did quick math: it would be just past five in the morning in Moscow. Puzzled, she set it down, and waited, but it did not ring again, so she turned off the brown lamp and pulled her legs under the brown blanket, curling into the back of the brown couch. The baby shifted within her, and the echo of her name spread in ever fainter circles through her mind. She felt warm and at peace, comforted in some vast, serene knowledge that she was not alone, that she was loved. She was just dozing off—or perhaps she had fallen asleep already—when the telephone woke her.

She answered, her heart taking off in her throat.

On the other end of the line, her mother was crying.

"Mama?" she said. "Mama, is that you? Mama, speak to me! Mama, what happened?"

But she already knew.

20. Bedroom

Conversation in the Dark at the Age of Thirty

"PAUL, IT'S YOUR TURN TO GET UP."

"Mmm . . ."

"Do you hear me? She is crying. It's your turn."

"Mmm . . ."

"Paul? Paul! Oh, never mind . . . The floor is so cold, I need slippers—or maybe a rug, maybe we should buy a rug—"

"Did you say something, honey?"

"Yes, half an hour ago. She wanted her bottle."

"I slept through it again, did I? Sorry, you know how it is . . . Are you just now getting back into bed? What time is it?"

"A quarter past four."

"Your feet are like ice. All of a sudden I'm wide awake. Hey, I can warm you up if you like—"

"I need to get some sleep, Paul."

"You're not mad at me, are you? You can nap with the kids during the day, you know. *I* have to go to work in the morning."

"I'm not mad. I'm just exhausted. They don't nap at the same time. Genie hardly naps at all now. Can we go back to sleep, please?"

"All right, all right . . . Hey, are you still awake?"

"I am."

"Listen, I've been thinking. The other day in the city I saw this girl walking along the street, she was pushing a stroller and she had a greyhound on a leash. She was wearing a little round fur hat, and she looked beautiful. Not as beautiful as you, of course."

"So?"

"So maybe we should get a dog."

"What?"

"Don't laugh. A dog. You know. A pet? People have pets. The kids would love it."

"Honestly, I don't think it's such a good idea right now."

"Do you ever wonder if you resist any kind of change so much because of all that preconditioning in your Evil Empire childhood?"

"Look, I'm not saying we can't ever have a dog. Maybe when the kids get a bit older . . . It would have to be a very small dog, though. We don't have enough yard for a big dog."

"And that's another thing. This house has gotten too tight for us, I think . . . Hey, are you asleep?"

"No."

"You've been silent for a while. Did you hear what I said? I think we should move to a bigger house."

"Paul. We just bought *this* house. I'm only now beginning to get used to it."

"So if you aren't used to it yet, you won't miss it. I mean, it's nice enough, but it has only two bedrooms, Emma can't even have her own room. With her constant crying right next to us, it's impossible to get a good night's sleep."

"You seem to manage with no trouble."

"You know how it is . . . Anyway, about the house—"

"Paul, this house is *fine*."

"You thought my one-bedroom rental was fine too."

"And it was. People don't just hop about from place to place every couple of years."

"Actually, that's exactly what they do. Did you know that an average American moves eleven or twelve times in his life?"

"Really? How terrible for the average American! That's, what, something like sixty rooms the poor fellow has to furnish? The horrors of having to buy sixty rugs!"

"Probably more like forty—it includes dorm rooms and studios and poky little houses like ours. Which brings me back to my point. This house is too small for us."

"Oh Paul, I don't know. I just hate the idea of moving again. And again. And again."

"What if we skip the remaining seven or eight moves, and just move this one time? What if we find ourselves a perfect place that we don't ever have to leave again? Just think about it—living in your dream house."

My dream house . . . Each room a different texture, a different mood, a different poem, and at its heart, a creaking ladder sliding along floor-to-ceiling bookshelves in a timeless oak-paneled room that smells of leather and eternity; and floor-to-ceiling windows that glow nightly with a soft, thrilling life, the laughter of friends and the strands of music and the sonorousness of words imbibed in the still hours before sunrise; and doors that open daily onto the world—the mountains to the north, the jungles to the south, the swaying of tall grasses to the east, and to the west, the islands of the blessed. And you can leave the house at any moment, go out into the unknown with nothing but a half-packed bag swinging lightly in your hand and a half-finished poem in your heart, and when you come back, it will all be waiting for you still, welcoming and unchanged and endlessly surprising, a warm place full of art and love and starry vistas, the volume you were reading just before you left still open to your page by your favorite armchair, your never-grown children safely tucked into their beds, your mother the mermaid in her turret singing songs and braiding her emerald hair, your father the sage eternally at work on his antiquated typewriter behind the closed door, and no one gone, and no one dead, and everything always the same and always different and always joyful. A dream house unfolding at some magical juncture of the past and the future, bypassing the dull, heartbroken, trivial present, born equally out of memory and promise . . .

"Hey, honey, are you asleep?"

"No. What do you mean, 'dream house'?"

"I mean a house with two stories and a finished basement, and a real backyard. A bedroom for each of the kids and a couple of guest rooms. A master bathroom with a whirlpool bath. Large walk-in closets. A fireplace or two. A kitchen where we can turn

around. A terrace where we can grill. Proper space for entertain-
ment. Perhaps an exercise room, a media room, a wine cellar—"

"I see. You want to dispense with the forty-room requirement
all in one fell swoop. I'm not sure I'm ready to live in something
out of *The Great Gatsby*. It's a moot point, though—you know we
can't afford it anyway. Of course you make good money, but I
don't work, and there are all your student loans, and your car,
and Genie will be starting preschool in the fall, and then Emma.
And I was hoping to get a car of my own someday too . . . Even
this place is a strain. Unless your parents help us, and we've
decided against asking them, I thought."

"Well, but we won't need my parents' help. That's just what I
wanted to talk to you about. Remember when I turned in that
proposal in the spring? Well, last week we actually . . . Hey,
honey, are you asleep?"

"Sorry, I must have dozed off. You were saying?"

"I'm saying I'm likely to become full partner by the end of
March. With the money we'd have we could get the perfect
house. We could start looking in the summer, move in time for
Christmas. Imagine having a real fire in a fireplace and the kids'
stockings hanging from the mantel. Eugene would love it, he
would be four, the ideal age. And you too, you could use some
happiness right now. How nice would that be?"

"That does sound nice . . . unrealistic but nice . . ."

"It will happen, you'll see. Hey, your feet are still cold. Let me
just—"

"Mmm . . . That's nice . . . mmm . . . mmm . . . Oh, Paul . . .
mmm . . . That was nice . . . But I really must get some sleep

now . . . Oh. Paul? Paul! She is crying again, wake up, it's really your turn now. Oh, no. Did you hear that? I think Genie's up too."

"Mama? I had a scary dream. There was a monster who ate all my socks. I'm thirsty."

"Paul? Paul! Oh, hell . . . Hold on, sweetie, Mama will be right there."

My dream house: a place where you can sleep.

Part Four
The Present

The New House

21. Ballroom

40. Entrance hall

22. Dining room

32. Kitchen

36. Garage

34. Living room

38. Library

37. Deck

30. Master bedroom

26. Guest bedroom

33. Son's room

23. Master bathroom

27. Master closet

25. Nursery

29. Laundry

31. Girls' room

24. Wine cellar

35. Bar

28. Exercise room

39. Home theater

21. Ballroom

Holiday Checklist

CARDS AND GIFT BASKETS FOR PAUL'S FAMILY. CHECK.
Tips for the mailman and the grocery man. Check.

New rug delivered. Check.

Fire burning in the fireplace. Check.

Silver garlands, bronze deer, gilded fir cones, red poinsettias, soft Christmas carols, smells of cinnamon and pine, trays of freshly baked cookies still hot to the touch, holiday cheer—all unpacked from various boxes, unwrapped, dusted off, aired out, arranged here and there. Check, check, check.

Four stockings suspended from the mantel, three of them identical, sporting names in green and red letters: "Paul," "Eugene," "Emma." Paul's was soft and worn-out, the wool, once white, graying with the accumulated soot of many Christmas fires; it had been knitted at his birth by an elderly great-aunt who was, miraculously, still alive nearly a third of a century later to present their children with matching stockings. The fourth stocking, her own, did not match and had no name on it, but, unlike the other three, it carried a small private memory with it. On a cold, windy day in November six years before, the two of them had wandered into a neighborhood antique shop; Paul had found the stocking in the dingy back room and, maneuvering it off the hook, had turned to her and, looking uncharacteristically nervous, said, "For when we have a mantelpiece." That evening he had asked, and, unsurprised, she had said yes. Check.

An enormous tree, the size of Paul with Gene standing on his shoulders. Check.

A room vast enough to accommodate said tree. Some months before, as they had followed the genial real estate agent on their first tour of the house, she had felt dazed by the stately succession of spaces—the entrance hall with its marble staircase, the living room with its blinding wall of windows, the expansive kitchen with the sunlit dining area separated by the curve of the granite island, the darkly paneled library, then yet another room, which appeared to be a second living room, with a spectacular chandelier she had just narrowly avoided walking into. "It's hung a bit low, I think," she said, flustered, and the agent laughed his agreeable laugh and said, "But naturally, there will be a table underneath." "Oh," she said, "I thought the dining room was back there." "No, honey," Paul said, smiling, "that was just the breakfast nook." "Oh," she said again. By then they had returned to the hall and the agent had stopped before the tall French doors on its opposite side. "And the best for last," he said.

She fully expected that they had come to the end of the house and would now find themselves outside, and so was unable to suppress a gasp when, after a dramatic pause, the agent pushed the double doors open.

"The ballroom," he announced.

She thought: It's like a house within a house—a house that is bigger on the inside than on the outside, like in some magic story. I will write a poem about a delighted little girl who discovers a fairy-tale ballroom, complete with candlelit mirrors and princesses twirling in a waltz, hidden in the middle of her suburban bungalow. But when she considered for another minute, she knew that there was no poem in it: the mere notion of living in a house that contained something called a "ballroom" left her too stunned for words.

"Just look at these ceilings," Paul said, tilting his head.

(Sudden money, and not as much as they suppose, the agent thought, appraising his clients with an experienced eye; the woman especially looked all agog with greed. The agent had "Peter Boggart" printed on his expensively embossed business cards, but his real name was Bogdan Petković, and he did not like big new houses, or the people to whom he showed them. His grandfather had kept bees in a small village in the Balkan mountains, and he himself dreamed of going back there once he had set aside enough savings. Whenever he felt drained, he imagined the drowsy droning of bees above a blue meadow, and a dark-eyed girl by the village well looking at him over her shoulder with a quick, saucy smile; the vision never failed to motivate him.)

"Twenty-two by thirty-two, with a fourteen-foot ceiling," the agent offered energetically. "You could almost fit the White House tree in here."

Check.

("It's perfect," Paul had said as soon as the agent had waved his good-bye.

"It costs much too much," she said.

"We can afford it. As long as we budget."

"The kids might fall down the stairs," she said.

"We'll set up childproof gates."

"I wouldn't be able to hear them at night," she said.

"We'll put monitors everywhere."

"It would take all my life to clean it," she said.

"So we'll hire a maid. Once I get my next raise."

"All the furniture we own would fit in that one throne room, or whatever he called it, and I wouldn't know what to do with the rest of the house," she said.

"We can get a decorator to help you. It will be fun. Please, honey, don't fret so much. This house is perfect for us. And we can finally get a dog. Or even two."

She thought: God help me, I love the house.

She thought: I no longer recognize the shape of my life.

Aloud she said, "You have a solution for everything, don't you?"—and, after a moment, remembered to smile, so it would not sound like a reproach.)

The penultimate item on her holiday checklist: a dozen children's presents to assemble under the tree in festive piles—check, check, check. They had promised to give each other no gifts that year: she had not yet mastered driving, and the new house was even farther out than the old one, with no stores to walk to; in any case, she had argued, the house was gift enough for both of them. On Christmas morning, still in her pajamas, she kneeled on the new rug and watched the children; four-year-old Gene whooped with excitement as he tore the paper off his puzzles, and one-and-a-half-year-old Emma lay cooing on top of a gigantic plush dog. Once all the presents had been unwrapped, dismembered, and discarded, Paul brought in mugs of hot chocolate with marshmallows, and she gathered both children into her flannel-clad lap and sat looking at the flames, while white wintry sunlight flooded the great expanse of the bare room. There is something so peaceful about a fire in the morning, she thought. Emma grew heavy with sleep, making her right arm numb; Gene stared at the wisps of snow that darted outside the still-curtainless windows.

"Tell us one of your stories," she asked.

Gene nodded and, not pausing to think, began: "Once upon a time a boy wanted to make a snowman, but it was fall, and there was no snow, so he made his snowman out of leaves. But in the morning he woke up, and the snowman was not there: the wind carried it away at night. But when Christmas came, the boy made another snowman out of snow, and it was so much fun. The end."

As she listened, her habitual worry loosened its hold on her heart, and she felt certain, almost certain, that this house was just what they needed—that here Gene and Emma would be sure to have a childhood no less magical than hers had been. But magic, she knew, was not born of place alone; she too would have to try harder. When Gene fell silent, she reached for the book of Russian folktales that had been her present to him, showed him the pictures of firebirds and bears. He seemed indifferent until his eyes fell on a reproduction of a painting she had loved as a child, which he studied in absorbed silence. "The rider has stopped at the crossroads," she explained, pleased by his interest. "See this stone? The words on it say: 'If you go straight, you'll find happiness. If you go right, you'll lose your horse. If you go left, you'll lose your life.' He is choosing where to go."

Paul guffawed. "Why would anyone choose to go right or left?"

"Hmm," she said. "I never thought of it like that. Maybe you need to be Russian to find it tempting."

"Or maybe he can't read," Gene said, sounding slightly disdainful; he had learned his letters in the fall. "I don't like it. It's scary."

"Scary?" she repeated, surprised, and looked at the picture again—and saw the empty yellow sky, the crows and the skulls, and the horseman, his face invisible, stooped before the gravestone; and now his pose did seem to her one of deep weariness, perhaps even defeat, and the entire landscape pregnant with an evil hush of ominous forebodings.

Gene leaned over to push the book away, and spilled his mug of chocolate on the Persian rug. Emma woke up wailing as a few hot drops landed on her wrist. But of course memories and enchantments aren't transmitted by blood, she told herself sensibly; it was only natural that their childhood magic would be different from hers. And as she rushed to take care of burns and stains, she strove to smother the dull throb of sadness deep, deep inside her.

That evening, when the exhausted, satisfied children had fallen asleep, the monitors crackling at their bedsides, she returned to the darkened ballroom and sat on the floor by the dying fire. After some minutes, Paul came to join her, a glass of spiced eggnog in one hand, a long velvet box in the other.

"A little something for you," he said, setting the box gently in her lap.

"But Paul," she protested. "I thought we'd agreed——"

"It's nothing. Just a token, really. Go ahead, open it."

Inside was a choker necklace of golden filigree.

"It's lovely," she said with a small sigh.

"Here, let me——the clasp has a trick to it . . ."

There sounded a sharp little snap, like a clang of rodent teeth. She looked at the shadowy woman in the nearest mirror, at all the women in all the mirrors around the room, then slowly lifted her hand to her throat. The necklace felt cold, heavy, and smooth under her fingers. She thought she saw a reflection on the edge of the crowd stand up and leave without a glance back, and was seized by a wild desire to follow.

She turned her back to the mirrors.

"This is just the way we imagined it," Paul said. "Isn't it?"

"Yes," she replied——but as she said it, she knew that she had never imagined anything like it. She had grown up in a world where the value of jewels had been measured in stories, not carats, and the castle she had dreamed of inhabiting as a little girl had nothing to do with owning property, or with drinking eggnog on a palatial (if somewhat stained) Tabriz: it had been merely a wish to live in the daily presence of beauty——the idea of beauty, as she had understood it in her seven-year-old mind. Yet this beautiful house was not an idea, it was real——too real; and she could no longer pretend, as she had in their low-ceilinged bungalow, that it was all temporary somehow, a flimsy, hastily assembled theatrical set, a prelude to a proper life she would lead someday soon.

But perhaps she was wrong to feel so apprehensive. There was an art of poetry, true, but there was an art of living as well, and, contrary to the beliefs of the nineteenth-century romantics, one did not preclude the other, did it? Perhaps it was time she learned something of the latter. And why should she not enjoy a comfortable house with two bright, healthy children and a loving husband? She emerged from her anxious reverie to discover him kissing her neck, a little shyly, whispering about christening this rug, this room—this house, actually, even though they had now lived here for almost two months—for it had been a while, a long while, a very long while, she kept putting him off, she had not yet had a chance to visit her doctor since Emma's birth, to talk about options, and he had grudgingly agreed that two was probably enough, yes, three would have been nice, three would have been his choice, he supposed, but he understood that two was just right for them. But maybe this time, just this one time, she could stop worrying and live in the moment, for what were the chances, and wasn't that what she wanted, a life of spontaneity, a life of experience—and the embers were glowing so cozily in the fireplace, and the tree was tinkling and sparkling above them, and the taste of eggnog was sweet on her lips, and of course in time she would write all the poetry she meant to write, and everything, everything, would turn out just fine.

The last item on her holiday list: happiness. Check. And a barely visible question mark next to it.

22. Dining Room

The Ghostly Conversation

"SALAD FORKS GO ON THE OUTSIDE," SAID PAUL, walking into the dining room with a stack of soup bowls and taking in the table at a glance.

"I know that," she replied with some irritation, and, turning, saw that she had indeed set the forks wrong: the smaller ones bumped the gilded rims of the plates at crooked angles. She did not remember placing them there.

"Are you feeling all right?" Having unburdened himself of the bowls, he paused on the threshold to give her a mildly inquiring look.

"I'm fine." She would not meet his eyes as she went around the table switching the forks. "Just a bit queasy. Something with my stomach."

"Or it could be nerves," he said with an easy shrug. "There's no need to feel nervous, you know. It's only my boss and his wife we're trying to impress. Only my entire future hanging in the balance. Well, I better go check on the sauce."

He beamed at her before vanishing into the kitchen, and she heard more sizzling and banging and the oven door swinging open and the refrigerator door swinging shut. I guess that was a joke, she said wordlessly to the afterimage he had left behind, I mean your comment about the future, because isn't all this, your partnership, this place, our children, isn't all this supposed to be the future already? . . . The meat smells so rich . . . Oh no, there it is again, that wave of sick feeling. I suppose I'm getting ill. Or else. Or else. But I can't think about that right now.

And she did succeed in not thinking about it while their guests arrived, and for a spell after that, give or take a nauseating stray thought. As the four of them sat around the table crowned by the radiant magnificence of the chandelier, she would turn her head to the left and converse, almost convincingly, about the merits of silk wallpaper, then turn her head to the right and discuss the Russian Revolution, all the while straining to catch the back-and-forth traipse of Mrs. Simmons, their new babysitter, on the ceiling and the hushed whimpering of Emma, who could not fall asleep. Paul's boss, a stout, round-shouldered man in his early sixties, had a rowdy laugh and the massive jaw of a bulldog. His forty-something wife talked softly, revealing a dazzle of perfect white teeth in a frozen face framed by long tousled locks of brittle gold. "But this is divine," the woman kept saying in a toneless voice every time she took another dainty mouthful of soup. Whenever she lifted the spoon to her mouth, her diamond bangles slid down her skinny wrist and clicked together discreetly.

They got through the soup course. She poked at the edges of her salad, unable to eat, nodding as Paul's boss held forth on the proper ways of stocking a wine cellar. Paul brought in the steaks, explaining his personal take on béarnaise sauce. When they began to debate some incomprehensible work issue, she played a silent rhyming game she had invented to help her get through the more mind-numbing chores of the day, constructing short stacks of words in her mind, moving from the tangible and present to the abstract and remote: "Fork—cork—dork—New York. Knife— wife—strife—life. Spoon—old prune—cocoon—doom . . . Wait, the last one doesn't fit. How did that jingle go, from the show Gene used to watch? One of these things is not like the others . . . All right, then: Big Bird—slurred—curse word— theater of the absurd—"

Paul's boss had turned to her and was asking her something.

"I'm sorry?" She tried not to look at a speck of brown fat that glistened on his chin.

"*Dacha*," he boomed. "Tell us about your *dacha*. You have a *dacha* back home?"

He mispronounced the word—*daka*, he said—though of course she did not correct him. But when she opened her mouth to reply, something happened to the guests, to the room, even to Paul himself: everything suddenly assumed a flat, two-dimensional sleekness of unreality, like some film she was only half watching. I must be getting sick, she thought again. Or it could be nerves, I suppose. Or . . . No, do not think about that, the gods would not be so cruel . . .

She blinked, caught herself, felt the awkward silence widening around her like a clumsy spill. All three of them were looking at her, their smiles becoming glazed.

Paul came to her rescue.

"But naturally they have a *dacha*," he rejoined, and she felt a sharp little shock when he echoed his boss's error, though he knew how to say it correctly. "It's a real log cabin in the middle of a forest. No running water, and conveniences in the yard."

"How quaint," the wife said, sounding faintly disgusted. "Like living in a Tolstoy novel." She stood up, her bracelets sliding and clacking.

Paul started to clear the table for dessert.

"Don't you get frostbite when you use your outhouse in the winter?" the boss asked, his mouth remaining agape even after he finished speaking. She smiled at him in anguish. His teeth were not perfect like his wife's, but pointed and yellowing, wolfish somehow. "Siberian winters and all that?"

"They don't go there in winter," Paul answered with readiness, bending to refill the man's wineglass for the fourth time, then, after a beat of hesitation, refilling his own as well. "Of course, in the summer you must ward off the mosquitoes and the wasps, no?"

He carried the empty bottle into the kitchen.

Could it be true, she wondered, that people got just the dinner conversations they deserved? She went on smiling, terror growing inside her.

"Hell," the boss cried, "if I were a mosquito, I would bite you!" He roared with laughter, and in the next instant she found his hand clamped around her knee. Stricken, she stared at his impeccable starched cuff, at his golden cuff link in the shape of an anchor; but the clasp had already turned into a pat, jovial and vapid, and the wife came back in, talking about this nice little shop she knew where one could get the best guest soaps, and Paul entered with a new bottle of wine and a platter bearing Casanova's Delight, announcing it to be the very thing that had made his wife fall in love with him, and the evening proceeded on its limping, unreal course.

After coffee, Paul offered to take their guests on a tour of the house. "But I must warn you, it's a work in progress," he said. "Apart from the dining room, none of it's furnished. As you can see, we started with the most important room."

"You should keep it this way," said the boss's wife, rising from her chair. "I always say one can have too many things. Don't I, Mark? Don't I always say to you, one should be able to waltz through one's house without tripping over all these silly antiques?"

It was obvious from her tone that she meant precisely the opposite.

"Coming, honey?" Paul paused in the doorway, swaying a little.

"You go ahead," she said. "I'd like to clean up a bit."

But when she was alone, she did not move from her seat. She heard their voices echoing in the entrance hall, Paul's boss guffawing—"And what about a bed, surely you have a bed!"—adding something she could not make out that caused the men to gargle with laughter the entire way up the stairs. Now their voices grew indistinct, and two sets of manly footsteps thumped broadly above her head, while a third set tapped like a delicate hammer driving delicate nails into her temples, which made her realize her head was throbbing, had been throbbing for some time. Then she no longer heard them at all; but oddly enough, she continued to hear the flow of some ghostly conversation taking place just a breath away, not behind the wall but right next to her, yet sounding distant, as if reaching her ears through a thick veil. Several voices wove in and out, discussing with quiet passion things of inestimable interest and everlasting importance, though she could catch only a snippet now and again—something about a ruined temple in a tangle of vines in a jungle, and a sky over a western sea darkly aflutter with a thousand migrating storks, and a herd of wild horses running breast-deep through wind-blown steppe grasses. She listened for a long, entranced minute. Perhaps, she thought, in some parallel dimension, infinitely close and infinitely far away, another house existed alongside theirs, and in that other house lived fascinating people who did fascinating things and held fascinating talks over their dinner table—and though there was no doorway between the two places, one could occasionally stumble upon glimpses and echoes of that other, brighter place, and, for one single moment of miraculous serendipity, one could feel almost complete. She could write a poem about it . . . And she forced herself to go on, to think about the poem for another full minute; but all along she understood, of course, that what she was really doing amidst the fingerprinted crystal, the smeared china, the crusted silver—the wreckage of a sumptuous, laborious, vacuous meal—was trying to ward off her nausea, to distract herself with frantic imaginings from what, deep inside, she already knew to be true.

Presently Paul and the others returned, and soon after, their guests were taking their leave. The boss said, "A perfectly cooked steak is so rare," and laughed uproariously at his own pun. *(Poor thing, he thought kindly, she looks much prettier in that wedding photo Paul keeps on his desk. She seems so ill at ease, and always as if she is thinking about something else. I tried to cheer her up, but no luck. Some folks are like that, difficult to talk to. Or it could be the language barrier, I guess. But if she listens to Paul the way she listened to us, he can't be very happy. It's a shame all the same.)* "Look, if you ever need anything," he said, and he sounded sincere. The boss's wife, in parting, squeezed her hand and said, "I'm so sorry about your father," and her voice was no longer toneless, and her eyes glistened. "Courage, my dear."

But they are not as I thought they were, she registered with mild surprise; but she was distracted, and when the door closed, she forgot all about them. She followed Paul back to the dining room, began to stack up the cups. As Paul talked, slurring slightly, about the success of the evening, and his plans for the wine cellar, and Mark's lake house, she thought: It won't be real unless I say something. I don't have to say anything. I won't say anything. I can just pretend it's nothing. It probably is nothing. It was just that one time at Christmas, what are the chances, I've been late before, I've been nauseated before, it doesn't have to mean anything. I could just go to the doctor, and I don't have to tell Paul, I won't tell Paul, and even if it *is* something, it won't feel like anything if I talk only to the doctor, because when they say things like "first trimester" and "estimated date of confinement" and "induced termination," these are just words, they don't have to mean anything, as long as no one but the doctor knows anything about it. Of course I will know about it too, but it will be all right, it's only five or six weeks now, if it's anything at all, and it's probably nothing, and in any case it will be over soon, and I too will forget all about it, it will mean nothing—just as long as nobody thinks about tiny little toes that look like pink peas, and tiny little fingers curling around one's own finger in a surprisingly firm grip, and that sweet little fold in the back of the neck, and the warm smell of milk and sleep, and the toothless gums unsealed in their first smile—

She set the wobbling tower of cups onto the table.

"Paul?" she said. "Paul. I think I'm pregnant."

And within the cold immensity of her terror there already glowed a small, timid kernel of joy.

23. Master Bathroom

Death and Golden Faucets

"THERE ARE COLUMNS IN YOUR BATHROOM," said the plumber.

His voice sounded indifferent on the surface, as if he was just stating the fact, but she imagined she could detect hostility underneath, and meekly, almost apologetically, she offered, "We've only just moved in." She wanted to add: You could fit my entire childhood apartment in here; but he looked at her with a stony expression, and she said nothing else, only smiled to hide her discomfort and sat down on the vanity bench, awaiting his verdict. She took shallow breaths to avoid gagging.

"So, no blockages, then," the plumber said, unrolling his tools. "Just the smell."

"Just the smell," she confirmed, then continued in a helpful rush, "Something must be wrong with the pipes. I mean, I understand that in my condition all smells seem stronger than they really are, but you can smell it too, can't you?"

He did not respond, did not glance up at her, did not ask about her due date, or whether she was having a boy or a girl. She had felt a little disappointed when she let him in the door, a flabby, sour-looking man past fifty with the hard bristle of a sandy mustache not quite hiding the downward turn of his mouth, and her initial assessment had proved right. The other plumber from the company, the one she had dealt with on the previous two occasions (there had been a leak in Emma's bathroom and a dripping faucet in the kitchen), was an amiable, garrulous young fellow who would surely ask her how she was feeling and whether they'd picked a name yet. But this man went about his business in silence, tapping here, peering there, and she knew, just by looking at his stiff back, that he resented her presence in the bathroom and would have much preferred her to leave.

Pulling herself together, she made a new attempt.

"So," she said brightly, "do you have any children?"

He grunted into his mustache, whether a "Yes" or a "No" she could not discern, and set about rolling his tools back up. *(Sean O'Reilly's only daughter had drowned at the age of eleven. Now she often came to him at night. They walked the deserted streets of his neighborhood side by side, talking about nothing much, the weather, a new hardware shop around the corner, their old cat. Her sneakers squeaked with water, her voice never aged. The following morning his pajamas were often muddy and his heart lagged exhausted in his chest. He suspected that each nocturnal visit was shaving days, if not months, off his life, but he did not mind. Aching with hope, he wondered if she was going to come tonight, then reluctantly turned his attention to the rich lady with the slight foreign accent and needy eyes.)*

"Nice faucets you've got here," he said, standing up with an audible creak, brushing off his knees. His tone, once again, carried a brusque undercurrent of hostility.

"I'm sorry?"

"Your faucets. Gold-plated. Very nice."

"These faucets are gold-plated?" she echoed, incredulous. "I had no idea."

He gave her a sullen look and walked out of the bathroom.

"But what about the smell?"

"The pipes are fine," he said. She waddled after him across the bedroom, down the stairs. "You've got a dead animal in the wall. I still have to charge you for coming out, though."

"A dead animal? You mean, like . . . a mouse?"

He turned to her in the entrance hall. "Judging by the smell, something larger. A rat or a squirrel, I'd guess, maybe a raccoon."

"A rat? But . . . what do I do now? Do I call an exterminator?"

"I don't know what you people do in such cases," he said with a shrug, and opened the front door without waiting for her help with the lock, "but I'd call one of those animal trappers. No need to exterminate anything, it's dead already."

"You people," she thought, stung—what did he mean by "you people," I don't have any "people," one should never judge by appearance only, my real world is far away from here . . . Resisting the urge to chase the dour man outside and set him straight, she locked the door behind him and puffed her way back upstairs, stopping at the bathroom threshold, peeking in. When she had first seen the house, the whirlpool bath with its swan-shaped faucets, submerged in the deep basin between the two columns, beneath the two chandeliers, had struck her as the most marvel-ous of all the marvels here. Now, hidden behind its lustrous gray marble lay the decomposing corpse of some rat crawling with maggots—and so troubling was the image, and so unshakable her sudden sense of the entire house weighing down upon her, demanding to be maintained in a manner she was beginning to suspect beyond her, that she found herself reeling. Crumpling onto the gorgeously veined floor, she pressed her forehead against the cool side of the bathtub and burst into tears; and as she cried, she remembered last night's dream, heroic and primary-colored, in which she had fought in some medieval battle in a green meadow under blue skies alongside fierce youths with lions' manes and undying courage; and the memory of the dream made her cry all the harder. But it's nothing, it's only hormones, stop it this minute, she thought after a moist, confused moment, all at once angry with herself.

At least she had not been cowed into giving that unpleasant man a tip.

She called Paul, but he was in a meeting.

"Are you feeling all right, Mrs. Caldwell?" his secretary asked, her voice oozing solicitude. "Do you want me to page him?"

"No, no, I'm fine," she said. "Maybe he could call me back later?"—but just then Emma woke up from her nap and Gene needed a snack, and her free half-hour was over.

The trapper arrived on Wednesday. He was a cheerful black youth dressed in a neatly pressed khaki-colored uniform with his name, some unpronounceable combination of d's and b's, embroi-dered over the breast pocket. He took the matter in hand with

great efficiency, considered the angle of the roof, even went outside and climbed a ladder to probe around the skylights. "This is
where it gets in," he said, returning to the bathroom, pointing.
He spoke confidently, flashing bright teeth in a dark face agleam
with sweat, his words like solid blocks of wood, sturdy with some
accent she could not place. "I must break the wall to pull it out.
I'm sorry I do not fix the wall for you. Your husband, he will fix
it, yes? It is easy, just drywall here, then paint over."

She made a mental note to call a handyman as soon as the
trapper was gone.

"You should leave now," the young man said merrily. "Bad
smells for a lady in your state. Boy or girl, you know?"

He looked smiling at her belly, and instantly she felt a rush of
gratitude so strong it made her eyes sting a little.

"Actually, it's two boys," she said. "Twins. Identical."

As always, when she said it (and she did not say it often, mainly
to workmen who came to the house, and only if they were curious
enough), she experienced anew that heady mix of terror, disbelief,
pride, and wonder—just as she had felt when the doctor, studying
the small black screen on which some white cobwebby lines
shifted and curved, had said, "Ah, there it is, a nice, healthy heartbeat," and frowned slightly, sending her own heart into a frightened lurch, then, an excruciating second or two later, beamed and
said, "And here, surprise, surprise, we have another heartbeat," so
that in her first moment of pure incomprehension, she said stupidly, "The baby has two heartbeats?"—and as she was saying it,
realized what the doctor had meant. She wept in the taxi on the
way home. That evening, when she told Paul, dry-eyed but even

more panicked, she wanted him to console her; but he only whooped and grabbed her and lifted her up, as though to whirl her about, then, recalling himself, set her down gently instead as if she were porcelain. "If one of them is a boy," he had cried, "we should name him Richard. Dad would be thrilled!"

"Twins," the trapper said, inclining his head in what seemed a small bow. He was no older than twenty-two or twenty-three. "You are blessed, Mrs. Caldwell. Twins are special. Sacred. Poets sing songs about twins. In Africa, I am a twin also. My father was king of my tribe, and my twin brother is king now. One day I will find a poet and tell him my life, and the poet will make me and my father and my brother into songs."

Another delusional royal, she thought with a quick flash of disdain—and then, surprising herself, opened her mouth and said, "*I* am a poet," and, flushed with instant embarrassment, hastened to add: "But I'm not yet published or anything."

"Published? But poets are not published, Mrs. Caldwell. You do not put a song in a book. Being a *jali* is a gift you carry to the people. You walk among your people singing them alive, keeping their roots nourished, teaching them who they are. The word *jali*, do you know what it means in my language? Blood. Yes. That is what it means. Poets are the true blood of their people." He was silent for a moment, a still look on his sculpted face, as though lost in some memory. *(He was seeing the night settling in the clearing, and the drums beating and beating, and his father twirling in the circle of the dancers, their eyes shining darkly in the slits of horned and feathered masks, and the wisdom of past generations deep in his being like the slow flow of rich ancestral blood, a part of him forever. The world, he knew without ever putting it into words, was so much more wondrous than most people here ever suspected.)* Then his lustrous eyes rolled over her, lit up with another smile. "But now I open the wall, so you go someplace with no death, it is no good for you here."

She wanted to continue talking to him, but of course there could be no conversation while the animal (a squirrel, not a rat, as it turned out, much to her relief) was being extracted, and in any case, she realized with a start that Emma had been screaming in her crib for quite a while now; her ability to tune things out had become truly astonishing. Well, the drywall man will be coming in a day or two, she thought as she hurried down the corridor toward her daughter's high-pitched wails. She wondered what he would be like, and felt a small thrill of anticipation.

When the trapper left, she gave him a sizable tip.

24. Wine Cellar

The Cask of Amontillado

HER HEART FLIPPED LIKE A FISH WHEN SHE answered the doorbell.

"Please, please, come in," she said.

He stepped inside, a bouquet of nondescript flowers in his hand.

"Not gladioli, I see," she said with a nervous little laugh. "You haven't changed at all."

Adam smiled with his lips only, glanced around the entrance hall.

"Nice place," he said, his voice flat.

His jacket was shabby, she saw, and his shoes cheap.

"Oh, would you like a tour? I'll ask Dolores to put these in water," she said, and, flushing for no reason, abandoned the flowers on the marble-topped console and fled ahead of him without waiting for his reply. "Please, this way. Paul likes to show people around"—she spoke over her shoulder, not wanting to fall silent, not wanting to slow down—"but he won't be back from work for another hour. I'm having the living room redone, do watch out—oh, sorry!"

He had barely avoided stepping into one of the pans of paint her contractor had left for her to review. As she maneuvered him into the ballroom, the telephone rang, and for an insufferable minute she tried and failed to extricate herself from a discussion of cushion upholstery with Felicity, her decorator, while his level gaze pursued her through the mirrors, judging her, judging her. In the kitchen, Gene was helping Emma with a puzzle, and Squash and Pepper tangled panting in their legs. "The enthusiasm puppies have for the world!" she said, laughing, and again saw Adam's cheap shoes, and was all at once conscious that, deep underneath the awkwardness, she was almost enjoying this chaotic display of the full, prosperous life she had managed to build for herself out of nothing. Upstairs, in the nursery, she grew likewise conscious of the fact that she had once wondered about having children with the very man who was now commenting politely on Emma's doodles framed above the cribs; it caused her to coo over the twins in a fussy manner not her own, which made Mrs. Simmons raise her eyebrows slightly. In the bedroom, she was conscious of other things yet. To avoid lingering by the enormous king-size bed, whose elaborate carved posts Dolores was brushing just then with a duster, she pulled him into the bathroom.

"Nice place," he said again, in that same polite, flat tone. "Orchids and swans."

Their eyes met, and a brief silence settled between them.

"Can you believe it," she exclaimed wildly, desperate to dispel the hush, to say anything, anything at all, "these faucets are actual gold, isn't that silly!"

Dolores crept in, a spray in her hand, her gaze cast down with disapproval, muttering, "Excuse me, ma'am"—probably hoping to spy on us, she thought in sudden agony. *(Dolores did not notice the strained pauses in the conversation between her employer and her employer's guest. She paid no attention to them whatsoever. She was thinking of the bells ringing in an ancient bell tower in her hometown, and of herself as a fifteen-year-old girl, and of the bell ringer's son taking her night after night up the winding staircase of the tower, and the bells ringing within the stone walls, and the two of them holding hands as they rose higher and higher, past the bells, past the roof, until they were climbing the endless celestial ladder among the stars. One time, when the bell ringer's son was not looking, she sneaked a small star into her pocket, and when her son was born nine months later, she gave it to him. She had not seen her son in twenty years, but she was sure she would always know him, for once you touched a star, you were marked for life.)*

"Why don't I show you the wine cellar next?" she offered brightly.

"Please," he replied, his voice reserved.

On the stairs to the basement she paused, turned to glance up at him.

"But you haven't changed at all," she said again, hoping that this time he would return the compliment; but, as before, he said nothing, only looked down at her evenly from a step above. In truth, she was not being entirely honest herself. In the decade since they had seen each other last (a decade—was it truly possible?), he had lived in Paris, Vienna, Prague, and Rome, had traveled through Asia and South America, had composed several well-reviewed shorter pieces and a symphony that had been performed in a concert hall in Boston, and there was talk of a teaching position at Juilliard. He looked young still, but his cheekbones had become more pronounced, imparting a sterner cast to his features; his halo of golden curls had subsided, flattened, darkened; his face had gained a deep, assured stillness over which his painfully familiar expressions skimmed lightly, without, it seemed, touching his essence—a face of someone who knew he had already accomplished something in life and was bound to accomplish much more.

She wondered what changes he saw in her, what he thought of her now, a thirty-three-year-old mother of four. She was not as thin as she used to be. Did he still find her beautiful? Was she still beautiful? Her heart caught with a small, discrete ache. Without another look at him she resumed descending the steps.

"Here it is," she said, pushing the door open, switching on the dim overhead light. Together they stepped inside a shadowy room packed with a dry, cool smell of wood and earth, and carefully she closed the door behind them—Paul was forever reminding her to pull the door shut, to maintain the proper temperature within. "Always kept at a constant fifty-six degrees," she said as they walked along the walls. The honeycomb of wine racks was still three-quarters empty, but was filling up at a steady pace. "Paul is really into wines nowadays, he has even taken a wine appreciation course at a local winery. The reds are here, the whites there, you see—"

They stopped, stood side by side, their shoulders close but

not touching, looking at the dull gleam of the dozens of bottles before them.

"So," he said, "this is where you invite me to taste your rare Amontillado, and while I stumble about inebriated, you chain me to the wall and abandon me to starve to death for all my sins."

For the first time since he had crossed her threshold, his voice lost its dullness, quickened with life.

"I'm afraid the sins are all mine," she said, starting to laugh, and the brittle sound of her laughter was like a tinkle of broken glass falling all around them.

He turned to face her.

Suddenly she was no longer laughing.

"What are you thinking?" he asked, and the long-forgotten gentleness in his voice made her heart thump, pushing into her throat, her wrists, her temples, until she felt her entire being filled with her heart's troubled thudding. She shivered in the chill of the cellar, drawing her cardigan tighter around her shoulders.

I'm thinking: Once you love someone, how do you unlove them?

I'm thinking: Kiss me.

"I'm thinking of a poem I wrote when I was twenty," she said. "One of the ones I burned on the day we met. I translated it for you later, though it isn't nearly as good in English."

He waited in silence. She too was silent for a moment, unsure whether she was going to do it. Then, meeting his eyes, she began to recite, stumbling a little, the heat of her insidious intent creeping up her neck. *"In the coldness of an autumn night*—no, 'coldness' is not right, was it 'darkness,' yes, I think it was 'darkness'—

"In the darkness of an autumn night
I imagine golden beehives of a fireplace
Where the embers' honey slowly ripens
And a cat is snoring by the flames . . ."

The cavernous cellar caught her voice and echoed it ever so slightly, as if adding a second dimension to the sounds, amplifying and deepening the meaning.

"And I am, once more, my own grandmother,
I am knitting an eternal scarf,
And my life is pasted in an album
In a row of brown old-fashioned photos.
As I knit the scarf, for my granddaughter,
In the resonance of solemn hours—"

She broke off. She looked at the wine racks, at the tiled floor under her feet, at her hands twisting the button on her cardigan— anywhere but at him. The unfinished poem lay like a damaging secret between them, the unsaid words crowding in her throat, pushing against her lips; she felt them on her tongue, shapeless, soundless, but she could not bring herself to release them into the cool, expectant stillness of the cellar.

"I . . . I don't remember any more," she began to say, all at once frightened—but he was kissing her already.

She felt suspended for an instant, then leaned into the kiss, her eyes fluttering closed. Everything forgotten was back in the kiss—their youth, their love, their future. The smells of earth and wood in the cellar became the smells of the outside world, the smells of mushrooms and flowers, the changing of seasons, the joyful, heedless tumbling of the universe through rushing, dazzling space—for when you closed your eyes tightly and fire coursed through your soul, you were free to inhabit any place you willed into miraculous being, a place with no walls, no thermostats, no neatly arranged rows of expensive wines . . .

"Come away with me," he whispered into her neck.

"How can I?" she asked, pulling away just a little so she could see his face.

And for one slow, deep-thudding heartbeat, she believed that she had truly intended it as a question—had wanted him to tell her, had hoped he could tell her.

Releasing her, he turned away, stepped back.

"I understand," he said.

No, no, you don't, she nearly cried out, wild with panic, kiss me again, do you hear, I want you to kiss me again—but she stood unmoving, and so did he, his face now closed, almost cruel-looking, and it was suddenly over, the moment was over, and she knew that he had not meant it, not fully, not at all. And she knew too that in that one confused, liberating, false moment she had risked robbing of meaning the entire past decade of her life—and the near loss of her past made her weak with shame.

Did you only want to pay me back for breaking your heart all those years ago? Did you want to make me feel that my marriage, my children, my life—that all of it was worthless, that nothing real had happened to me since I had left you, that I would give it all up at the drop of a hat if only you called? Well, let me tell you,

I wouldn't—you could never have given me a life like this, and I'm happy with what I have, with where I am, do you hear me? And the kiss—the kiss was nothing, nothing at all, just a moment of insecurity, do you hear—and I don't care how handsome, how impossibly handsome, you look—

There were steps running above their heads now, and Squash, or was it Pepper, choked on excited barks, and the bottles jingled anxiously as someone—Gene—thumped down the stairs hollering, "Mama, Mama!"

Paul was home.

"We might as well pick out some wine for dinner," she said, readjusting her cardigan as she moved to face the bottles. "We are having snapper Veracruz."

"Could go either white or red," he said. "The whites are over there, yes?"

The door to the cellar opened, and Paul strode in, wide-shouldered in his custom-made gray suit, his head almost touching the ceiling, his easy smile at the ready. She flew at him with an exaggerated, frantic kiss. "Aren't you going to introduce us?" Paul said, laughing as he shook her off. But they already recognized each other from an anthropology class they had both attended in their sophomore year. Everyone stood smiling at everyone else with the shared consciousness of being broad-minded and civilized and mature, and achingly insincere.

"We were trying to choose a bottle for the main course," she hastened to say into the small breach of silence. "Chardonnay, perhaps?"

"No, that's too obvious. Why don't we let our guest choose?"

The two men began to talk about sauces and pairings. It now transpired that Adam knew his wines every bit as well as Paul, and quite possibly better, and they soon fell into an amiable banter of old acquaintances, comparing the qualities of Pinot Noir, Chenin Blanc, and Pouilly-Fuissé. He had not cared two figs about fine wines in the past, she thought—back when they had been young, and free, and so full of joy, living in that dreary basement studio, no bigger than this cellar, spending entire days in bed, listening to jazz, reading poetry to each other, drinking whatever sour piss they could come by—

"How about Amontillado?" she said, cutting in.

Paul laughed dutifully, looking a bit puzzled, but Adam only smiled a fleeting smile without taking his eyes off the racks.

"Riesling would be another possibility," he said smoothly.

For another minute, her heart tight as a clenched fist in her chest, she listened to the two of them discussing grapes. Then, unnoticed, she slunk away, making sure to close the door behind her, mindful of forever maintaining the steady chill of fifty-six degrees.

25. Nursery

The Jungle Theme

RICH HAD CRIED SO MUCH DURING THE NIGHT that she had moved his twin brother over to Emma's room and had spent the hours before dawn dozing fitfully in the armchair next to Rich's crib. Now his fever seemed to have broken, but a rash bloomed all up and down his pudgy arms. Might be roseola, she decided—she had been through enough childhood illnesses, midnight vigils, emergency room dashes, to keep a mental catalogue of various symptoms, pink eyes and earaches and inflamed throats, at a well-thumbed ready; except that this was an odd sort of rash, tiny red blotches under his skin, like pinpricks of blood. Probably nothing to worry about, just hives or a heat rash, she thought as she inspected him closer in the morning light—but worth a visit to the doctor all the same. She checked the clock above the dresser. Paul would have already left for work—vaguely she remembered his shout of "Bye, honey!" reaching her from the edges of the house—but Mrs. Simmons was due to arrive shortly. She would have to ask her to take the boy, and Mrs. Simmons would purse her lips and act all put-upon, and she would end up offering extra for Mrs. Simmons's trouble.

Suppressing a sigh of exasperation, she reached for a fresh diaper, and Rich gave her a toothless smile and aimed a warm yellow stream at her hands, just as Emma burst through the door, wailing over a missing button on her favorite frock, the one with pink lollipops. Suppressing another sigh, she wiped her hands dry, pacified Emma with a set of wooden blocks, and, casting a wistful glance out the window—the sun lay in bright yellow slabs on the flagstones of the winding garden paths—went to get her sewing kit. No sooner had she settled in the armchair with the dress than Rich began to cry in his crib, and George woke up and joined him a room away, and Emma began to bang her blocks on the floor, not to be ignored, and when the delivery man rang the doorbell downstairs, Squash started to bark.

"Oh, be quiet!" she shouted, and, after a calming intake of breath, shouted again, "Be quiet, Squash!"—for she did not want to be the kind of mother who shouted "Be quiet!" at crying babies and peeved little girls, as much as she felt like it at times. For in truth, her exhaustion was making her irritable, not to say angry. Mrs. Simmons came to lend a hand three days a week, and Dolores helped with the cleaning every Wednesday; but even with their capable assistance, taking care of four children, two dogs, Eugene's fish, and a house stuffed full of things that needed constant dusting, washing, updating, and repairing took its toll. It was like a never-ending sentry duty—or, as it seemed in her grimmer moments, a prison sentence with no chance of parole. Apart from an occasional dinner outing with Paul—and these were becoming increasingly rare, subject to Paul's demanding work schedule and Mrs. Simmons's migraines—she never even left the house, and she was never, ever alone.

(She calmed Rich and George, called the doctor, dressed Emma, explained matters to the newly arrived Mrs. Simmons.) She thought of the kiss in the cellar, half a year ago now. Troubled as it had made her feel at the time, inconsequential as it had proved to be since—Adam was back in Paris, and they were not in touch—she found herself returning to it again and again. While knowing that this chapter of her life was finished, she felt nonetheless sustained by the secret fantasy of another, happier woman who had been released into being by a different answer— "Yes!"—at that dazzled instant in the cellar and who had walked out of the chilly gloom into a full, three-dimensional existence of moonlit romance, sunlit adventure, daring art, and, yes, guilt and regret; for unlike her, this imaginary woman, whose parallel existence ran like an intermittent ghostly thread through her mind, was an unnatural mother who *had* abandoned her children. (Mrs. Simmons called from the doctor's waiting room; they would be seen next. She finished reading a book to Emma, folded the laundered clothes, and commenced scrubbing the changing table.)

Still, her confinement was only temporary, of course. First would come the driving: it was essential to be able to leave the house. She was hoping to start her lessons in another month, a month or two, as soon as Eugene had adjusted to his new school routine. (The doctor's office called; Dr. Peck's rumbling baritone came on the line, asking her if he had her authorization to perform a simple blood test, merely a precaution, he just wanted to be sure it was nothing. Of course, of course, she said, and, hanging up, changed George's diaper and moved on to sweeping the detritus of broken toys from under the cribs.) Yes, first the driving, then a membership at the library, a reading club, perhaps, even some classes at a local college. Not right away, for she was still needed at home—but in only four years the twins would join their older siblings at school, and she would have a glorious window of freedom, from ten in the morning until two in the afternoon five days a week (minus the holidays and the summer vacation and the spring break and the winter break and the snow days and the sick days and the dental appointments and the plumbing repairs and the visits to the vet). She would still be young then, only thirty-eight, her whole life before her, or no less than three-fifths of it, or at any rate more than half. (She gave George and Emma their snacks; the dogs needed walking.) Then Eugene would leave the house altogether to go off to college, and Emma would follow three years later, and finally the twins—and thus in seventeen years, a decade and a half, really, she would be free at last to live her life to the full. Fifty-one was nothing in this day and age, at fifty-one anything was possible still. She would travel, she would meet fascinating people, and most important, she would—she would—

Mrs. Simmons entered, carrying Rich. She leapt up from the armchair in which she had just collapsed, and rushed to take him. His face was blotchy from recent tears, and a bandage with blue balloons bulged in the crook of his plump little arm; but his forehead was cool to the touch of her lips, and his eyes had lost their dull sheen of sickness.

"I'll let the dogs back in," Mrs. Simmons said from the doorway, "and give lunch to Emma and George. Rich will sleep now, I think. Dr. Peck asked you to call him when you have a minute."

(Mrs. Simmons, who had left Hungary as an eight-year-old girl well over a century before—for Mrs. Simmons was much older than she looked—still kept to the old ways. At night, in the solitude of her small apartment, empty save for the tent she had set up in the middle of the floor, she read tea leaves and peered into crystal balls and chatted with the moon; she was no longer hoping to see a handsome dark stranger in her cards, but she had some modest investments on which she liked to keep her third eye. On occasion she would receive, unasked, glimpses of other futures, intimations of other lives. Poor dear, she thought as she walked to the kitchen. The things we deem important are so fleeting. I do hope she survives the birth pangs, for if she ever comes into her own, it will be something to see. Perhaps I will stay a bit longer, help her through the pain.)

She settled Rich in a nest of fresh blankets and, still unwinding the spool of a different, brighter life in her mind—her fantasy fifty-one-year-old self sipping absinthe at a sidewalk café in Prague, her pen poised in her hand, her companion, his face rather vague, playing with her foot under the table—dialed the doctor's number. The doctor came quickly. Too quickly. There was nothing definitive yet, he hastened to reassure her, it was only a preliminary result; they would know more in an hour. As she listened, the sidewalk café dimmed and receded, became a ghost of a wisp of a thought—and the present sped toward her, until here it was, looming large and solid, threatening to crush her below its sudden weight.

"But you shouldn't be alarmed," the doctor said before ringing off.

She stood with the telephone clutched in her hand, then punched in Paul's number. "I think you better come home," she said.

"I have a client meeting at noon. Couldn't you just talk to the doctor when he calls? Or . . . do you think it might be serious?"

"No. Maybe. I don't know. There was just something in Dr. Peck's voice—"

"I'll come," he said.

He arrived less than an hour later; he must have run a few red lights. She was sitting on the floor, her fingers white around the receiver, her face against the bars of Rich's crib. She was watching him sleep.

"Have you heard anything yet?" he asked.

"No, not yet," she said.

"You know it's probably nothing," he said, "they just have to—"

The telephone rang in her hand.

She looked at it.

"Well, answer it, answer it!" he cried.

"Hello," she said, and her voice sounded all tinny to her ears.

"Yes," she said. "Speaking."

"Oh," she said after a minute. "Yes, I see."

"Oh," she said a little later. "So the oncologist will be there when?"

"Yes," she said. "Of course. We'll be waiting for your call."

"Yes," she said then. "Thank you. I understand."

But she did not understand, not at all. Her eyes still, she repeated what the doctor had told her.

"So they don't know," Paul said fiercely. "They don't know for sure. Honey. Listen to me. Listen to me. This doesn't mean—"

She sank to the floor, the telephone slipping onto the carpet. The carpet was green, and all along its border, monkeys, elephants, and giraffes with tails sticking up trudged clockwise one after another. The nursery had a jungle theme. There were blue monkeys climbing up and down the vines on the curtains, and green and orange monkeys on the sheets, and the clock was the grinning face of a lion with two thrusts of jaunty whiskers for hands. The clock showed eleven minutes past one. The lion grinned as its longer whisker moved down a notch, and now it was twelve minutes past one, and the lion's grin looked evil, and its eyes were demented slits. Fifteen minutes, the doctor had said. Shouldn't take more than fifteen minutes. Half an hour at most.

The demented lion's whisker moved down another notch.

There was a swarming of hot wasps in her head. But I don't understand, she thought dully. This isn't happening. This can't be happening. This can't— With dry, feverish eyes, she stared around the nursery, at the two matching cribs, one of them empty now, sliced in half by a slanting ray of sunlight; she could hear George's giggles bouncing like spilled peas somewhere downstairs. In the other crib, Rich slept peacefully. His pink lips were partly open, and his shirt rose and fell with his slow, even breaths. He lay on his back, as he often did, his arms and legs spread out wide, as if he had fallen into a tranquil doze while making a snow angel—or a bed angel—or an angel soon to be.

No. This isn't happening. Why him, why me, why? It was all a mistake. It made no sense—like opening a gift wrapped in cheerful floral-print paper to discover some rotting horror inside, something vast and nameless from the underside of reality that reared up and swallowed you whole—the nursery's stuffed animals with their vapid button-eyed faces and blue plush hides turning on one another, tearing out one another's innards in the hot darkness of the jungle, the reek of guts and feces in the air, the vicious pulse of life and death, and her children, her own flesh and blood, wandering lost and frightened, so sweet, so innocent, so defenseless—

Her jumbled thoughts rose to a pitch inside her, a hot silent howl. This isn't real, if this happens, life will be over, nothing will matter, time will drag on and on from year to year, empty, empty. A phrase Hamlet liked to repeat in some unimaginable past fell like a cold little pebble into the turmoil of her mind: *Art is a haven from misfortune for mankind.* Some ancient had said it, Seneca or Menander, one of those stoic philosophers or sage playwrights who strode about wrapped in their neatly pressed togas, proclaiming that nothing human was alien to them. She felt she was choking. Haven from misfortune—what mockery that was, what mockery . . . No, if this happens, I will be silent forever, for this suffering will not fit into any words, into any poetry—who can even think of poetry when it's Rich, my Rich, my special Rich, so full of life, so full of future, why? But the horrifying knowledge had already stirred inside her, uncoiling its slithering length. I did this. *I* did this. This is my punishment—my punishment for always thinking this isn't enough, my punishment for always dreaming of a life I will lead once I am free, once I am an artist, once the children are *gone.* This is the gods throwing it back in my face, this is the gods, yet again, granting the most evil of my wishes, answering the darkest of my prayers. You wanted your children gone, and so they will be, one by one by one, so now go stuff yourself full of your fucking freedom, full of your fucking art . . .

She grew conscious then of her sobs, and of Paul on the floor next to her, gripping her shoulders, repeating, "Honey, please, honey, we don't know for sure——" With a jolt she remembered him, her big, safe, cozy giant of a husband who always knew just what to do, whose love for her had always been there. Something deep in her seemed to give way at last, and her soul rose in her mouth, heavy with gratitude and love and terror. Gods, oh gods, I swear, if only you avert this, if only you take this cup of suffering away from me, I will be happy, I will never want anything more, I will never ask for anything more, just this life, just this small life, because it isn't small, I understand that now, it is enough, it is all I want, this family is all I want, all I ever wanted, my husband and my children and my home, I swear, I will prove it to you, I swear, just let it be the way it was and you will see, please, please, if you let me, I will even——I will even . . .

They sat on the floor, holding each other, while the lion whiskers crept forward on the wall, and the telephone lay inert and deadly between them, and their baby slept in his crib with the orange monkeys, and outside the closed door their other children squealed with laughter, and spots of bright sunshine slithered like fat yellow slugs across the giraffes on the carpet, and some other, normal life slipped farther and farther away, sliding over the edge, year after year, decade after decade, falling into nothing.

The lion's whiskers now pointed to twenty-nine minutes past one.

The telephone rang.

They looked at it.

"Paul," she mouthed. "I can't. Paul. Please."

He answered, his face blank, his voice a wire.

"Yes? Yes, Dr. Peck. Yes. Yes."

She held his free hand, crushing his fingers, watched his face split open with relief. She felt herself going slack, and hid her own face in his shoulder, and cried with happiness unlike any she had ever known. They were reprieved, the door that had cracked open onto the monstrous blackness had swung closed, this time at least—but she would never let there be another time. And when he finished telling her, and when they stopped laughing and shouting and kissing the bewildered, sleepy Rich long enough to catch their breaths, she snuggled deeper into his arms and whispered, "Let's have another baby."

The expression on his face was suddenly hard to read.

"We have a wonderful family already," he said a long moment later, and leaned over to kiss her—but she knew by the way he looked at her that he would change his mind in time, that she would change his mind for him.

26. Guest Bedroom

The Only Poem Written at the Age of Thirty-five

"NATURALLY, THESE ARE ALL IMPORTANT DECISIONS," the decorator said, shutting her purse—a hard-edged affair taut with some reptile's skin. "And while most of our options are not inexpensive, you must keep in mind that, if done properly, they will last you forever." In the doorway she paused. "Also, Mrs. Caldwell, you should consider cutting down that tree in front, it makes the room quite dark."

"Yes," said Mrs. Caldwell. "Thank you for coming, Felicity."

Alone, she dreamily stroked the rise of her stomach and contemplated the two bare windows, dimmed by the oak's giant shadow. Felicity's right, I should call our tree service, she resolved—and was, for the briefest of moments, visited by a disorienting sensation, a memory, or perhaps a thought, brushing by her only to flee out of reach. Just then, on the exact same spot in a neighboring dimension, a woman who looked much like her, but who had no baby with glowing pink fingers close to her heart, stood gazing out of her study window, thinking about a poem she would write next. It would be a long poem set entirely in an old tree, even bigger than this one—like the magnificent oak that grew in a forest clearing beyond her childhood dacha. There would be fairies living in its vertiginous upper reaches, elegant, haughty, and treacherous, weaving subtle byzantine intrigues over sips of pollen-sweetened dew from perfumed petal cups; and nameless birds, bees, and squirrels working their lives away in the middle thicket, scurrying in and out of nests and hollows, storing honey, gathering acorns, raising their young, ensuring by the daily accretion of minute labors the eternal rotation of the seasons, the steady passage of time; and, in the damp, black interstices of the underground tunnels and roots, secret societies of gnomes pursuing with dark obsession some mysterious, closely guarded purpose of their own, and a lonely mole scribe entrusted by generations of moles before him to continue the Sacred History of the Tree, to record with diligent devotion each drought, each near strike of lightning, each furry death, each feathered birth, to write the world into existence while himself remaining blind, unappreciated, and unknown, year after year after year. But the most marvelous thing about the tree would be its leaves, for the leaves—the leaves . . . And just as the woman at the window of that other, haphazardly furnished, much smaller house reached for her pen, Mrs. Caldwell looked once again at the notes she had jotted down in her agenda, under the heading "Convert study into guest bedroom":

Curtain rods: fluted or smooth?
Antique pewter or ancient gold?

Double-pleated or double-ruffled?
Finials: square or round?
Rings: leaf-carved or plain?
Paint: Inner Balance or Paris Rain?
And what width should the rods have?
And what shape should the brackets be?
And how much will the tassels cost?

Eugene's school bus screeched to a stop outside their gate. But I shouldn't rush into anything, Mrs. Caldwell thought as she set her notebook aside and went downstairs to meet him. Because whatever choices I make, these window treatments will be forever.

27. Master Closet

The Secret Life of Mrs. Caldwell

THE LARGE WALK-IN CLOSET, UPHOLSTERED IN striped damask of pale beige and cream, had a satin-covered settee at one end, beneath a wall of precisely arranged shoes, and a second settee at the opposite end, by a floor-length mirror. On the left, Mr. Caldwell's suits and shirts hung in a neat procession of muted grays and blues; on the right, somber bags of sturdy plastic concealed the bright plumage of Mrs. Caldwell's evening dresses.

Her most recent acquisition, a long gown of crimson velvet, had matching high heels, which sparkled with tiny crystals along delicate crisscrossing straps. Mrs. Caldwell finished struggling with the left clasp and took a tentative twirl in front of the mirror. She had chosen the dress for an evening of gambling at a Monte Carlo casino: the dark red velvet would look dramatic, she thought, against the backdrop of green-clothed tables and tuxedoed men. "Shaken, not stirred," she said in a throaty voice to her reflection, narrowing her eyes in the manner of a dangerous woman who might or might not be an enemy secret agent. After taking a few more twirls, she stepped out of the heels, pulled the gown off in fits and starts, and, somewhat flushed with the effort, ran her hands down the luxurious fabric before zipping the plastic cocoon back up. Then, sipping at her vodka tonic, she listened for baby cries or toddler steps.

All was thankfully quiet.

She looked with renewed deliberation down the long row of garment bags, selecting her next outing, her next adventure. Should she have cocktails under palm trees on a Caribbean beach (the light silk sheath hand-painted with flowers, and the pineapple-shaped bag that cost a small fortune)? Or go yachting off a Greek island (the turquoise beaded tunic, with the golden gladiator sandals)? Or indulge in a romantic evening at a Paris restaurant where soft jazz would mix with the aroma of lobster bisque and she would look so enticing in a tight black number with a plunging neckline?

Ever since Cecilia's birth, Mrs. Caldwell found herself engaging in fervid bouts of late-night shopping, compulsively clicking the "Complete your purchase" button after Paul had gone to bed. She bought only special-occasion dresses, stiletto heels, evening bags—fancy things of useless, extravagant beauty, of which she had not the slightest need (and which hardly even fit her properly: she chose all her clothes two sizes too small, for when she was thin again). She liked to envision a specific occasion before each new acquisition, the particular place and time she would use it if she led the kind of life that called for the use of such things; and she was then free to imagine the outings in the privacy of the closet, a well-deserved drink close at hand, posing before the mirror in that short, blissful interval after her five children had fallen asleep and before Paul returned from the office and one, or two, or three of the children awoke, wailing with wordless hunger, or asking for water, or frightened by a nightmare, or needing to pee.

Sometimes she thought: Perhaps, when I am ninety years old and my mind is failing, I will find a trunk crammed full of chiffon and glitter in the attic. I will stare at the moth-eaten gowns and the dusty shoes with dimming eyes, and I will mistake my long-ago closet fantasies for actual memories. For what, after all, is the difference between a memory and a fantasy? Are not both a succession of imprecisely rendered images further obscured by imprecisely chosen words and animated only by the wistful effort of one's imagination? And who is to say that a vividly imagined moment of happiness is not, in the end, more enriching to the spirit than a hazy semi-recollection of some pallid pastime?

She had just squeezed into a full skirt of iridescent peacock-blue taffeta (she had to leave the zipper half undone) and was searching for a suitable top when the telephone shrieked. Frantic, she groped in the pile of discarded shoe boxes. One ring, two rings—and, panting, she grabbed at the receiver, gasped a breathless, slightly slurred "Hello?"

The woman's accented voice on the other end was unfamiliar.

"Wrong number," she said curtly, and was hanging up already when the voice resolved into Olga's briskness.

"Did I catch you at a bad moment?" Olga asked.

Mrs. Caldwell felt a sudden surge of hostility. She has all the time in the world, she thought, so why must she intrude upon what little time I have to myself? But the house lay still; the children, mercifully, went on sleeping; she resigned herself. Clearing the nearby settee of gauzy accumulations of scarves, she settled down and, clutching her half-finished drink, spent a few minutes taking stock of her life. Paul was well, the children were fine, Emma was reading far beyond her years, Eugene enjoyed science, the twins really did have their own language, Celia had not yet begun to sleep through the night. Having dispensed with the obligatory questions, Olga plunged into chatter. Her latest relationship was over but she had just met someone new, she was planning to quit her job and travel for a while, go to Egypt, to Argentina . . . Mrs. Caldwell barely listened, as ever on the alert for the sounds of her children waking; and when, in an offhand, "Oh and I nearly forgot" manner, Olga delivered her real news at last, Mrs. Caldwell caught only the tail end of the sentence.

"What do you mean, three years ahead of schedule?" she had to ask.

"With my novel," Olga replied. "Remember how I always said I'd write one when I was forty? Well, it's coming out next spring."

"Really? That's great, congratulations . . . Oh no, the baby is crying, I must run . . . Talk soon!"

She finished the vodka tonic in one gulp and sat frowning at her half-dressed reflection in the mirror, and in another minute Paul strode in, shrugging off his jacket. She had not heard him come home.

"God, what a day!" He bent to peck her cheek. "They fired two more guys, and now Mark's worried that—"

"Paul," she said. "Remember how we were going to go to Thailand or Greece or China for our honeymoon, but my passport still hadn't arrived, and anyway you had too much work, so we just went to that bed-and-breakfast in the middle of nowhere instead, and you told me we'd do the real thing later? We never did, though."

"You got pregnant," he said, inspecting his tie for stains.

"I know." She glanced at her reflection, gave the skirt's zipper a surreptitious upward tug. "Do you . . . do you ever think about that place?"

"What place?"

"The bed-and-breakfast. We were there for three days, and we never even left the room, remember, we had all our meals brought in . . . Well, no, we did drive down to the only bar in town on our first evening, but we were afraid to show our faces there again after we beat all the local high scores on their trivia machine. Oh, we had such a wonderful time—do you remember, Paul? The bed was too soft and too narrow, and it made the floors creak, but we didn't care." She laughed a small laugh, gave her empty glass a shake, watched the ice cubes shift and resettle. He was busy sorting through a cluster of suits. She sighed. "And the railroad, remember the railroad?"

"What railroad?"

"There were railroad tracks running just a street away, surely you remember. And I've never told you this, but every night, after you'd fallen asleep, I stayed awake for hours listening to the freight trains go by. They were so loud, like huge metal boxes being dropped again and again and again. Of course, you slept through everything. But every time one of them rattled by, I wanted so badly to wake you up. I imagined us dressing in the dark and sneaking outside and hopping on one of the cars together, leaving all our luggage behind, not even bothering about the final destination, because anywhere out there would be new, anywhere would be thrilling. I never did wake you, though—I didn't want you to think I was disappointed. But maybe I should have. I mean, who knows where we'd be now if we had really done it . . . Paul, are you even listening?"

"I'm sorry, honey, I'd love to reminisce, but with this work crisis, my mind just isn't . . ." He had finished surveying his clothes and was now pulling shirts and jackets off hangers. "Besides, take it from me, travel is overrated."

"Wait—are you packing your bag?"

"Honey, I've just explained to you, I have to go to Texas tomorrow, back on Friday . . . Shall I fix you another drink? I'm going downstairs to make one for myself in a minute. If ever I needed one—or three—"

"Sure," she said after a moment's pause.

When she stood, the taffeta pooled stiffly around her feet, making her stumble.

He looked up, seemed to take in her drab maternity bra and the unzipped skirt for the first time, and said smiling, "Maybe you should buy yourself some nice new clothes while I'm away. Something . . . custom-fitted."

She winced and opened her mouth to reply and closed her mouth again.

"One vodka tonic coming right up," he said, already walking away—and then Celia wailed as she always did, without any warning: asleep one instant, rending the air with bloodcurdling screams the next. In the blink of an eye Mrs. Caldwell wiggled out of the skirt, tossed it onto the hanger, threw on her robe, and was flying out of the closet. In the doorway she heard a faint metallic rustle and, glancing back, discovered the skirt crumpled on the floor, the hanger, bereft of its weight, swinging lightly; but she did not return to pick it up, vanishing instead around the bend of the hallway.

The woman on the other side of the mirror stared after her thoughtfully. It was sad, she considered, what some lives came to when all was said and done; yet in truth, she failed to muster much sadness on behalf of Mrs. Caldwell. She moved her eyes around the closet shelves, studying the haughty lacquer of red-soled pumps, the soft sheen of cashmere shawls, the dry luster of snakeskin clutches. What if some catastrophe erased at one go all the cushioned comforts of that woman's oblivious life—some devastating natural disaster or, better yet, a bloody revolution? Her husband would be one of the first to get shot, and she would have to rely on herself alone to feed her brood of starving children. She would have nothing left to her name but a pile of expensive trifles, shards of a beautiful, idle life that could no longer be imagined in the new world of military fatigues, food rations, and sudden death; and she would have to trade each ruffled gown, each jeweled bag, for a crust of bread, for a spoonful of milk, for a sliver of life-giving medicine. There might be a poem here, she thought, happy as always when things shimmered with potential in her mind; but as she glanced again around the closet, she decided against it, already bored with the meaningless clutter of the costly ephemera—bored with Mrs. Caldwell. She picked up her notebook, rubbed the bridge of her nose in a small gesture she had inherited from her father, and left to search for ideas in the wider world.

28. Exercise Room

Conversations with the Dead

"AND DON'T ARGUE WITH ME, CHILD," her grandmother said in that habitual tone of disapproval Mrs. Caldwell remembered so well. Whenever she lifted the cigarette to her unevenly painted lips, the pale, expressionless cameo women on her bracelet clattered down her mottled arm. "Your life is unhealthy, I tell you. At your age, you need to meet people, go places, have experiences. You need to be *greedy*."

Again Mrs. Caldwell did not answer, hoping that such a demonstrable failure to uphold her end of the conversation might put a stop to the tedious dream. She did not remember falling asleep. She remembered herding the children to bed and mixing drinks and feeling better after the first martini and worse after the second. She remembered Paul, who had again returned from work in a foul mood, lecturing her about the state of the economy, asking whether she had not, of late, spent much too freely, carrying on unintelligibly about mortgages, budgets, overheads and underwrites, or was it overheaders and underwriters, then glancing at her waistline mid-sentence, and glancing away just as quickly. She remembered setting her jaw, making a silent, angry resolution, abandoning her barely touched third martini to change into her workout clothes, and stumbling downstairs to the exercise room. She even remembered plopping down onto the weight bench to tighten her shoelaces—but after that there was a disconcerting blank, and now here she was, running on the tread-mill, just as she had intended, except that her late grandmother was sitting on the treadmill's handlebars, wearing her old purple robe of faded velour and felt slippers the color of dusty roses, and, in turn, lecturing her about life, pulling on her cigarette between admonitions.

"Let me tell you something, child," her grandmother began anew. "A woman arrived among us recently, and not an old woman either, not a day over sixty—"

"Arrived where?" Mrs. Caldwell interrupted, forgetting her decision not to encourage the unnerving apparition. "Heaven?"

"Never you mind where," her grandmother replied with irrita-tion. "Anyway, this woman, she spent the last fifteen years of her life lying in bed. Nothing wrong with her, mind you, she just didn't feel like getting up. Had a live-in nurse bring her meals and clean her messes and tend to her bedsores. Now she'll be stuck where she is forever. You have to pay to move up, you know, and the currency is memories, stories of your life you must give away, like a kind of scouring, a gradual peeling of onion layers, do you see, to reveal the core within. And no, before you start to argue, there is a *world* of difference between memories and fantasies. But anyway, this woman, she is like a potato instead of an onion, all bland and mealy inside, so she has nothing to give, nothing whatsoever."

"Oh, is it like purgatory, then?" Mrs. Caldwell panted, curious in spite of herself.

She had finished the first mile, and was doing the second mile uphill.

Her grandmother ignored her question. "There is an even sadder case, a woman who sat on her toilet for years, refusing to stand up, until her skin actually grew around the seat. Mind-boggling, it is, but I tell you"—and she stabbed the glowing cigarette perilously close to Mrs. Caldwell's face—"this is exactly where you are heading if you are not careful. Can't you just stop this senseless trotting in place and listen to me? No matter how fast you run, you won't run away from yourself, you know."

Mrs. Caldwell clamped her lips tight, and furtively increased the speed and the incline of the treadmill, hoping that her grandmother might fall off; but the old woman held on.

"It's not healthy, I tell you," she repeated. "You need to learn how to drive, you need to get out of the house, you need people around you. And by 'people' I don't mean anyone below the age of ten, or anyone whom you pay, either. Otherwise, before you know it, you'll start talking to yourself or imagining things that aren't there, or worse, not being able to tell the two apart. You're too young to spend your life within four walls."

At this, Mrs. Caldwell had to speak, had to object.

"I'm thirty-eight, Grandmother. Almost thirty-nine. Hardly

young." To herself, she added: In this place, aging begins early. And earlier still when you have five kids.

"Child, you don't have the slightest idea of what aging means. And who forced you to have five kids?" her grandmother grumbled, just as though Mrs. Caldwell had voiced her thoughts aloud. She should not have drunk that third martini, she scolded herself dully. "And did you have any of your children for the simple reason that you wanted to have them?" the old woman continued relentlessly. "Indeed you did not. You had the first one to console a sick parent, the second to provide a playfellow for the first, the next two by accident, or maybe out of some self-destructive impulse—let a council of psychiatrists puzzle over that one—and the last, the last out of guilt. Children are not some stoppers you can wedge in wherever your life springs a leak. Next you'll be having one to fix your failing marriage."

"My marriage isn't failing!" Mrs. Caldwell exclaimed with indignation.

Her grandmother was the one to stay silent now, but her silence felt full of gloating.

"Oh, what can you possibly know about it?" Mrs. Caldwell cried, nettled. "You divorced both of your husbands, and only ever had my mother, and you didn't even raise her, you left her to Grandfather and his second wife to raise, while you went off somewhere, I suppose to have experiences and to be greedy. Well, I have all the experiences I need right here. Of course, I could have had a different life, I could have gone hopping from Paris to Rome to Vienna with that—that genius wannabe who didn't love me nearly enough and who was so self-absorbed he probably would never have wanted children. Instead I chose to create a real home, to have a family with a man who makes me feel safe and whole, who will always love me, no matter what—"

Her grandmother's small eyes glittered like a crow's, and her voice grew sharp with wicked triumph. "And if he will always love you no matter what, then tell me, my dear, why are you huffing and puffing like that on this infernal contraption?"

And all at once grief was upon her. The monstrous notion of growing old, of losing her husband's love, of finding herself alone—of having her entire life fall apart—took hold of her roughly. Was it indeed true that she had spent her best years as a fairy-tale princess locked away in a tower—a confinement of her choosing, a confinement with many comforts, but one with barred windows and locked doors all the same? And now, seeing the gates inexplicably open, had she wandered outside, only to find herself, dazed and helpless, in the midst of a dark, frightening forest where wild beasts crouched in wait in the shadow of the night and she herself was no longer young enough, no longer pretty enough, to count on a rescue by a passing knight?

Gods, my gods, how did I come to be in this desolate place, where did my sunlit garden go, did I take a wrong turn somewhere along the way—

"There, there, no need to mope like that," her grandmother said, patting her sweaty hand. "Bad things happen whenever they get a mind to, but good things don't happen at all unless you go looking for them. Remember the story I told you about the tree? Why did you stop with those nice little poems you used to write? You shouldn't give up trying, you know. Go ahead and rhyme a line or two—start with your own small life if it makes you feel better, but do remember to aim higher and higher as you plod along." She cackled, her crow's eyes sparkling. "Why, if you take me as your guide, you could become a modern-day Dante some-day. Oh, the things I could tell you about heaven and hell . . ."

Abruptly she ceased cackling, dropped her cigarette onto the floor, and glanced over her shoulder, looking half annoyed and half alarmed, as if she had done something wrong and someone was calling her now to come and be chastised. *(In the end she would be forgiven yet again. Silly woman, God boomed in her ear, sternly but not unkindly. Why must you always run on so? You told this poor girl enough fairy tales when you were alive. Come now, Gabriel has called everyone to evening tea, and we will be serving your favorite gooseberry jam.)*

Mrs. Caldwell looked where her grandmother was looking, but there was nothing there. "What tree, Grandmother?" she asked, turning back, but her grandmother was gone, and she was finish-ing her second mile on the treadmill, out of breath, crying for some reason, the mirrors all around the exercise room crowded with unmistakably middle-aged women who had swimming, in-ebriated eyes and unsubtle hints of double chins. The air held tell-tale traces of smoke. Mrs. Caldwell wiped away the tears with her sleeve, turned off the treadmill, and stepped down, swaying. If Paul finds out that I've taken up smoking, he will be upset, she thought, bending to pick the cigarette stub off the floor. Of course, I only ever smoke down here, where he never sets foot, but still . . . She was about to slip the stub into her pocket, to bury it in the depths of the trashcan later, when she noticed that it looked oddly unfamiliar, steely gray instead of the speckled gold of her own preferred brand, and ringed with peach-tinted lipstick. Why, oh why, did she have to start on that fourth martini? Averting her eyes, she tossed the cigarette back on the floor and pushed it under the treadmill with her foot. There, all out of sight now, and everything was well, and no reason to feel so unsettled.

She turned off the lights, and, to her relief, the middle-aged, double-chinned women vanished obediently. "So what if I'm no longer twenty," she said aloud, arguing with an invisible someone. "So what if I'm no longer skinny. My husband will love me no matter what."

She slammed the door on her way out.

29. Laundry

The Laundry Cycle

FRIDAY WAS MRS. CALDWELL'S LAUNDRY DAY.
Unlike some things, it did not become more enjoyable with repetition.

Occasionally, as she threaded collar stays through shirt collars, buttoned cardigan buttons, and ironed creases into Paul's pants, she pondered a certain paradox: An average woman—or at least an average married woman with children, which, for all she knew, no longer signified an average woman; to rephrase, then, a woman average for most of human history—almost certainly devoted more of her time to the pursuit of laundering than to the pursuit of love; yet for all the thousands and thousands of poems written about love, only a handful had ever been written about laundry. Without a doubt, laundry, as she had learned rather exhaustively, was in its essence not a poetic matter, and most poets were men and knew little about it; but was not imparting beauty and meaning to the mundane and the meaningless one of the most vital missions of poetry?

One day in January, after she had hurried to cram the washer full of her husband's shirts, she tried her hand at a limerick. She stumbled almost instantly: there seemed to be nothing that rhymed with either "Moscow" or "Russia." She grew stubborn and for a couple of minutes paced the stuffy laundry room, now and then bumping the ironing board with her hip, until the last syllable fell into place.

> There was a young woman from Moscow
> Who bought laundry detergent at Costco.
> But her clothes turned to mold,
> And then she grew old,
> That no-longer-young woman from Moscow.

This, of course, was neither beautiful nor particularly meaningful; but every Friday from then on, as she folded and ironed in the small, steamy room with its stacks of damp underwear and pastel-hued seascapes on the white windowless walls, she continued to toy with words—just to while away the time—until, without writing down a line, she had half composed a collection of laundry poems across the genres.

She resolved to set them down on paper when she was done.

February she devoted to the epic and the folk song. The epic installment, written in measured Homeric rhythm, sang of the dawn of the world—rosy-fingered Eos rising over the wine-colored sea, Nausicaa and her handmaidens on the shore stretching linens and laughing, the linens fluttering in the wind, white and fresh like Nausicaa's purity, and Odysseus, watching her, pierced with an unaccustomed regret, the sheets spotless, the virgin smiling, the words unspoken, the cool air brisk with the flapping of taut cloth, the sweetness of what might have been and what never would be: the recently violent world of war and rapine reined in by the civilizing restraint of a young girl's domestic perfection. The folk-song fragment was a medieval dirge, the lament of a peasant woman at a half-frozen river, scraping blood off the mail shirt of a conquering Mongol who had burned down her village and slaughtered her husband. In the last week of the month, she dashed off a quick fairy-tale tribute—a happy little ditty trilled by an ever-hopeful, ever-misguided Cinderella over her tub of soapsuds.

In March, she composed some erotic couplets—a courtesan in Renaissance Venice humming to herself as she perfumed her red satin pillows—and a longer tragic poem set in Paris, the whispered prayer of a mother in a dark, rat-infested attic bending over the tiny soiled underclothes of a dead child as revolution swept through the streets outside. While in the French mood, she also amused herself with a short Molière-style comedy, in which sly maids and greedy servants exploited their masters' bedroom secrets gleaned from love tokens unearthed at the brushing of gold-trimmed petticoats.

She rounded off the month with a quick haiku.

God from his white cloud
watches angels soaping souls,
scrubbing off our sins.

In April and May, she paid cursory tribute to a variety of minor genres, including:

anthropology: a fiercely rhymed chorus of old women gathered in the village square the morning after a wedding to inspect the sheets and stone the errant bride;

religion (or possibly satire, she could not decide): a meditation on Protestant ethics with a prodigal son who returned home in rags to smell milk, bread, and linen in his mother's kitchen and fell on his knees, his face buried in her crisply ironed apron, while she admonished him gently: "Cleanliness, my boy, is next to godliness";

and, finally, autobiography: Paul doing his first-ever laundry load, in the early days of their marriage—and, far from separating the reds from the whites, indiscriminately picking up the entire pile of dirty clothes he had dumped on the floor in the hallway and throwing it into the washer, trapping in the midst of the mess her favorite, her only, pair of black leather boots (which she had lined up neatly by the door). The boots had been ruined, and she had been vexed. She had never let him approach the washer again. Now, after having devoted what must have translated into solid weeks of time to laundry duty (a conservative calculation: at three hours a week, fifty-two weeks a year, thirteen and a half years of married life: some eighty-eight *days* of nothing but laundry), she wondered whether the boot fiasco had been as scatterbrained, as innocent of intent, as she had supposed it in the heat of the moment. Yet the poem was devoid of any traces of anger: it had turned out oddly tender, nostalgic almost.

She did not think it one of her more successful efforts.

In the middle of June, two weeks before her fortieth birthday, she was hunting down the twins' mismatched socks while working on a children's song:

The sock monster through the house
Tiptoes quiet as a mouse.
Doorknobs turn and drawers creak,
But you won't see him if you peek.
He will crawl into the laundry,
He will—he will—he will . . .

And it was while searching for the insistently escaping rhyme to "laundry" that she looked directly at the telltale stains on her husband's collar, the glinting peach-colored traces resembling a woman's lipstick—smelling of a woman's lipstick too, as she verified in the next, unthinking moment, lifting the shirt to her nose before she could divert her attention. And, of course, she had seen them before, these now obvious signs—had glimpsed them, but had not wanted to inspect them closely, thrusting the clothes into the washer with increasingly frantic movements, explaining away the faint whiffs of perfume and the most conspicuous spots—a splash of ketchup on this sweater's shoulder, a dash of mayonnaise on those pants' zipper, he had always been an enthusiastic eater—and, on that January day, when she had peered an incautious instant too long at another peach-tinted smear on a shirt's cuff and found the truth looming dangerously close, occupying her mind with a limerick, then a dirge, then a haiku . . .

And yet, for all her hectic poetizing of the past few months—

whether an attempt to break through the mundane to a deeper reality or to escape the reality altogether—was it not telling that most of her laundry poems had ended up being love poems after all?

Her hands trembling, she pushed the shirt under other shirts, pressed the "Heavy Soil" button. "'Laundry'—'husbandry.' 'Laundry'—'quandary,'" she repeated, but neither was a very good rhyme, and abruptly she abandoned the composition. She already knew that she would never write any of the poems down, but that was not important, not important at all. And the thing that *was* important, the thing that had gone so horribly, so inexplicably, wrong—it could still be fixed, could it not, it was not too late to fix it, all they needed was a fresh start, yes, she was certain that everything would be fine, everything would be back to the way it was, if only they could have something—someone—someone new and wonderful in their lives to remind them how much love there really was between them.

If only they could still—if only she could still—

30. Master Bedroom

Conversation in the Dark at the Age of Forty

UNHAPPINESS THIS IMPENETRABLE IS LIKEWISE silent, but the silence lasts longer.

31. Girls' Room

A Grimm Fairy Tale

"'MY DEAR CHILDREN,' SAID THE OLD KING, 'I WILL give you three trials, and he who wins shall have the crown. The first trial is to bring me a cloth so fine that I can draw it through my golden ring . . .'"

It was the girls' turn at book hour. Mrs. Caldwell had made sure that Eugene had finished his homework and Rich and George had brushed their teeth, and had settled in the girls' room with a volume of the Brothers Grimm tales, a spiderweb and a glossy red apple on its cover. She read mechanically, pausing now and then to listen for the sounds of her husband's arrival. She promised herself that it would be tonight. Tonight she would tell him. She had meant to tell him every night for weeks, but every time, her nerve would fail her at the last minute. He would come home late, looking harried or morose, and stomp down to the bar to mix himself a drink without checking on the sleeping children first, not asking her about her day. At times she imagined she caught wafts of floral perfume. He was never unpleasant to her—it was more like he did not remember her presence; his eyes slipped past her, his thoughts slipped past her. Tonight she would make him stop and look at her.

Tonight she would tell him.

"'And so the king embraced his youngest son, told his servants to throw the coarse linen of the older sons into the sea, and said to his children, "For the second trial, you must bring me a little dog, so small that it will fit in a walnut shell."'"

"Well, that's just stupid," Emma declared. "The first trial was not so great either, not like battling a giant or finding a sorcerer's stone or anything, but at least you can make something useful out of cloth. Why does the king want an itty-bitty dog? It can't hunt or defend anything. And how does your ability to find a tiny dog make you good ruler material, exactly?" She had her blanket tucked neatly under the mattress and drawn below her chin in a straight line; her bed was free of stuffed animals, and the books on her nightstand were arranged by size in perfect order. Mrs. Caldwell imagined that inside Emma's ten-year-old mind things were just as organized and logical and uncluttered. Emma possessed a clear-eyed, levelheaded need to make sense of the world, and she usually succeeded. Mrs. Caldwell did not worry about Emma.

"It's *not* stupid," Celia said in an impassioned voice from her side of the room. Her bed barely had space for her, crowded as it was with teddy bears and dogs and elephants, her favorite one-eared bunny dressed in her old baby nightshirt. "I think the king just loved pets. Like I love Squash. Like I loved Pepper before he went to dog heaven." Her mouth curled downward, and Mrs. Caldwell hurriedly resumed her reading.

Mrs. Caldwell worried about Celia.

She read in English because the girls did not know Russian. Eugene was the only one who understood it, albeit imperfectly, for she had sung him Russian lullabies and told him tales of her own childhood; but when she had spoken Russian to the infant Emma, Emma had cried, as if sensing something amiss, and as a toddler she had flatly refused to submit to the pointless torture of learning some made-up word that no one but her mother understood for every normal word used by everyone around her. By the time the twins were born, Mrs. Caldwell had switched fully to English.

"'The older princes brought many pretty little dogs, but none could fit in the walnut shell . . .'" The room flared up in a car's headlights, and Mrs. Caldwell paused to glance out the window; but the car did not slow down by their gates, passing out of sight down the darkened street. "'And so the old king again embraced his youngest son, told his servants to drown all the other dogs in the sea, and—'"

"Oh, Mama, does it really say that?" Celia cried, her lips turning down once again and beginning to tremble. Mrs. Caldwell looked at her without comprehension, then ran her eyes over what she had just read. She was in the habit of softening the harsher truths of the Brothers Grimm stories, omitting certain details, changing executions to exiles and deaths to prolonged absences— when she paid sufficient attention.

"No, sweetie, of course not, I read it wrong," she hastened to say. "The king told his servants to release all the dogs by the sea."

"Because the dogs will enjoy playing on the beach," Celia said, and, nodding with understanding, subsided back into the pillows.

Emma snorted.

Mrs. Caldwell gave her older daughter a warning look, and returned to the book. At the account of the third task, that of finding the most beautiful girl, her thoughts wandered again, and by the time it came to the king's ordering the entire crowd of second-rate ladies "to be thrown into the sea and drowned," she neglected to amend it. Celia sat up in bed, blinking.

"So ladies who aren't beautiful are drowned? What if I'm not beautiful when I grow up?"

"You probably won't be. To be beautiful," Emma said helpfully, "you need to be really skinny and at least eight feet tall."

Celia looked alarmed.

"No, no, sweetie, Emma's joking," Mrs. Caldwell said, snapping the book shut and turning off the lamp, then gently pushing the bunnies and the bears aside to perch on Celia's bed. "And in any case, I'm sure all the ladies knew how to swim and were perfectly all right in the end."

Except for the old ones and the fat ones, a voice inside her added with bitterness.

Squash growled in uneasy slumber in the hallway, and she listened for a moment, but all was quiet again. It was almost nine o'clock. The girls' room lay shadowy and warm, illuminated softly by a single nightlight shaped like a pale pink seashell. "Why don't I tell you some stories from my childhood instead? How your grandfather and I used to hunt mushrooms, or about the brownie who lived in our dacha attic, or—"

"I don't want real life," Celia said. "I want a fairy tale about a princess, but only with a happy ending."

Mrs. Caldwell looked over at Emma, but she had already fallen asleep, probably as soon as the light had gone out. *(In her dream, Emma walked through a city, barefoot, still wearing her cherry-studded pajamas. It was a place she dreamed about often. The streets were straight, the squares wide and empty, the houses made of brightly polished white stones. There were no people around, only statues dressed in what looked like cascading sheets, but Emma was happy there; it seemed to her serious and good. Whenever she found herself visiting, she tried to commit to memory the gleaming geometry of the place so she could build a city just like it when she grew up.)*

"All right," Mrs. Caldwell whispered, stretching along the edge of Celia's bed. "There once was a princess."

"Was she beautiful?" Celia asked, snuggling closer.

"She was. But she was not one of those silly princesses who sit in front of their mirrors all day long combing their hair. The most beautiful thing about her was her voice, and above all else in the world she loved to sing. One day the princess decided to leave her home."

"Why? Didn't she live in a castle? Were her parents not nice?"

"She lived in a very small castle. Her parents, the old king and queen, were kind and noble, but their kingdom was tiny, and the princess wanted to see new places and learn new things. When she went to say good-bye to her parents, her father gave her a gift—a box that looked plain on the outside but had seven precious songs inside. And he told her to treasure these songs and to keep them secret from everyone. For her voice would stay beautiful and true only as long as the songs stayed hidden, the king told her, but if she let the songs out, she would no longer be able to sing at all. So the princess took the box, thanked her father, and traveled to a distant land across the sea, and in that land she met a prince."

"Was he nice?"

"He was very, very nice. And he lived in a lovely castle that was much bigger than the castle where the princess had grown up. The prince fell in love with the princess, and the princess loved how nice the prince was, and she loved his castle too. So they got married, and the princess felt so happy on their wedding day that she opened her secret box and sang the first song to her new husband the prince. And the next morning her treasure box had only six songs left in it, but some time later a beautiful baby boy appeared asleep in the cradle, and the princess was happy—so happy that she opened her box and sang the second song to her little son. And then she had only five songs left in the box, but some time later a beautiful baby girl appeared in her cradle."

"And did the princess sing a song to her baby girl too?"

"She did. In fact, she sang two songs, one to her new baby girl and one to her firstborn boy, to show that she loved them both equally. And then she had two new babies, and only three songs left. And this happened two more times—two more times the princess felt so happy that she sang one of her special songs—and so in the end she had six precious children, and only one song left in her secret box."

"Six children, how nice," said Celia sleepily. "You only have five. And did the princess sing her last song away too?"

"No, that one she kept for herself," Mrs. Caldwell said.

"So the last baby didn't make her happy?"

"Oh. No, no, it's just that she wanted to keep one song for herself."

"So she was selfish." Celia yawned and closed her eyes, and mumbled into her pillow, "Or maybe the last song was a bad one. Or maybe her father forgot to put it in the box and gave her only six. Or maybe the princess lost it when she opened the box the time before. Or maybe—"

Mrs. Caldwell sighed. "Maybe," she said. Bending over the drowsy girl, she smoothed the matted blond locks on her forehead, then whispered, her lips against the child's warm cheek: "Would you like a little sister?" Celia did not answer; she too had fallen asleep. *(Celia dreamed that she lived in a house just like their house from the outside but completely different inside. There was no furniture anywhere at all, and the empty rooms had clear glass walls; through the walls she could see disappearing vistas of tantalizing, brilliantly colored places—gardens, mountains, amusement parks with the most delightful carousels—to which, however, she could discover no entrance, for when she walked through the doors, she found herself in other glass-walled rooms that were just like the rooms she had left. The floors were likewise glass, and when she peered closely, she could see roots and insects stirring in the soil under her feet, though she could not touch them through the thick transparent plate. None of the rooms had ceilings; no matter what floor she was on, wherever she looked up, she saw white curly clouds scurrying across the skies and, in one spot, a gathering thunderstorm. A few times she thought she glimpsed, through the glass of the walls, her mother passing slowly, rooms away, her eyes cast down, her face pale—but she could never get close to her. And once, a man appeared before her and looked her over thoughtfully. So you are one of the brats for whom your mother the princess has given up her songs, he said. I wonder if you're worth it. He smiled at her then, but it was not a nice smile. She felt a little afraid, and fascinated at the same time.)*

Mrs. Caldwell slipped off the bed and sat down in her reading chair to wait. All five children and the dog were sleeping now. Outside the girls' room, the house shifted, settling deeper into its mysterious nocturnal life, filling with odd creaks, groans, and murmurs—the sock monster rummaging through the laundry basket, the cantankerous ghost of her grandmother muttering in the exercise room, two shadowy lovers embracing among the bottles down in the cellar—but inside the girls' warmly glowing pink-and-white room there reigned a tranquil stillness, not altogether soundless, and yet separate from the rest of the world, as if they were sheltered within some luminous rosy seashell, and while the seashell hummed gently with the rumble of the ocean, the ocean's chilled, roiling vastness was reduced in the seashell's pearly, blushing spiral to something toylike, and soothing, and remote. Mrs. Caldwell watched her daughters sleep—Emma lying still and serene on her back, her dark hair framing the solemn clarity of her profile, Celia tossing, pulling the covers on, throwing them off, revealing the scratches on her arms and the scabs on her knees, hugging her bunny closer to her chest, muttering something with a quiet but fierce conviction—"Yes, yes, I am, I swear," Mrs. Caldwell heard, or thought she heard. Two small, self-contained worlds, two perfect, unknowable mysteries, and down and across the hallway, three more—and she loved each of them completely, loved them more than anything else in the world, more even than her songs.

Another pair of headlights flooded the inside of the seashell with a cold, sliding glare, but this time the car did slow down, the gates glided open, gravel crunched under the tires. She did not rise to meet him—she had chosen this room for their talk, had meant to stay within its rosy safety. When his ponderous steps thumped up the stairs, she called him in an undertone, and called again, louder. The steps hesitated on the landing before turning toward her. Then he stood in the doorway—an imposing, impeccably dressed man with the heavy face of a tired stranger.

"Come," she said, "look at them. Look how sweet they are."

"Yes," he said from the threshold, and was silent. She saw his face harden with a sudden resolve. He took a step into the room.

"Sit down for a minute," she said, and while her voice was low with tenderness, her stomach lurched with worry.

She could smell whiskey on his breath from where she sat.

He remained standing, looking away from her, at the girls in their beds.

"Time has flown," he said. She wished she could see his eyes. "It's hard to believe Cecilia is turning five in another week. Not a baby any longer . . . Look, there is something I've been meaning to tell you."

Panic split her asunder. She had prepared for their conversation with care, had watched her face in the mirror as she had practiced saying the loving words leading to the hinting words leading to the shocking words to be followed up quickly by the calming words—but there was no time for it now. He was going to tell her about the other woman, she knew, and then he was going to leave her, leave her and the children, because none of them were babies now, because they would manage——

"Wait, I have something to tell you too," she cried. "I'm pregnant!"

The seashell nightlight glowed, the girls' breathing was peaceful in their sleep.

He looked at her stonily, without speaking.

"I'm pregnant, Paul," she said again, softly, and forced herself to smile.

The expressions shifted in rapid succession on his face, like a shuffled deck of cards, until the one that settled on it was anger.

"How is that possible?" he said. His tone was even, but she felt the boil of his fury beneath. Her smile flickered out. She could no longer tell what expression her own face bore. "How is that possible? It's only been once or twice in the past few months, if that. And I thought you were taking the pill——"

Her panic grew. She had not practiced for this.

"But I am," she pleaded, untruthfully. "Accidents happen."

He sat down on Emma's bed, placed his hands squarely on his knees.

"Look," he said. "Things aren't . . . We already have five children. You only ever wanted two. I wanted three. The twins—the twins were a blessing, of course, and little Celia . . . Well, you know I was against it, but you talked me into it, and I wouldn't have it any other way, that goes without saying, but this time . . . We're both forty years old, my job security isn't what it used to be, and—and things are different. You have to talk to your doctor——"

"Paul." She was crying. "I can't. I can't now. It's too late."

"What do you mean, too late?"

"Do you remember that night—the night your father told you he needed surgery—"

"Do you mean," he began, and stopped, and stood back up, towering over her, staring down at her as she pressed, feeling small and frightened, into her chair. "That was almost five months ago."

"Five months and a week," she whispered.

"You are five months pregnant, and you haven't told me?"

"Don't shout, please don't shout, you'll wake them up . . . I didn't know. Please. Paul. I didn't know myself. I thought I was just . . ." (*Old. Fat. Say it.* The cold voice inside nudged her, but she disregarded its promptings.) "I only just found out myself. Paul. It's going to be a girl. A healthy girl. Look at them. Look at them!"

And there were the upside-down mermaids floating on the wallpaper, and the warm seashell nightlight, and Emma's papier-mâché model of a human heart on her desk, and Celia's one-eared blue bunny hanging half off her bed, and two heads on the pillows, one blond, one dark. And as he stood before them, the big hulk of a man, the big husk of a man, his shoulders drooped, his mouth sagged, and she saw defeat in his eyes, and underneath it, possibly, just possibly, the touch of old warmth, of old kindness.

"Oh, honey," he said.

And though he did not move to scoop her into his arms, but took a step back and, sitting down again, stared at the carpet, an immense exhalation of relief shook her. Her panic abated. It would be all right now, she knew. She sighed, and rose, and, going over to him, placed her hand lightly on his hair, ruffling it, willing him to raise his head and look at her, look at her, until he did at last.

"Let's name her after your other grandmother," she said. "It will make your dad happy. He needs all the happiness he can get right now, you know?" She smiled her tremulous relief down at him, then picked up his big, limp, unresisting hand, and pressed it to her stomach.

"Margaret," she said.

32. Kitchen

After Thanksgiving

THE DINING ROOM STILL OVERFLOWED WITH THE festive chaos of cutlery clicking, glasses ringing, younger children screaming with laughter as they licked the last of the pecan pie mush off their plates, but the meal was over now, the table half cleared, and the voices had already begun to spill into the living room and, from there, to fan out all over the house. Mrs. Caldwell could hear her mother's incredulous "But how we could eat so big bird so quick!" and her mother-in-law's decorous laughter as she replied, "It happens every time—of course, there are so many of us," and even a room away, Mrs. Caldwell thought she detected a slight dipping in her polite voice.

They were one fewer this year: Paul's father had died in the spring.

For a minute Mrs. Caldwell stood still in the deserted kitchen, listening to the noises from the other rooms, surveying the piles of dirty plates, the puddles of cranberry sauce and the chunks of sweet potatoes solidifying on the bottom of serving bowls, the graying remains of the turkey. She had cooked the entire feast with her own hands; since they had stopped indulging in frequent takeout meals (Paul's new job did not pay quite as well), she had discovered in herself an unsuspected culinary talent. The dinner was a success, she thought as she rolled up her sleeves, turned on the hot water, and soaped the first plate. This was her in-laws' special wedding china, which Paul's mother had given them after Dick Caldwell's passing, and it had to be washed by hand; but Mrs. Caldwell did not mind. She liked the sensation of warmth running over her fingers, liked seeing her immaculate kitchen gradually emerge from beneath the disorder, plate by gleaming plate, glass by sparkling glass, pot by scoured pot, liked hearing the sounds of her well-fed family all around her while being alone, free to—not think, exactly, for she was too full and tired to think—free, then, to feel at peace.

Of course, her solitude never lasted long. Squash and Snuggle, the new puppy, padded into the kitchen, slashing their tails back and forth in whimpering excitement, and she put a couple of greasy trays on the floor for them to nose. Celia burst in giggling, followed by Maggie, who, at two and a half, liked to hurl herself in endless, heedless pursuit of her siblings. Distracted by the sight of her mother's legs, Maggie swerved aside and stood clutching at Mrs. Caldwell's skirt, cooing up at her. Mrs. Caldwell's heart dissolved. She gave the girls caramel apples, even though they had undoubtedly had enough sweets already—but this was part of Thanksgiving, was it not, everything in excess, everyone generous. They settled at the kitchen table slurping and chewing noisily, just as Eugene wandered in to ask whether she had seen his *Brief History of Time*. She had indeed: he had left it on top of the toaster oven during breakfast, as he was forever leaving a stream of objects behind him in his absentminded, cogitative, preoccupied progress through the house—mainly books and pencils, but also gloves and hats in winter, rocks and bugs trapped in jars in summer, and socks, and homework, and, of late, scraps of paper with phone numbers scribbled on them. "Oh, thanks," he said, and, picking up the book, perched on the nearest stool and proceeded to read, oblivious of the clamor of cleaning all around him, oblivious too of the prospect of caramel apples. Rich and George, who had just run in, bickering about some game score ("I did!"—"You did not!"—"I did too!"—"You so didn't!"), were not oblivious of the apples; Rich tried to take a bite from Maggie's but she snapped her caramel-smeared teeth at him like some feral beastie, and Mrs. Caldwell hurried over to give the boys their own. Both of them, she noticed, had cranberry sauce splattered up and down their new white shirts; she chastised them out of habit, but everyone knew she did not mean it. Emma, gliding in next, the only one of the children to keep her clothes entirely spill- and spot-free after the two-hour meal, declined the apple and offered to help with the dishes instead; Mrs. Caldwell gave her the delicate task of drying the crystal. Her mother tried to take up a towel too, but Mrs. Caldwell would have none of it, bustling her over to the table with a cup of coffee, which she presently dispensed to Emma the elder as well (she had long stopped thinking of Paul's mother as Mrs. Caldwell).

Paul was the last to enter the kitchen.

"So that's where everyone is," he said. "I can finish with the washing."

"I'm almost done now," Mrs. Caldwell said. "Here, pass me the carving knife."

He stood behind her at the sink, surveying the crowded kitchen.

"I do believe we need a bigger house," he said.

She whipped around, and discovered him smiling, and laughed herself, to make sure that they both knew it was a joke; for she would not be moving anywhere.

She liked this house, and she liked this life, just as they were.

Her sense of contentment had crept up on her. After Maggie's birth, more and more often, she had felt as though she was finally growing into her days. Perhaps the house had simply been too vast for her and she had needed every last one of her children to fill its empty rooms with disarray and light, and, in doing so, to put a stop to her uneasy, strained sensation of being a grain of sand falling through chilly expanses of the hourglass in a place, in a life, not her own. At times she thought of it, half seriously, in terms of destiny: Maybe each person was intended, by God, or the position of stars, or one's biological nature, to achieve a given number of feats, be it children or scientific discoveries or works of art or anything else of merit. Destiny was not the same as fate, of course, and one was free to fulfill it or to ignore it as one saw fit, but until—unless—all the discrete internal hollows yawning empty with potential were filled, one was bound to feel loose, restless, incomplete, not at ease in one's own skin. Maybe, according to some mysterious reckoning, she was meant to have six children, and now that she did, she could take a deep breath at last, enjoy the fruits of her labors, embrace her hard-earned role of the capable matriarch, dispenser of food, warmth, and love, the irreplaceable heart of a large, happy family in the bosom of a welcoming house.

Or maybe she was just too busy to wallow in discontent, and too wise to yearn for the unattainable.

As for Paul, he now came home early on weekdays and stayed home on weekends, and she no longer cared to sniff his clothes, or worried about the size of her own—just as, having learned at long last how to drive, she no longer dreamed of finding a highway and disappearing into the sunset in a convertible, its roof down, the wind in her hair, but merely used her minivan to transport the children from baseball to ballet.

"I was only joking about the house," Paul said, and she could see his mouth growing thin, as it did whenever he thought of their recent financial setbacks. He lowered his voice. "Have you spoken to your mother?"

"Not yet," she whispered back. "I will as soon as I get her alone."

Later that evening, when everyone else had retired upstairs, she asked her mother to join her for tea. She served it in the familiar porcelain cups of her childhood, which her mother had brought as a gift on a previous visit; though when she had first produced six misshapen bundles from her suitcase and proceeded to unwrap the thick layers of woolen stockings, all the while smiling slyly, like a magician about to bestow some momentous surprise, Mrs. Caldwell had looked at the row of hatching cups and failed to recognize them. They were not as she remembered them from the countless teatimes in the dark, tight entrapment of their Moscow kitchen. There, radiant with gold, bright with paradisiacal flowers and birds, they had stood out as something singular, something precious, that had required conscious handling and admiration amidst the mundane oppression of grimy pots and aluminum forks. Now they were only half a dozen gaudy cups, one of them chipped, lost in her light, spacious kitchen, whose every glass-paneled cabinet glittered with much finer china. All the same, she thanked her mother profusely, and afterward made sure to use the crudely painted cups whenever the two of them had tea together.

Old people, she knew, became so attached to their old things.

"Have you thought more of our proposal?" she asked, and blew on her tea. "There is no one to take care of you in Moscow, and at your age . . . Of course, seventy-four isn't old, but I worry."

"I know it makes sense," her mother said smiling, "but I'm so settled there—it's my whole life. Did I tell you, by the way, they finally finished with that construction across the road. Only took them half a century. It's a giant parking garage now, lots of silver Mercedes going in and out. But I sometimes wonder: What was it supposed to be, I mean in the beginning? Something else, don't you think? Remember, your father used to joke—"

Mrs. Caldwell waited for her chatter to subside.

"Yes, but our proposal?" she asked again.

"Well, I just hate the idea of our apartment lying empty, going to ruin, your father's books and pipes gathering dust—"

"Oh," said Mrs. Caldwell, "but of course the apartment would have to be sold."

Her mother blinked at her.

"But you see, it can never be sold," she said, speaking with exaggerated slowness, as if to someone foreign. "Because it's our home. And then, your children—it's all I can leave them, you see. I know it's small and poor, nothing like this—"

Mrs. Caldwell gently moved her hand over her mother's.

"Mama," she said. "It's over, that part of life, it's just—it's like one's childhood or youth, you will always remember it, but you can't, and you shouldn't, ever go back. And my children don't even speak Russian."

"But I don't understand. What do you mean?" her mother muttered, and looked at Mrs. Caldwell with frightened eyes, as though she might have misheard the entire conversation. "You want me to sell our apartment?"

"I think that would be best," Mrs. Caldwell replied softly.

(Her mother thought: Does she not remember? Does she not know? Any place is only a place, four walls, a door, a window—it's the accumulated living, the weight of memories, that make it magic, that make it yours. The air you breathe within your four walls is like no other air, and your past is not past, and the love you have felt all your life is bright within, and you never age, and you never, ever forget. But she left, and she has forgotten. I shouldn't have given her my cups. No one can have a future without a past. She is only forty-three, but she has misplaced her childhood and now she looks so old.)

She looks so old, Mrs. Caldwell thought, and lowered her eyes, her chest tightening. The silence hung thick between them.

"This needs to be sweeter," her mother said in a tone of abrupt disapproval, and put a sugar cube into her cup, and stirred it without looking up. Mrs. Caldwell waited for her to speak, but she said nothing else, just drank her tea in silence, her face askew. Having taken the last sip, she stood up, carried the empty cup to the sink, and set about carefully scraping the soggy tea leaves into the trash.

"Please, just leave everything," Mrs. Caldwell called out. "I'll take care of it."

But her mother was still standing by the trash, staring into it.

"You threw away the turkey leftovers again?" she asked. "You promised not to."

"But they were mostly bones," Mrs. Caldwell replied with a slight shrug. "No one would have eaten them tomorrow."

"I would have," her mother said, and now her voice was oddly close to weeping. "Why, why must you always throw everything away? It's not becoming. It's a wasteful person's habit. It's—it's a sin."

"But Mama—" Mrs. Caldwell began, deeply shocked.

Without another glance at her daughter, the old woman quit the kitchen.

33. Son's Room

The Wheel of Time

AS SHE GREW OLDER, MRS. CALDWELL NOTICED A
curious thing: time moved differently in different parts of the
house. In little-frequented rooms, where living was thin, it pooled
like calm, standing water, hardly ever changing; when you peered
inside, it would give you back a reflection of yourself at another
age. Thus, from the ballroom's threshold, she sometimes glimpsed
a young woman, almost a girl, sitting on the floor by the flames
that had turned to ashes many years before, lifting a hesitant hand
to the golden choker on her neck, awed by the splendor of it all,
afraid to be happy. Other places served as frames to a single bright
moment, a flash of desire or pain or fear. The moments themselves
were in the past, and the rooms had flowed by on the current of
years, obscured by layers of subsequent, dimmer living, no longer
supporting the memory precisely; the earthy gloom of the wine
cellar had been banished in the glare of new fluorescent lamps, and

the twins' bedroom had long shed its giraffes and monkeys, the cribs replaced by the efficiency of bunk beds, the twins themselves gangly teenagers now. But there time had stopped in its tracks, briefly blinded, and to this day, whenever she entered the cellar to pick a bottle of Riesling for dinner or happened to glance at a clock hanging above Rich's desk, she felt touched by an emotion—only an echo of the past emotion, to be sure, yet always there.

She preferred other rooms, where life had not gouged out a permanent scar and where several layers of time coexisted in peace: recollections overlapping, comforting her with a steady knowledge of now and then, nothing lost yet nothing over—a good life having been lived, a good life being lived still. In the girls' room, she imagined she could see the vanished mermaid wall-paper as a playful shimmer under the current green paint, Celia's earlier stuffed animals sharing the shelves with her later piles of books, Emma's elaborate architectural drawings hanging over her kindergarten stick figures in their houses of squares and triangles. She thought her firstborn's room like that too—a decade and a half of warm, innocent memories present at once, from a tod-dler napping cheek to cheek with his toy hedgehog to an eighteen-year-old arranging, with shy pride, his chess trophies on the dresser, all visible simultaneously in her mind's eye, reassuring her with a sense of a happy, wholesome childhood she had helped shape and protect; and when, in his sophomore year, Eugene brought Adriana, his Romanian girlfriend of the past three months, home for a short Christmas visit, it was solely out of reluctance to muddy the memories, not out of any sense of old-fashioned pro-priety, that she gave Adriana the guest bedroom.

On the last night of their visit, Mrs. Caldwell went up to her son's room. She knocked before entering, but it was a cursory knock: she had left Eugene foraging for a snack in the kitchen, and assumed the room empty. She had misplaced her glasses earlier that evening, and rather suspected that she had forgotten them on his nightstand, resting in the crook of his book, which she had leafed through in a surreptitious moment. All through his stay, she had made mildly disparaging comments about his choice of reading matter whenever she had caught him absorbed in it, and was now hoping to retrieve her glasses before he stumbled upon them, as she preferred to conceal her curiosity about the novel. Secrets, even minute, trivial ones, did not come easy when one was nearing fifty, burdened as one was with failing eyesight and increasing absentmindedness.

The telltale glasses were indeed there, on her son's bedside table, sprawled with abandon across the open pages of Olga's most recent book. She did not, however, notice the glasses, because Adriana was lying in a come-hither pose on top of Eugene's faded Star Wars duvet, naked but for a tiny triangle of black lace between her startlingly white thighs. That much she had time to glimpse, her hand frozen on the doorknob, Adriana's inviting smile frozen on her lips, before the girl began to scramble madly, grabbing for her clothes, crying, "Mrs. Caldwell!"

"I'm so sorry!" Mrs. Caldwell cried in turn, and, leaping back into the hallway, slammed the door shut. Once outside, she stood staring at the doorknob. Twenty-some years before, from the other side of a slammed door, she had assumed that Mrs. Caldwell— the original Mrs. Caldwell of the tweed suit, the pearl necklace, and the rigid haircut—had felt shock and distaste when coming upon her in a similar state of undress; yet she herself felt neither. She was saddened by the loss of the room where stuffed hedgehogs had lived in the shadow of a peeling solar system, and, at the same time, relieved that her bookish, abstracted boy was progressing through life's stages in a manner befitting a self-sufficient adult male. Then, too, she could not help feeling a bit jealous at being supplanted in her son's affections, as well as fleetingly bitter— because at her age of forty-six she knew that she would never again inspire that tug of desire in a man, because her days of lolling about in skimpy lingerie had been over before she had known to treasure them fully . . .

And every single one of these feelings is a cliché, she thought as she stood in the hallway, staring and staring at the doorknob. In our youth we believe ourselves so unique and our stories so original, yet we are all stuck running like hamsters on the wheel of time, all acting in the same play, and the roles of the play stay the same, only the actors switch places: one minute you are an ingénue charming an affable heir—the next, a matron used for comic relief in a scene of which you are no longer the protagonist. Emma Caldwell must have known it, just as this lovely girl will know it in her own Mrs. Caldwell moment two or three decades from now.

And yet maturity offered other consolations, so much so that Mrs. Caldwell supposed she would choose not to relive her twenties if presented with the option. Among the varied advantages of middle age, you knew enough to accept being ordinary and to find much comfort in it, just as you knew enough to recognize the clichés for what they were and be able to laugh at them. For of course the thing was funny, too funny. She waited another minute, twisting and retwisting her string of pearls. All was silent within the room now, but she sensed that the girl was standing still on the other side of the door, straining to hear the sound of retreating footsteps. Poor thing, she must be mortified, thought Mrs. Caldwell; but she too will learn to take life lightly, given time.

With a slight sigh, she turned and walked down the hall, making sure to stomp, debating whether to find Eugene and allude to the incident. But she suspected that the girl would keep quiet about it, just as she herself had kept quiet about her mishap nearly a quarter of a century before; and in any case, by the time she reached her bedroom she had already set her heart on a long, lazy soak with an aromatic candle and a glass of red wine, and so let the matter rest.

Family life was fraught with minor embarrassments, and some things were better forgotten.

34. Living Room

The Antique Mirror

THE STEINWAY HAD MADE HER ANXIOUS—WOULD the angles of the room accommodate it, she had wondered on more than one sleepless night—but when the movers stepped aside, she breathed a sigh of relief.

"Almost done, ma'am," said the man with the chipped front tooth. "Are you sure you don't need help unpacking the boxes? We can do it in five minutes flat and haul away all the trash for you."

"No, no," she said, "just set them down here, I'll go through them myself."

She was rather looking forward to unearthing all the treasures from their padded cocoons. Again she glanced at her watch, impatient for the men to leave; she had only two hours remaining until the first of the school buses returned. The electrician, she saw, had just finished with the last sconce. It would all be ready by the time Paul came home.

"Well, all right, then," said the man with the tooth. "If every-thing is to your satisfaction, sign on the line here, please . . . Ah now, thank you, ma'am, your kindness is much appreciated."

Alone at last, she slit the boxes open, taking a quick inventory—silver here, china there, lampshades separate from the lamps, everything as it should be. She set to work. As she handled the precious objects, inspecting them one by one with subdued flur-ries of something approaching delight, her thoughts drifted and she found herself wondering about time. Like a train taking off from a station, which, after an initial leisurely stretch, starts gathering speed, time now passed more and more quickly, and the landscapes outside the windows flickered with increasing vagueness until merging at last into an indistinct blur, perceived in the most general of terms: a city, a field, a forest—school proj-ects, home projects, the dizzying succession of holidays and birth-days, the smooth running of the household, the middle span of middle age—until life just flew by, reduced to unmemorable and unremembered, albeit pleasant, routine brightened by discrete flashes of rare events. (And "brightened" was really the wrong word, Mrs. Caldwell reproved herself as she discarded the last empty box; for at her age the events themselves had become pre-dictable and rather sad, consisting mainly of departures: the younger generation setting off toward life, the older generation leaving in the opposite direction, for regions unknown, the mid-dle generation seeing off both, struggling to stay in place amidst the flux.) Did it not seem like mere months since they had shared that happy Thanksgiving meal with Paul's mother? Yet here they were, five years later, and Emma was gone, and the Caldwells' stately ancestral furniture had just been installed in her own living room.

The living room was her concession to Paul's grief. The Caldwells' New England house had been sold and most of its contents auctioned off, but his parents' living room held a special place in Paul's childhood memories, and he had wished to preserve it in its entirety, down to every candlestick on every table, every cushion on every chair, every photograph on every console, all of which had thus been carefully dismantled, boxed up, and dispatched to them in a behemoth of a truck. Some weeks earlier, in preparation for its eventual arrival, Mrs. Caldwell had stripped her own meticulously assembled living room bare. She had been sad to see her lamps and pictures dispersed and swallowed up by random corners of the house, and her adored green sofa carted off altogether; but, sensitive to Paul's feelings, she raised no objections, of course, despite being quite upset every time she chanced to glimpse the dismaying eyesore of a void gouged out at the heart of her beautiful home.

Yet now, as she stood surveying the handsome new layout of the room, she had to admit that the overall effect was rather pleasing. The dark mahogany antiques lent an air of blue-blood distinction. She found herself, to her surprise, loving the faded Aubusson rug, the richly tasseled French draperies, the magnificent collection of Cecilia Caldwell's Meissen in the ceiling-high buffet; and the enormous Venetian mirror in its eighteenth-century frame made her feel almost giddy. She paused before it now, smiling at her well-coiffed, recently blond reflection—and was startled to see a tall, dusky shape rise behind her. For the duration of one wild heartbeat, she imagined that the mirror held an olive-skinned gypsy in swirls of fiery skirts, but when she swung around, the vision resolved into Mrs. Simmons in her somber widow's clothes, standing just past the threshold, her old-fashioned black handbag in the crook of her arm.

"I didn't hear you come in!" Mrs. Caldwell exclaimed with a flustered laugh. She had forgotten that it was a Thursday, had thought herself alone in the house. "You move like a cat. Are you on your way out?"

Paying no heed to Mrs. Caldwell's question, the housekeeper in turn studied the room. "It looks different," she said at last, her austere, thin-lipped, long-nosed face without expression. "The furniture is fancier. And there is more of it."

"This is really a memorial to Paul's parents," said Mrs. Caldwell. Her heart still had not subsided all the way.

Keeping firm hold on her bag, Mrs. Simmons walked over to a painting on the far wall, touched the top edge of its gilded frame, peered at her darkened finger.

"Lots of new knickknacks to dust," she said.

Mrs. Caldwell noted disapproval in her housekeeper's voice. On Mondays and Thursdays, ten to two, it would indeed fall to Mrs. Simmons to do the dusting, and Mrs. Caldwell felt a light itching of guilt, which, however, she was able to dismiss with relative ease: Mrs. Simmons received more than adequate wages.

"I'm certain it can be managed," she said, a little dryly.

Without looking at her, Mrs. Simmons moved about the room, prodding here, poking there. "Do you ever wonder why it is so hard for the rich to enter the kingdom of heaven?" she suddenly said. Mrs. Caldwell stared at her. "It's because the rich have so little time. Time, you know, is what you give up to own all the things you own. Because every new thing you let into your life eats a tiny bit of your life away. The rugs need cleaning, the chairs upholstering, the silver polishing, the china washing—and even if you do none of it yourself, maids and handymen need supervising and keeping in line."

"I believe I've always treated you with fairness," Mrs. Caldwell said stiffly. She had never heard Mrs. Simmons offer any opinions on anything other than household matters, or say more than a few words at a time, and she was beginning to feel quite appalled.

Mrs. Simmons did not appear to have heard her. "So the more things you have," she continued, and her ordinarily imperceptible accent came and went, making some of her words sound harsher, more foreign, "the faster your time runs through your fingers. In case you were ever wondering why that was. And then you have no time left to think about things that are distant and hard. Like God. Or death. Or poetry." Mrs. Caldwell looked at her sharply, but the old woman seemed busy inspecting the sconces. "Well, but it must be worth it to you, or things would be different."

Completing the circle of the room, she stopped in front of the mirror.

"What—what do you mean by that, Mrs. Simmons?" Mrs. Caldwell managed.

"Please, I'm no more Mrs. Simmons than you are Mrs. Caldwell," the housekeeper said with growing irritation. "And you know perfectly well what I mean."

For a moment their eyes met within the silvery pool of the

priceless mirror. In spite of the old woman's ill-tempered tone, her direct black gaze held no strife, only sadness and, underneath, some vast, vast disappointment. Mrs. Caldwell saw what the old woman was seeing—a plump, beautifully dressed forty-eight-year-old blonde with large pearls in her ears; the blonde's painted mouth appeared to be working in soundless outrage, chewing, chewing on itself . . .

Mrs. Caldwell's eyes thrashed and leapt away, like two slippery fish twisting free of their hooks and falling back into the rippled depths.

The old woman shrugged and, turning away, began to rummage through her monstrous black bag. "I've watched you for years and years, you know. And every day I kept expecting you to do something different. Just waiting for you to wake up one day and say: Now. Today. But you didn't, and you haven't, and you won't. I must have misread your fortune, happens to the best of us—"

Mrs. Caldwell drew herself tall. Even at full height, she was a good head shorter than the old woman. "You forget yourself," she said.

"No, I fear it's you who forgot yourself," said Mrs. Simmons, not glancing up from her bag. "Well, tell the children I love them. Especially Celia. She's a bright little spirit, I'll miss her. I'll miss them all. Now, where in the world did I put them—"

"Are you giving notice, Mrs. Simmons?"

"Yes, I believe I am, Mrs. Caldwell . . . Ah, there they are. I will leave them right here for you."

Mrs. Caldwell lunged to intercept the keys before they scratched the surface of the seventeenth-century table, and caught herself in mid-motion, and drew back, biting her lip. The old woman was looking straight at her, and her face was severe, and her eyes young and knowing. Mrs. Caldwell grew hot inside.

"I will send you your monthlong severance by mail," she said.

"Good-bye," said Mrs. Simmons whose name was not Mrs. Simmons.

Mrs. Caldwell heard the front door open and close, but she did not move to see the housekeeper off. She was shaking. There had been an instant when their eyes had met within the mirror and she had felt *seen*—and felt, too, that in that one instant she had seen herself, seen herself with an absolute, pitiless clarity, and had found herself lacking, and had shrunk back from the fullness of her knowledge.

She turned to the mirror.

Had her longing for art and beauty somehow, without her noticing, become a longing for Aubusson rugs and Venetian mirrors? Or had it been that all along? Had her first-grade teacher been right after all—had her childhood yearning for a fairy-tale palace been nothing but bourgeois rot? Was that why she had chosen to trade her home, her language, her aging parents, for the land of walk-in closets and golden faucets? Was that why she had left the man she had left, and married the man she had married? And later, after her marriage had become what it became, was that why she had not let her husband go, binding him tighter to herself with yet another child?

Horrified, she looked at the blonde in the mirror.

When Paul returned from work that night, the house lay swollen with winter darkness, torpid and still.

"Hello?" he called out.

"I'm here," she said.

He stopped on the threshold of the unlit living room, peered into the dimness, saw her sitting on the shadowy couch against the shadowy wall in the cavern of shadows.

"What are you doing in the dark?" he asked, taking off his coat.

"Waiting for you. It's all finished. Turn on the light, go ahead— it will make you less sad."

He flipped the switch, and saw the room, and gasped.

"Just like home," he said; but he did not look less sad. "The piano is a perfect fit. And the buffet. And the mirror—oh no! Was the crack always there, or did the movers damage it?"

"It was always there," she said, standing to straighten the photographs of sepia-tinted children on the side table. "But don't worry, I've spoken to the restorers already. They have some period glass they can use to replace it. They are coming to do the measurements on Monday."

As she pushed the photographs about, a bit to the left, a bit to the right, she suddenly saw, in a serious, wide-eyed, beautiful face of one of the boys, the face of the hurt man before her. She stared at it for a long moment, careful to keep her bandaged hand out of sight.

35. Bar

Conversations Between Friends and Strangers

SHE WAS BAREFOOT WHEN SHE CAME DOWN, stepping softly on the wall-to-wall carpet, and he did not hear her approach. He was sitting hunched over at the bar, cradling a half-empty martini; between the scoops of his big, still hands, the glass looked fragile and small, like a cup from a child's toy set. She stopped, feeling awkward, as if she were spying on something not meant for her eyes, invading a home not her own, and waited for him to notice her. When he did not stir, she cleared her throat.

"Oh, hey," he said, standing up. "How long have you been there?"

In the blurred erosion of his voice, in the loose way he moved the bulk of his body, she could see that the martini before him was not his first. She wondered if she should not invent some trivial reason for entering his domain—a question to ask, a child's activity to confirm—then quickly retreat to her upstairs quarters;

but he had already walked behind the bar and was reaching for the shaker.

"Can I make you a drink?"

She did not want a drink—she drank almost nothing these days.

"Please," she said, tightening the belt of her robe as she climbed onto the leather perch of the stool next to his. She watched him go through the motions made fluid by hundreds, by thousands, of repetitions—watched his large hands deftly manipulate ice and crystal, watched the back of his head, his hair still abundant and dark, no trace of gray, watched his face as it appeared and disappeared in the mirror that ran behind the bar, sliced into slivers by the reflections of the bottles. He would turn fifty at the end of the month. His hair was that of a younger man, his face that of an older.

"So," he said, sliding the martini over to her. "To what do I owe the pleasure?"

She wanted to say: I felt lonely tonight. It's different in the house these days—only four kids left, and the boys are seventeen and out so much, and Celia always has her nose in a book, and our baby—our baby is nine and so independent, sometimes it feels like she doesn't need me at all. Of course, my days are still brimming over, so many things to take care of, always—but every night now, there is this odd sort of emptiness that can't be filled, a stretch of emptiness before me, and you never even come upstairs until after I'm asleep. I just wanted to see you. To talk to you. The way we used to talk.

"I just—I felt like having a drink," she said.

"You've come to the right place," he replied without smiling.

They sat in silence for a while, drinking side by side. It was nearing midnight, she knew, but there was no clock in the bar. The lamps above the counter were turned down low, the shelves with the bottles mirrored, the wall behind the shelves mirrored as well; she kept catching oblique glimpses of the two of them at alluring or unflattering angles, reflections of reflections—a profile, a double chin, a slanted glance, a green bottle, a blue bottle, a bottle in the shape of a skull, a bottle in the shape of a bull, the dull glint of a wedding band on a hand raising a glass. An odd sensation took hold of her and grew, that of sitting in a real bar next to a real stranger; and as she neared the bottom of her drink, it stopped being a sad feeling and became one of possibility instead. She studied him out of the corner of her eye, wondering whether she would still find him attractive if she met him now— and then he turned to her, and immediately the sensation of strangeness dissipated, and she saw the good-natured giant of a boy who had made her feel safe all those years ago.

"Oh, by the way, I've always meant to ask you," she said, as if continuing a conversation. He rose to make the next round of drinks. "The first time we met—well, not met, technically, but the first time we spoke—"

"The time in the library when you made me feel like a complete idiot."

"Well. You wore a Grateful Dead shirt, remember? It puzzled me later, because you never seemed the type—I mean—"

"You mean that even at eighteen I was too staid and boring to listen to music or smoke pot. A management consultant as a young man. No novel there, I suppose."

"I didn't mean it like that—I just—"

"No, you're right. The shirt was a gift from a girl I dated for a couple of months. I ditched it when we broke up."

He put the freshly made drinks on the counter and sat back down.

She stared at the olive bobbing in her vodka.

"Paul," she said. "Where did we go wrong?"

He was quiet for so long that she thought he was not going to answer.

"Do you know what I liked about you?" he said then. "Well, I liked everything about you, but you know what I liked best, why I fell in love? I loved how different you were from everyone I knew. I thought it was your foreignness at first, but it wasn't that, it wasn't only that, it was something else. The way you would grow still and seem so far away, the look that would steal over your face, like you were seeing something special, even when you did something as trivial as—oh, I don't know, writing grocery lists. You looked so beautiful then, like you knew something about life that was worth knowing. And I wanted to find out what it was you knew, but I worried it was like one of those fairy tales where the dumb prince spies on his magic princess and she turns into a swan and flies away. So I never pressed for it—I wanted you to tell me. No, that's not even right—it wasn't that I believed there was anything *to tell*, not like a concrete thing or anything. It was just a sense I had that you were different, marked out by something or someone, and that if I married you I would have a life that would be—I'm not sure of the right word. Deeper, I guess. Charmed. Special."

"You told me once that everyone was special."

"Did I? I don't remember. Isn't that just the lie you feed your kids when they suspect, for the first time, that they too are just like everybody else? But who knows. Maybe it's true, maybe everyone *is* special—maybe it's just very few who manage to do something with it. It's not so easy to measure all the things wasted."

"So then you haven't," she said softly. "You haven't had a special life."

"No," he said. "I haven't. And look, this is a good life. We've been richer than most in our children, I've been luckier than most with my career, we live in a beautiful place, and you—you even iron my pajamas for me. It's just that . . . I keep having this feeling that it could have been *more* if only you'd trusted your dumb prince with your frog skin or your swan wings or—or whatever it was you turned into when you were alone. Because our life often felt—I don't know—less than real somehow. Like you weren't all here."

She was almost done with her second martini. The bottles were winking and weaving on the mirror shelves. Her head swam. She wanted to cry, to beg his forgiveness—or else pull him toward her and kiss him, kiss him deeply, to dispel the need for stiff, inadequate words. Instead she heard herself asking: "When you were a child, what did you dream of being?"

"Oh, that's easy. I wanted to be a chef."

"The celebrated chef Paul Caldwell!" she cried.

"No, I didn't want to be celebrated. I didn't have any delusions of grandeur, I just liked the idea of feeding people. My restaurant was going to be different. There would be no menus, and every day I would serve only food that was white, or only dishes that started with the letter *p*—paellas and pumpkin pies—or only desserts, whatever mood I was in. You would come and you would never know what to expect that day, except that it would be delicious—and a surprise. I wanted to make people happy."

"But you don't ever cook at home," she said. "Not like you used to."

He shrugged. "You seem to manage so well by yourself . . . So what about you?"

"What about me?" she asked, though her heart was already skipping.

"What did you dream of being?"

She had not said certain things—not even to herself—in years, many years. She finished her drink before speaking. He waited patiently.

"Do you know, my mother once told me that women in my family liked to keep secrets. I guess that's true. My mother had her share of secrets—I remember odd little things from when I was very small. There was, I think, another man. Maybe. Maybe not. I asked her once, after my father died, but she pretended not to hear. My grandmother had secrets too, as did my great-grandmother before her—there was something about a Grand Duke, or maybe a gypsy, I forget now . . . Anyway. I wanted a secret of my own. I wanted to have something deep and unreachable by anyone else, all to myself—a kernel of light or dark, I could never quite decide which, at the very heart of things. But I think maybe I chose the wrong thing to keep secret. It's dangerous to make a secret not of something you *do* but of something you *are*, because if you go about wearing a mask for years and years, you may end up becoming what you were only pretending to be all that time— you may find that there is no face under the mask." She knew she was tipsy now, but it felt marvelous to talk, and her words flowed with the easy eloquence of an oft-imagined speech. "And as time passes, you forget you ever even had a secret. You know, like when you hide something in case there is a break-in or to keep it safe from your maid—say, you put your diamond necklace in some pocket of an old coat or some shoe you never wear—and then you completely forget where you put it, and you look for a while, but then you think, well, anyway, it's in the house somewhere, I'll find it some other time, except you keep putting off the search until you forget that you ever had it, because honestly, how often do you have an occasion to wear a diamond necklace? So for months you go about without remembering it even once, until a year or two later, out of the blue, in the middle of the night, you wake up from this nightmare you keep having, this dream in which your house slowly eats you, and you sit bolt upright in bed and break into a sweat and scream: Oh God, where the fuck did it go?"

"I'm not sure I follow," he said. "Are you telling me you lost the necklace I gave you on our twentieth anniversary?"

"Oh," she said. "Oh, that. No, no, I'm sure it will turn up some- day. Someday soon. I'm sorry, I think I'm a little drunk now. Anyway." She upended the empty glass into her mouth, licked her lips. "I wanted to be a poet."

And then she sat still for several thrilled, inebriated, frightened heartbeats, waiting, waiting for something—but the lightning bolt did not strike, and he did not tumble off the barstool, or mock her for her failure, and the ceiling did not split open to spill out torrents of heavenly light with Apollo riding a white steed and strumming a lyre as he smote her for having squandered her gift.

"Did you?" asked the young, friendly, curious boy from the library whose smile was so kind and who was so eager to talk to her. "Did you really? How come you never told me? You actually wrote poems?"

She wanted to laugh and laugh, astonished at how simple it had been, how simple it was. "Yes!" she exclaimed, then sobered up enough to add: "A long time ago."

He swung the barstool around to face her. Their knees jammed together.

"Read some to me."

"I can't," she protested, giggling. "I don't remember any, it was decades ago . . . But wait, I remember this—" She looked away, recited all in a rush:

"Taking a shower in small golden earrings,
Well after midnight,
Washing smoke out of my hair."

She stopped. He waited, smiling.

When she did not speak again, he prodded her lightly. "Well, go on."

"That's all."

"That's all?"

"That's all. It was supposed to be a haiku, you see. It was the first poem I ever wrote in English. Well, maybe not the first one ever, just . . . one of the first ones." She wondered if she was blushing. "I was nineteen. And the funny thing is, I had no idea what a haiku really was, so of course the syllables turned out all wrong, and when Apollo read it, he was quite amused—"

"Who?"

"Who what?"

"You said when Apollo read it—"

"Did I? God, I'm not used to drinking this much, it's hard to keep up with you . . . I meant to say Hamlet. You remember. John. The guy who—"

"Yes," he said. "I remember." But his face had darkened, and he appeared every bit his age again—a man of fifty with eyes grown opaque and a voice hardened by decades of success and pressure. He pushed his unfinished drink aside. "I'm sorry. Sorry things have turned out this way. But God knows, I loved you." He was silent for a moment, looking at her. "Did you ever love me?"

And all at once her thoughts were a disturbed nest of wasps, darting around with swift menace, all dangerously capable of stinging. She thought of confessing to the shattering loss of her youthful love, and her conviction, born in the solitary darkness of the following months, that she could never again give herself fully if she wished to remain faithful to her art. She thought of telling him of that time, shortly after his mother's death, when she had seen herself in a new, stark, ugly light and been flooded with remorse, and blamed herself for everything that had gone wrong between them. She thought of asking him about the smell of perfume on his shirts. She thought of asking for another drink.

She became aware of the silence spreading wider and wider between them.

"Of course I did," she said, speaking with something much like desperation—and, just like that, the wasps fell silent, and she knew it to be the absolute truth. "Of course I did. I still do. It's almost as if—you know how you don't choose your parents or your children? Well, after twenty-three years of marriage you don't choose your spouse either."

"Such passion," he said, but he was smiling now, and as he put his hand over hers, she thought: And this too was easy, and it's not too late, nothing is too late—and for another minute they sat, no longer drinking, in companionable silence, until she brushed his cheek, quickly, almost shyly, and said: "I'm going back upstairs. Join me soon, before I fall asleep."

In the shadowy mirror above the bar, among the splintered reflections of tumblers and decanters, the dimly glimpsed middle-aged couple were having a conversation of their own. They talked about Rich's difficult adolescence—they suspected him of dabbling in drugs, there was trouble at school. He was in favor of harsh disciplinary measures, but she wondered whether they shouldn't take a family trip instead. They had never done it; of course, for years money had been tight, the house had sucked away everything, but they could try to do it now, could they not? Granted, his inheritance was not quite what he had expected, but wouldn't it be worth a one-time splurge, it might bring them all closer together. He did not think much of the idea; how quick she was to spend his parents' money, he said, what little there was of it. Hurriedly, before things veered off in an unpleasant direction, she mentioned Emma's being less communicative of late, not returning her phone calls with the usual promptness, which she found a bit worrisome. Must she always be so oppressive, he said—the girl was entitled to cut loose in her college years. So they moved on to Eugene's girlfriend; things were clearly serious between the two. She thought Adriana lovely, but he said that he doubted she'd make their son happy; she might be nothing but an Eastern European gold digger, he said. Conversation lapsed briefly after that, until she thought to mention her mother's fragile health. She was hoping, she said, that they could persuade her to leave Russia and move in with them at last. He did not reply. She nursed her one drink. He was drinking steadily. His eyes were becoming bloodshot. After a while, he started to talk, staring directly ahead, past the bar, past the bottles, at whatever he saw in the mirror, beyond the mirror. Much of what he said made little sense to her, but he seemed to imply that her life had been easy, that he wished he too could stay home all day long drifting from room to room, playing peekaboo with babies, overseeing the domestics. She could not begin to imagine the stress of providing for a wife and six children, he said, she took things for granted, she took him for granted, she never asked about his work, did she even know what he did, she found him boring, he supposed—but she should take a long, hard look at herself instead. She held on to her silence with the tenacity of a drowning woman clinging to a log, until she could stand it no longer, until she found herself crying out that he—that he should drink less.

He turned to consider her, his reddened eyes bulging.

"When did you stop dyeing your hair?" he asked, his tongue slow in his mouth. "You are showing your age."

She stood up and walked away, leaving him hunched over the

bar—the man who had made her feel safe, the man whom she loved. In the doorway, she paused to look at him. His back was toward her, the broad back of an aging athlete, obscuring the martini glass she knew to be trapped between his hands. He was, she realized, still wearing his suit and tie. They will be wrinkled tomorrow, she thought, I'll need to drop them off at the dry cleaner's in the morning, I must remember to defrost the chicken too, I know I should try harder, but everything will be fine in the end, we just need to work on some things.

As she trudged up the stairs, she wondered which of the two conversations had been real—or had it been both, or had it been neither? She found she could not decide; though she had her suspicions, of course.

36. Garage

A Taxonomy of Neglected Possessions

1. Things that will be used someday soon (if, that is, one doesn't forget they are there): spare batteries, extra lightbulbs, extension cords, a shriveled-up pair of gardening gloves, a second hose, a box of candles, a tower of plastic cups. One tends to think of them as reserves maintained against the gray forces of entropy—if something breaks or runs out or gets lost in the house, there is a replacement waiting in the wings; yet as time passes and the batteries and cords turn dusty and drab, becoming an ingrown part of the garage shelves and corners, they may end up contributing to the encroachment of entropy rather than holding it at bay. But not if they get used first, of course.

2. Things that don't appear to be of much use in the foreseeable future but may come in handy next year, or at some point thereafter: three and a half cans of Paris Rain paint (in case

they repainted the since repainted guest bedroom in the old color), converter plugs (in case they decided to take that trip overseas after all), portable heaters (in case the furnace malfunctioned) and fans (in case the air-conditioning broke down), a guide to the restaurants of Venice (see above), a giant fish tank, a yoga mat, a ski mask, a pair of hiking boots, a set of golf clubs, and on, and on. True, they do take up space, but one can't just throw perfectly good things away. And one never knows.

3. Things that are broken but may be fixed someday: an old vacuum cleaner, four or five expired computers, two maimed bicycles, a box full of cameras and phones, a microscope, a flashlight, a nineteenth-century porcelain cup with its handle knocked off and preserved in two separate pieces.

4. Things that are ontological mysteries: nuts that fit unknown bolts, keys that open no doors, an unlabeled homemade videotape that gets stuck every time one tries to play it. Throwing them away would be tantamount to admitting that one no longer expects anything unexpected to happen in life. Though that may be a good thing.

5. Things that will be discarded in due time, but not just yet: a baby monitor, a toddler's bib, a child's bike helmet, a child's pair of goggles, a child's telescope, a hedgehog that looks like a bear, its nose spilling plush of a muddy brown color, once beloved by a boy who got married last March; a saltshaker in the shape of the Taj Mahal; an empty plastic case that once housed magnetic poetry tiles. On second thought, the last item is best tossed out without further delay. Even clutter has its limits.

6. Things that are the only remains of one's childhood home (sold last year, gone decades before that), brought over by one's mother, not yet sorted: a shoebox filled with papers, and a duffel bag containing a handful of pipes wrapped in a thick gray-and-white sweater. These are, for the moment, relegated to the darkest corner of the garage, behind a battalion of cleaning supplies. There is no need to rush, there will be time enough to decide where to put them later—once one is able to look at them properly, without breaking into tears at the sight of the familiar handwriting, at the ghostly smell of tobacco, reaching one from another country, another century, another life.

37. Deck

Forty

THERE WERE SIXTEEN LARGE FLOWERPOTS ON THE covered deck, positioned at regular intervals along the wall, and a separate tray with cooking herbs on the table. They had been her mother's pet project: upon moving in with them two years before, she had declared their house too much like a museum, no greenery anywhere, and had set out to remedy the situation by assiduous gardening. Unwilling to brave the steep stairs down to the yard, she had spent most of her days on the deck, pruning and clipping and talking to herself.

Nearly three full weeks after her mother's death, she remembered that she had neglected to water the plants, and came out to look at them. Most were, indeed, beginning to turn brown, especially the ones at the deck's western edge, inundated as they were for hours with the afternoon sun. The farthest on the right was the only one that appeared to be healthy; it had even sprouted a disturbingly glossy, plastic-like red growth—could it be a flower?—amidst the swollen protuberances of its leaves. But the third from the left seemed dead, all black and brittle, and a few others fared almost as poorly. She stared at them for a long blank minute, then dragged the hose over and flooded each pot with water. She had no idea what any of them were, or how much moisture they needed.

When she returned to check on them some hours later, evening had already fallen. Here and there water was still standing in the pots, glistening with the pink of the sunset. The plants looked worse than before—dead with a final kind of deadness. She dropped into the nearest chair and began to cry.

"There, there," said her mother's voice. She lifted her eyes to see her mother bending over the pots at the far edge of the deck, hazily outlined by the setting sun.

She stopped crying, squinted against the light.

"Mama?" Oddly, she wasn't surprised. "Is that really you?"

Her mother was wearing her bright green gardening gloves. She did not look up, busy poking the crumbling plants with a rubber finger.

"Forty days," she said matter-of-factly.

"What?"

"Have you forgotten all of your people's traditions? Spirits loiter in places of their past for forty days, to say good-bye to all the things they loved before finally moving on. Or at least that's the idea. I suppose if one's spirit has nowhere better to go, it may hover about forever, or at least until it figures things out. But not me. I've always hated good-byes. Forty days—and I'm off."

Dimly she remembered the subdued gathering held on the fortieth day after her grandmother's passing; she had been ten at the
time. "Yes, I knew that," she muttered, shielding her eyes; the
brightness was spreading across the sky. Her mother was wielding a large pair of shears now, snipping in silence; it was difficult
to see her expression clearly in the sunset's shimmering glow, but
she seemed peaceful, smiling a little to herself, perhaps even
happy—happier than she had looked in years.

Mama has come to say good-bye to her plants but not to me,
she thought; after all, it's merely by accident that I happen to be
here. But then, it shouldn't seem so very out of character—hadn't
she spent more time with her pots than with her own daughter
while she was alive? Or—was it perhaps my own failure to pay
more attention to her, to let her reminisce about the past as she
tried to once or twice, when I had no time to sit and listen—
when I had a roast burning in the oven or Paul's shirts to iron or
Maggie's homework to check? Oh God, she talked to the flowers,
she must have been lonely . . . And because her eyes were beginning to brim over again and she was suddenly afraid that she
might fall apart, or worse, speak harshly, she asked the first irrelevant thing that came into her mind: "So . . . why forty? Why
forty days?"

"It's always forty," her mother replied, snipping, smiling. "Forty
is God's number for testing the human spirit. It's the limit of
man's endurance, beyond which you are supposed to learn something true. Oh, you know what I mean—Noah's forty days and
nights of rain, Moses' forty years in the desert, Jesus' forty days
of fasting and temptation. Forty of anything is long enough to be

a trial, but it's man-size, too. In the Bible, forty years make a span of one generation. Forty weeks make a baby."

"Oh," she said. "I see."

They were silent for a minute. Her mother would not stop her puttering, her back bent, her hands always moving, strands of white hair falling over her face, so she could never see her clearly, could never meet her eyes directly. In the evening stillness, the gardening shears went on making sharp little sounds, unpleasant like the clicking of teeth, the scraping of claws. Bits of greenery rained onto the floorboards.

"You've made a terrible mess of my little garden," her mother said at last, not altogether kindly, as she stepped back to survey the plants. "You are at an age where it would do you good to learn some particulars about the world. Making things grow is a kind of immortality too. But that's the trouble with people who prize words above all else—you don't know anything practical, anything useful. Your father is just like that too. Philosophy this and truth that, but I don't believe he could ever tell a cactus from a begonia. The world becomes obscure and remote when you look at it through a mesh of words, you know. Like those semi-transparent sheets of paper they used to put over illustrations in old books, to protect them—it just ended up turning the picture all hazy so you could barely make out what it was supposed to be in the first place."

And this was just like her mother too—she had never seemed to comprehend the urge to create things that had no tangibility to them, things that were not flowers or feasts or offspring.

"Words don't make things hazy," she said, feeling defensive. "They clarify."

"Well," her mother said tranquilly, "I suppose that depends on the words. The words that clarify don't seem to be your kinds of words. Too small for you, aren't they? What is this plant called, for instance?"

She looked at the spiky monstrosity in the pot, almost hoping that its name might pop into her head of its own accord, as if the name was its perfect essence, the summation of its nature, to be revealed to those who studied it closely. Hadn't Adam and Eve guessed at the right, God-given names of all the creatures and plants in the Garden through mere contemplation?

"I don't know," she admitted at last.

"You see my point," said her mother triumphantly. "Not everything is *soul* and *love* and *art* and *happiness*. In fact, very often, the bigger the word, the smaller the kernel of substance within it— it's been rubbed flat, worn-out by all the use. Maybe that's why it's harder to be a great poet than a great novelist. A novel can be full of little words, as fresh and particular and unlike one another as a meadow of forget-me-nots."

"I bet Olga would agree with you there," she mumbled, all at once disconsolate.

"Who?"

"Olga. You know. My best friend in Russia."

"Every other girl in Russia is named Olga," her mother remarked with a shrug, and turned her attention back to the plants.

She sighed, recalling how distressed she had been a year before by the very same conversation, the first sign of her mother's rapidly nearing senility: the first sign of many to come. She had mentioned Olga in passing over dinner, and her mother claimed not to have known her. "But you must remember!" she had cried in exasperation. "She came over scores of times. The two of us even spent three or four days at the dacha right after high school graduation, you and Papa drove us there, remember?" Her mother had given her a withering look. "Aren't you a bit old for imaginary friends?" she had said. "I remember perfectly well. After graduation, you went to the dacha alone. We dropped you off. That was your present—you told us you wanted a taste of adult life. I was against it, but your father said fine, it would be good for you. There was some boy you liked across the street, so naturally I worried, but nothing came of it. I remember. I'm not yet senile." Her mother's insistence had made her very upset; she had even gone up to Eugene's room to retrieve a couple of Olga's novels she had seen on his shelf, but the novels had gotten somewhere, and her mother had acted so stubborn and tight-lipped about the whole thing that she had quickly dropped the matter, just as she hastened to drop it now.

The shears continued to click, click-click, click-click, beginning to sound like the ticking of some rusty old clock. She wanted to ask her mother so many questions—about God, and death, and life, and whether she had ever been truly happy with Papa—but the sun sank lower and lower until it was gone from the sky, and as the halo around the borders of things dulled into shadows, her mother seemed to fade ever so slightly, and then a bit more. She was still there, fussing and clucking, humming under her breath, but now it was possible to see her only out of the corner of one's eye, moving on the very edge of one's vision, for when one turned to face her directly, she quietly passed out of sight, like the flame of a candle at the moment of flickering out, only to appear again, a vague afterimage of a frail old woman in green gardening gloves, when one looked away.

She kept very still, her face averted, to prolong her mother's faint presence.

"Do you mind if I snip off a bit of parsley?" her mother asked.

Her voice too was growing more distant, coming in and going out.

"What?"

"Parsley. I thought I'd make your father some roasted chicken when I see him in a couple of weeks—you remember, don't you, it's his favorite dish. I'm afraid the parsley's wilted, but it will have to do. Do you mind?"

Surprised, she turned, and her mother was gone. She rose, walked over to the row of plants. There were no snippets of leaves on the deck, and the darkened water was still standing in the pots, already beginning to look stagnant, to smell of decay—and yet she felt comforted, almost joyful, as if the world made better sense, after all, than she had any right to expect. For maybe, just maybe, the world is really like that, she thought, the way we imagine it as children, before we stop *seeing*: now it may seem only a mundane, finite place, but there are things moving just out of sight, at the very limits of our adult vision, and these things are every bit as real. And maybe big words do obscure ordinary things, but for these other things—the hints of things, the elusive presences of things, the great things we can't easily define—for these kinds of things, only big words will do. Maybe that is precisely the magic of true poetry: it looks at these retreating things directly and pins them down with big words before they can dart out of sight, making them visible, if only for the duration of a few verses. And maybe, after all my decades of blindness, I too will be able to see them at last—to see them again: maybe I just need to complete my own trial, my own forty—oh, not forty years, I'll be fifty-five next month, it's too late for that, and in any case, my trial would not be carried out on such an epic scale, it would be small, like my small life, a life within four walls . . . So perhaps— yes, wasn't there something about the average person inhabiting forty rooms in his lifetime? And didn't someone close to God, some saint or prophet, say that the soul has many rooms? So perhaps that is the desert through which I am destined to wander— forty rooms, each a test for my soul, a pocket-size passion play, a small yet vital choice, a minute step toward becoming fully awake, fully human; and by the time I have crossed my own wilderness of forty rooms, I too will be able to see the world as it really is—

With a start, she woke up from an unpremeditated nap on the deck of a large house, or else a small mansion. Her back was sore, and she was groggy from her dreamless sleep. She rose from the chair, walked over to the table with the herbs. The water, she saw, was still standing in the pots. Obeying some vague impulse, she took the plastic container with parsley in her bejeweled hands, rubbed the dying herb, smelled her fingers—and, amidst the chill of desolation, felt an inexplicable bloom of comfort.

Setting the parsley down, she wiped her eyes, and went inside to finish packing her mother's cheap, synthetic dresses, to be picked up by a local charity in the morning. When she was done, the clothes had not filled even half a suitcase. Prompted by another dim impulse, she flew to her own closet, scooped up, without looking, as many hangers as she could carry, and stuffed her own glittering garments, all the silk, all the velvet, into the suitcase as well, until it was crammed full. The zipper caught on something—a dress, or was it a skirt, of peacock-blue taffeta—but she jerked once or twice and freed it.

The suitcase zipped, she stood still for a moment, thinking, then ran to get another, bigger suitcase and returned to her closet.

38. Library

Lies and Idle Chatter

SHE WAS DOZING IN HER FAVORITE ARMCHAIR, a volume of Pushkin and a half-knitted scarf in her lap, when he strolled into the room. She had heard no approaching footsteps: one moment she was alone, the next he was there. She had forgotten him decades before, and, in the years since, had forgotten that she had ever forgotten anything at all; it took her a long, squinting moment to place him. He was still the same age as when she had seen him last, around forty, give or take a millennium; from the vantage point of her fifty-seven years, he appeared surprisingly young. He was dressed in nondescript clothes—gray jeans, a grayish shirt, graying sneakers; he was also rather less good-looking, less dangerous-looking, than she remembered, his features bland and smooth. He moved uncurious eyes over the imposing bookcases that lined the walls, nodded at her in a casual manner, as though they had parted only yesterday, and sat down in the armchair across from hers, throwing one leg over the other, crossing his arms behind his head.

"So," he said, "have you figured it all out yet?"

"I suppose I've figured out some things," she said mildly.

"If I'm not mistaken," he said, leaning back in his chair, "the last time we saw each other, you chose not to go back home, so you could be free. You were oh-so-eager to escape a conventional life. How did that work out for you?"

She smiled, secure in her elderly wisdom, happy with knowing her limitations at last. "Well, it didn't work out as I expected, but it worked out fine all the same. I believe I would have had this kind of life—an indoors kind, you know, marriage, children, home—no matter where I ended up. And yes, there were times, in my twenties, in my thirties, when it felt claustrophobic. The endless encroachment of stuff, it felt like, at times—things to take care of, people to take care of, the relentless thickening of matter . . . I used to wonder: Does it happen to others as well— do their lives change bit by bit, a new table here, a new baby there, until one day they wake up and look around and recognize nothing of their past in their present? But I grew into it. Learned to count my blessings. Learned to appreciate the small things. In fact, the older I get, the more I suspect that what we mistake for small things are really the things that matter. A child's happy smile on Christmas morning, that sort of thing. And it's not 'settling' if you are truly at peace."

"Sure, sure," he said. "Do remind me, though—unless I'm get- ting you confused with someone else—didn't you want immor- tality or something?"

"I don't mean to be rude," she said, "but those talks we used to have—oh, it was heady stuff for a girl of thirteen, but at my age I find that kind of fortune-cookie philosophy rather . . . hackneyed. Someone once wrote that the memory of man was the most likely location of heaven. If so, a mother of six is ensured her place among the angels, at least for a generation or two. And beyond that—well, no one who isn't Homer or Shakespeare has a right to hope for more anyway."

"All possibly true. Still, I thought you aimed a little higher than half a page in a grandchild's photo album."

She wondered whether she would tell him; she felt reluctant to revisit the follies of her youth. "Do you remember that time when I burned all my poems?" she asked at last, sighing. "Almost forty years ago?"

He nodded noncommittally, sprawled in the chair, his eyes half closed.

"It was only a dramatic gesture, you know, because I remembered them word for word. But I never wrote them down again. I believed them engraved upon my soul and I thought I would never forget them. But memory is such a funny thing. I did, of course—I forgot them with time, forgot them entirely, give or take a few lines. And as gradually as I forgot the words, I began to believe that they had been something special." She glanced at him for a reaction, but he appeared to have fallen asleep. "All the poems I wrote later, after my little bonfire, never felt quite . . . quite *in earnest*. When I looked at them with their ink still fresh, I always made excuses for myself: they were drafts to be reworked later, or mindless doodles, or prefabricated magnetic jingles, or rough translations from the original Russian. Oh, I knew myself capable of absolute brilliance, of course—the poems I had burned, now, those—those had been amazing . . ."

She was silent for so long that he opened his eyes and looked at her.

"Well?"

She studied her hands in her lap. "Well, after my mother's death, I finally got around to sorting through her things in the garage. I found two bundles of poems in a shoebox. Turns out my parents had saved the poems I had sent them while I was in college—"

"Ah, yes. On the Other Side."

She cringed. "Yes. So I sat on the floor of the garage and read through them right there and then. And see, I had remembered them as something luminous, something rare, something so much more than the sum of mere words on a page. But they were just stringent, hysterical, derivative little verses about nuns and angels and devils. And here is the truth: I was never very good, was I? I was nothing special." Again she looked over at him for a sign—a confirmation, or maybe, just maybe, an objection—but he only watched her politely, one eyebrow cocked, expecting her to go on; so, ignoring the slightest ache that had started somewhere deep in the hollow of her chest, she went on. "Which seemed a painful discovery when I first made it, but in the end, it's a relief, of course—I would hate to have wasted something real. As it is, my life has turned out to be just the right size for me—it simply took me a while to recognize it. Now that I'm too old to believe myself the center of the world, I'd much rather be a happy woman than a mediocre poet, and it's enough to know that the world is full of beauty made by others."

She nodded at the volume of Pushkin in her lap.

"Didn't you say there were two bundles of poems in the shoebox?"

"Yes. The poems in the second bundle weren't mine, but those— those were beautiful. Quiet, and wise, and—heartbreaking, really. They were about ordinary things: falling in love, falling out of love, children, death . . . They were in my mother's handwriting." She paused. She wanted to tell him how certain she felt that they had been written by the mermaid she had once met in her mother's bedroom, but his exaggerated nonchalance stopped her. He was inspecting his fingernails, seemingly indifferent to what she was saying. Something caught in her throat.

"Wait," she said. "Did you—you didn't by any chance know her?"

"Not closely. I can't quite recall. One meets so many people—"

There was something in his careless tone, in the glib readiness of his reply, in his refusal to meet her eyes, that made her heart throb. Since his eyes were cast down, she felt at liberty to inspect his face closely for the first time, to wonder, wildly, what it would look like if it ever had a mustache—but already, not wanting to see, she averted her gaze.

"Listen," he began.

His subdued voice was that of someone about to make amends; but just then Rose, the new maid, walked into the library with a feather duster and waved it once or twice at the nearest books before glancing over at her armchair and tiptoeing back out—and yet in that moment something had changed in the air between them.

"So," he said brightly, "what now? What will you do with the rest of . . . whatever you call this?"

She sighed. "I'm going to see Maggie off," she said, attempting to hide her disappointment in idle chatter. "She'll be finishing high school next spring, she has already been accepted at—"

He seemed dutifully interested if slightly bored, a well-meaning uncle; when he asked further questions, she found herself glad to return to the firm ground of her love for her husband and her children. She told him about Paul's recent successes at work; and Celia dropping out in her junior year of college to depart on a journey of self-discovery through the jungles of Asia, driving her mad with worry; and George striking it rich with some new-fangled technology idea; and Rich about to graduate from divinity school, such a good boy he had turned out to be, steady as a rock; and Eugene and Adriana moving to Romania, due for a visit at Thanksgiving; and Emma surprising everyone with her marriage and, mere months later, a baby girl, imagine that, she was a grand-mother now, she had even taken up knitting—

"Yes, yes," he said. "Well, that sounds pleasant enough. Finding happiness in the small things and so on."

He yawned and stood, brushing invisible dust off his denim-clad knee, taking a slow, lazy step away from her. All at once she knew that he was about to stroll out of her life forever, and she started out of her armchair, knocking her knitting to the floor.

"Wait," she cried, "wait!"

He paused in the doorway, his face a statue's eroded blank, his eyes pale and flat and devoid of expression, like painted marble faded by centuries in the sun.

"Tell me, did you—did you kill Hamlet?"

"But my dear," he drawled, "Hamlet is immortal. There are more things in heaven and earth, Horatio, than are dreamt of in your philosophy, and all that."

"What? Oh. No. I meant John. My first lover. Did you kill him?"

The slits of his eyes darkened with sudden life. He stood absolutely still—like a panther in the instant before leaping, she had time to think just as her heart dropped somewhere, her senses snapped wide awake, and every drop of her blood, every inch of her skin, every hair on her head tingled with the old fear.

He spoke, his voice a slow hiss.

"Do you really think that you are so important and that everything that happens to you, to those around you, happens for some preordained, divine reason? They had a good word for it in the old days. Hubris, it was called. Excessive pride before the gods. Gods have better things to do than meddle in the lives of every craven little nobody."

"Yes," she gasped, shrinking back.

"Next you will think that gods sit around counting hairs on everyone's head, cocking their ears for the sound of whimpering, ready to grant any prayer out of the goodness of their hearts. *Please take this cup of suffering away from me. Please make my child well. Please make my father live. Please make my lover leave. Please spare me any real pain, any real joy, any real shame, any real life—yes, please make my life as smooth, as shallow, as easy as it can get, because all I want is to tiptoe on the surface of things, composing little ditties as I do laundry, not*

knowing gut-wrenching love, not knowing life-shattering loss—and in
return I promise I will give up my passion, the only thing that makes me
any different from millions upon millions of others, I will throw away
every last crumb of inspiration I am granted, every last chance of becoming
an artist, I will never break out of the circle of time, I will live a silent life
and die a silent death, please, oh please—"

His tone was mocking, and furious underneath. She stared at
him, stunned. His face was not the smoothly attractive face of a
mortal man who had come into the library an hour before, but
the achingly handsome face of a wrathful angel. She stepped back,
and, tripping against the armchair, crumpled into it, and squeezed
her eyes shut, expecting to be consumed by his burning ire. And
then all was quiet, for almost an entire minute all was quiet—she
could hear the rushing of blood in her ears.

She kept her eyes closed, but dared to draw a breath, to stir a
little.

"Listen," he said. His voice was scarcely above a whisper, and
terrifyingly near. "Very few people are born great poets. Talents
are a drachm a dozen, but nothing can be had for nothing. I told
you this when you were young, but you didn't pay attention. Or
maybe you just didn't want it badly enough. You must earn your
right to say the things that truly matter—and for that, you pay in
years, you pay in sweat, you pay in tears, you pay in blood. Both
yours and other people's."

And then, just as she cowered, fearing the rip of a barbed
arrow through her heart, she sensed the smile back in his shockingly compassionate voice.

"Oh, and finding happiness in the *small* things, my dear, that's really nothing to brag about—it's the last consolation of those whose imagination has failed them."

She felt her lips lightly brushed by other, smiling lips, and their touch was ice, and their touch was fire—and she was ambushed by the memory of all the times when she had lain in bed at night, always exhausted, often pregnant, occasionally wondering about her husband's whereabouts, and as her thoughts would stray, she would imagine the soft, sneering curve of someone's mouth, the light, circling touch of someone's hand on her neck, and these thoughts would spin out into a tightrope on which she would balance for some minutes over an abyss of loneliness and approaching middle age, until momentary oblivion overtook her. Why, oh why, did you stay away for so long, she thought with a sudden contraction of anguish, not daring to look at him still; and though she did not ask aloud, he whispered against her cheek, so softly she could barely hear him, his words a gentle breeze that seemed to move through her mind: "You realize, of course, that I may not actually be here and that our little chats may be only as illuminating—or as *hackneyed*—as you are able to make them yourself? And if I live in your head alone, the real question you need to ask is why you haven't called me for so long."

Her eyes flew open. "No, I don't believe that—you—"

The library was deserted.

She felt that the fierceness of regret, the knowledge of all the things wasted, the sorrow of a life half lived—a life not lived—would consume her whole.

"No, wait!" she cried. "Tell me just one thing—are you saying that I got it wrong—that I could have been—"

But already she heard the maid's footsteps in the next room, and knew that, like all revelations, this too would soon be forgotten, and she let her voice die a death of resignation in the dark-paneled, leather-padded, respectable silence of the book-filled room. Her old volume of Pushkin still lay in her lap, opened to his poem "The Prophet." Her eyes trailed over the words, underlined, with excessive exuberance, by an elated fifteen-year-old in another place, in another age.

Exhausted by spiritual thirst,
I wandered in a gloomy desert,
And at the forking of the roads
A six-winged seraph came before me.
His fingers light as dreams,
He touched my eyes,
And the sibylline eyes unsealed
Like those of a startled she-eagle.
He touched my ears,
And clamor and ringing filled them,
And I heard the shuddering of the heavens,
And the lofty flight of angels,
And the underwater movement of sea beasts,
And the languishing of a lone vine in a valley.
And he clung to my mouth
And tore out my sinful tongue,
Given to both lies and idle chatter,
And with his bloody right hand pressed
The forked tongue of a wise serpent
Into my stilled mouth . . .

"I see you are awake now, Mrs. Caldwell," said Rose, entering the library with the duster and vigorously setting about the books. Clouds of ancient gray pollen rose into the air; no one had touched most of these volumes in years, if not decades.

She found herself sneezing, her eyes filled with tears.

"Sorry, sorry," said the maid. "So much dust."

39. Home Theater

A Small Foretaste of Death

SHE DID NOT WANT ANYONE TO BE IN THE HOUSE when she watched it. If she watched it at all—and she was not sure she would—she would be alone. She waited until Paul departed on another of his business trips, and Rose had finished with the afternoon chores. She ate a light supper—an apple, a handful of blueberries, she was never hungry these days—then walked through the rooms, picking up a misplaced magazine here, a teacup there; but the endless drift of books, clothes, phones, keys had ceased since the last of her children had moved away, and the house had lost its daily mutability—everything tended to stay in its place now, unchanged and unchanging for weeks on end. It was not yet eight o'clock when she found nothing but time stretching before her like an open sea—inviting, deadly. Even then, she was not sure she would watch it. She pretended not to think about it for a while, but no matter what she occupied herself with——perusing a cookbook in search of next Sunday's dinner, watering plants——she was always aware of the movie in its sealed case lying on the table at the foot of the staircase, waiting, waiting.

Giving up at last, she descended to the basement, scooped the movie off the table, and, tearing the plastic wrapping as she walked, proceeded to the home theater. The movie cover showed an imposing glass-walled office high up in a skyscraper, and, propped on a leather armchair behind the desk, the top half of a human-size *matryoshka* with the photograph of the famous actress playing the lead role pasted over the doll's rouged, round-eyed face. The doll's lower half lay tipped on its side on the plush carpet, and three or four smaller dolls had spilled out of it——the next-largest bearing the heavily made-up, obscene face of a young stripper, the smallest one that of a serious dark-eyed girl of about five. Quotations in square red letters, all the R's backward to signify the Russianness of the proceedings, promised "НЕАЯТ-STOPPING EXCITEMENT!" and stated underneath, in less prominent print, "Original screenplay by the award-winning author of——"

She parted the curtains that separated the movie room from the rest of the basement, maneuvered through the rows of built-in chairs. When she had first seen the house, thirty-two years ago now, she had been struck dumb by the cup holders in the armrests and the golden tassels on the decadent velvet of the curtains. Now everything appeared vaguely dated, and musty, and neglected. Paul and the children had watched numerous movies here, eating the inevitable popcorn, making shadow puppets with their hands in the beam of the projector during the credits; but now the children were gone, Paul was busy, and she herself could recall suffering through only half a dozen films in all her time in the house. She had no affinity for sitting in the dark, invisible and passive, following the peregrinations of someone else's life—it felt to her like a small foretaste of death.

Except this time, it would not be someone else's life: it would be her own.

For when she finally switched off the lights and settled into one of the rigid-backed chairs to watch the movie, she saw the view of the eternal construction site from the window of her Moscow apartment, and a caricature of her bearded, pipe-smoking father, who spoke in somber truisms, and a mother who collected porcelain cups and came across as superficial and insensitive, and a dacha neighbor for whom the heroine decorously pined while reading Turgenev. She stared at the screen in disbelief, her hands gripping the armrests. The actors sported laughable accents, the teenage heroine cavorted under onion domes and birch trees—and yet it was, undeniably, her childhood, her youth, at least up to a point. For after a particularly ham-fisted, cringe-worthy scene in the country, in which the heroine mused about her impending adulthood, the story veered off: the girl went on a moonlit walk with the dacha boy, and there followed her first kiss in the shade of an old oak tree and a subsequent anguished romance in the streets of Moscow, which scarred her deeply and made her swear off marriage and children, and move to America. With that, the exposition sequence over, the dreamlike sepia tone gave way to harsher colors that signified the present day and place, and the movie proper began. She found herself watching a thriller she could not follow, its fast-paced, intricate plot involving a corrupt American politician, and the Russian mafia, and the heroine, now a courageous New York lawyer, doing something brave yet sexy with a briefcase full of incriminating documents, and a manly colleague who resembled the dacha boy just enough to justify the lengthy backstory—

She stopped the movie, backtracked, watched the beginning again. Her heart felt crammed into her chest, its every beat a painful scrape against her rib cage. When the heroine burst out of her door and ran across the dirt road, hurrying to her first assignation with the dacha neighbor, she screamed and flung the remote control hard against the wall. It broke apart with a dry plastic crack, and the screen went black.

She sat unmoving in the dark, her temples damp, her mind full of poison.

Bitch, you bitch. How could you do that to me? You think you can steal from people like that, gut them, betray them, as long as you claim to do so in the name of art? But you are no artist—just a cliché-ridden hack, driven by nothing but the urge to escape from the emptiness of your own life. Because your life *is* empty, and you are alone, you have no husband and no children and no proper home—you have nothing, you *are* nothing, nothing, nothing, do you hear me . . .

The fury wound tighter and tighter in her chest, until something within it seemed to give way, to sag sidewise. Suddenly frightened, she pressed her clammy fingers to her forehead and took a shallow, labored breath, and another. All at once the darkness of the room was stifling her, threatening her somehow; she

wanted to turn on the lights, but she felt queasy, and oddly exhausted, and the image of herself stumbling through the black
void, bumping into unseen corners and edges, made her press hard
into the back of her chair and close her eyes against the darkness,
and for one moment give all her attention to the sweating, melting,
skipping, somersaulting thing that her heart seemed to be doing
against her will, of its own volition. Perhaps, she thought, I really
ought to stand up and get hold of the telephone, call an ambulance
or something; and the thought sent a stab of terror through her,
which radiated like pain from her chest and deposited the telephone neatly in her hand. Yet when she dialed, it was not the
ambulance, it was Olga's number instead; and though she had long
forgotten the number, if indeed she had ever known it, her fingers,
flying over the buttons, magically summoned the right combination to life—and though the number could have changed, and
though Olga was never at home, if indeed she had ever existed, she
answered on the first ring.

Why did you do it to me? Mrs. Caldwell demanded, not bothering with small talk; for there was no time for that. Is it because
your father drank, your mother slapped you, your childhood was
a low-ceilinged, dismal trap? Did you think the poverty of your
life gave you the right to steal from me, as you have done for
years—for I see everything now, all those books of yours with
their ballet dancers and precious heirlooms and cuckoo clocks,
even the names, even the faces, you used my friends, you used my
family, you used me, turned me into a cipher on a page, on a
screen—why, why? Was it not enough for you to have taken the
boy I liked all those years ago, must you now try to take my past

as well? Olga sounded apologetic but firm, sure of herself. She talked about art, no, Art—Mrs. Caldwell could hear the solemn rise in her tone each time she said it—and the illusory nature of memory, and the purgative power of the autobiographical impulse, and the greater artistic truths revealed sometimes by borrowing, sometimes by distorting, what might be called reality; not to mention the fact that whatever she might have borrowed from Mrs. Caldwell was now immortalized, an indelible footprint in the sands of time—

But already, tiring of the imaginary conversation, she released her immaterial hold on the nonexistent receiver, and briefly opened her eyes—and the darkness of the room crowded her still, and the dizzying pain was still there; so, closing her eyes, she thought, fighting through the chaos of her mind: But this does not matter, this isn't important, I shouldn't waste another moment thinking about it, for no one can take my past away from me, it's mine alone, and it's here, it has always been here, and if I float away from this pain that has narrowed and sharpened until it has become the piercing needle on whose tip the universe is spinning so quickly—if I walk away into this glowing mist, into this welcoming warmth, I will once again feel the trickle of lukewarm water down my back, and hear my grandmother's voice, and smell the sweet tang of the soap, and see the tree, the great ancient tree at the heart of the world, and sense the boundless promise of the future unfolding before me, and no one, no one, will ever take that away from me . . .

Overwhelmed by confusion, I stare at Mrs. Caldwell slumped over in her chair. I do not quite know how I got to my feet, nor do

I remember turning on the lights, yet I see things so surely, down to the smallest of details—the beige carpet stained by countless soda spills, the tassels on the velvet curtains tied into messy knots by the busy hands of restless children, the strands of Mrs. Caldwell's hair plastered over her moist forehead. Everything is bright and clear and precise and, at the same time, slightly off, as though every object has moved an inch to the side and now shimmers with a doubled contour—the way things appear sometimes when your eyes are brimming over with tears, in the second before you blink them away.

For a moment my world totters on the brink of falling over, as vast, invisible things strain to burst into light. Then the moment moves on. I am overtaken by a marvelous sense of an unexpected, unhoped-for liberation. I am free, I am somehow—finally!—free of this woman who is not me, who has never been me—free of the complacent, materialistic, dim oppression of her timid spirit. Light-headed with the immensity, with the joy, of this new freedom, I look again at Mrs. Caldwell. She continues to sit slumped over in her chair, her face covered by the fallen hair. She is, I imagine, still fuming over the irrelevant movie, insisting that her past is hers alone, planning perhaps to set her husband's lawyer on her treacherous friend . . . I am wondering if I should speak to her, when I am seized with a sharp, almost animal panic at the thought of lingering another instant in her oddly immobile, heavy-limbed presence.

Jerking my eyes away from the woman, I pass out of the room.

I feel another, lighter prick of panic when I realize that I cannot recall having parted the pompous curtains as I stepped over the threshold, but I dispel my fear quickly: I am, it is true, a little hazy about what has happened—about what is happening—to me, yet I am certain there will be plenty of time to sort it out later. For now, it is enough to know I am free. I am ready to go and live fully at last. I have so many plans, I think in a fever of joyous agitation. I will leave this house, I will travel, I will cross unfamiliar roads and turn blind corners without trepidation, I will look up old friends and talk to strangers, I will capture every moment of joy, every crumb of discovery, as I write all the poetry I have ever meant to write.

I do not remember the last time I felt so alive.

40. Entrance Hall

Departures

AND SO I HAVE MADE UP MY MIND TO LEAVE. I TOLD
Paul I intended to go to Russia for a while, spend a few months in
the countryside reliving my childhood, and he did not raise a single objection; in fact, he appeared distraught about something
and did not seem to hear me at all. His indifference saddened me
a little, but I reminded myself of the journey ahead and felt
restored to happiness. I will not go to Russia just yet; I will save it
for last. For now, I will follow religious processions through the
ancient streets of Spanish towns, I will sit on mud floors in African huts listening to the midnight roar of lions, I will taste unknown fruits in the floating markets of Asia. I will walk through
the mountains, the valleys, the forests of the world, all-seeing and
all-hearing, greedy for every tiny morsel of life. Perhaps I will
come back, perhaps not.

I have already decided what to bring with me on my travels. I will take almost nothing—just a thick sweater, a pair of sturdy walking shoes, my passport with its pages virginally clear of stamps, a handful of pens, a notebook, my dog-eared volume of Annensky, and Celia's lopsided blue bunny. I have not actually packed—in truth, things have developed a somewhat disconcerting tendency to pass through my fingers, but I choose not to dwell on such matters; I cannot leave just yet, in any case. Three and a half decades of maternal habits cannot be discarded so easily, and there are still a few loose ends to tie up before I can go: the birth of my second grandchild in February, followed by Eugene's homecoming over Easter, followed by another reunion in July—

In between family visits, I wander the house. As often as not, I end up in the entrance hall, and there I sit, going over the packing list in my mind, dreaming of escaping soon, so soon, almost any day now. The entrance hall is a grand space inscribed into the stately arc of the marble staircase, crowded with stuffy, lion-pawed chairs and consoles. One's entrance hall—my decorator told me once, a third of a century ago now—should serve as a perfect introduction to the house that follows; to the world of people forever kept on its doorstep, peering wistfully over the homeowner's shoulder (a delivery man, a gardener, a Jehovah's Witness, God visiting incognito), it should offer a tantalizing hint of the wonders that await the lucky few allowed within. When we first saw the house, I remember the awed sense I had upon entering—that of an immense place, full of possibilities, unfolding inward, like that magic house from a childhood fairy tale that was bigger on the inside than on the outside.

Now I know it to be the other way around. On the inside, the house is much, much smaller than its sprawling, many-columned façade would lead one to believe.

As I sit in the entrance hall, revising my list (I will not, after all, need that sweater), I stare at the enormous double doors of brilliantly polished oak reflected in the expanse of the brilliantly polished marble floors. I never throw the doors open, for fear that temptation will move me to make a dash for it before I have quite disposed of the last of my matriarchal obligations. Sometimes I do feel a surge of frustration, as though I am a clockwork toy that has been wound up and cannot act of its own accord until it completes the predetermined range of its mechanical motions. In other, darker moments, my throat tightens with panic—what if it is simply too late, what if over the years I have sprouted such thick roots that I will be unable to walk away? But such thoughts are only signs of weakness, so I force myself to breathe, and busy my mind with shaving more unnecessary items off the list (I decide I do not want the walking shoes either), and muse on my past, on the decisions I have made in my life, on the roads I have followed and not followed. I imagine having had five children, or two, or none; I imagine having left Paul or never having married him; I imagine having gone to Paris with Adam; I imagine not having stayed in America, or not having left Russia; I imagine having crossed that dirt road and kissed that boy; I imagine having never given up my poetry. I remember a little girl who lived in a faraway country with long, cold winters and bright summer stars—a girl who had a mermaid for a mother, a sage for a father, a god for a guide—a girl who loved life and played with words and looked out of the small window of her small room to behold the whole world. And when my memories start crowding my chest with something much like sobs, I distract my attention with the comings and goings of people around me.

For the house, even as it lies fallow during Paul's business trips, between my children's and grandchildren's visits, is never entirely empty. If I sit still enough, letting my mind drift free until it bursts the imprisonment of matter, I begin to see the riches of things that skip, slide, and dance beneath the surface of the world—and I can then sense ghostly women moving through the house. All with their own versions of my elderly face, they walk through the rooms on their different errands, possessed of varied degrees of presence and persistence—some mere echoes, glimpses, faint wisps of holographic lives, others coming through so clearly, so tangibly, it seems as if I could reach out and truly touch them. I understand that they are not really here, of course, for they are only a vast, cosmic branching of endless possibilities, of numberless outcomes—all of them variations on my own fate, passing through mirror dimensions, brushing by me, fading in and out of sight—an endless theater of myself, parading before me as I sit in the entrance hall, ruminating on the packing list (I can do without the passport, I think), dreaming of all the poetry I will compose once I am away.

The woman I see most often is an absolute bore, an expensively dressed phantom of a person with not an original thought in her exquisitely coiffed head. She spends her days straightening the rooms and leafing through magazines; her visitors are of the most prosaic sort, electricians and rug cleaners and dog walkers; in the evenings, when her husband's car pulls into the driveway, she dabs a touch of lipstick on her faded mouth before the entrance hall mirror, and waits, smiling meekly, tilting her head at the sound of his key in the lock. Paul is kind to her, if ever so slightly dismissive.

A more disturbing presence is a Mrs. Caldwell who has only five children and whose husband abandoned her for his secretary two decades before, though leaving her in full possession of the house. She dyes her indecently long hair blond and has dabbled in plastic procedures. Every time the doorbell rings on a Friday night, she clatters across the marble floor in her stilettos, and I catch a terrible glimpse of my features drawn on a sixty-five-year-old flesh-colored balloon, stretched and bloated. I hurry to avert my eyes, just as she is letting in her much younger boyfriend, to whom she then glues herself in a long, slurping kiss. I believe the man is no good; he is after her money. She has started to write love poetry, too. I find her frankly embarrassing.

There are a few others here as well—a thin-lipped, dieting, strident Mrs. Caldwell who has gone to work at some downtown office doing who knows what, as well as a flighty Mrs. Caldwell who occupies herself with trying to translate her mother's poetry and is prone to bursting into tears whenever any of her children visit. My favorite Mrs. Caldwell is plump and energetic, young at sixty-seven, with a bristle of unkempt hair and a marvelous touch with her grandchildren; her house is always overrun with them (Emma is divorced now and living here with her two daughters while she studies for her architect's exam, and Eugene and Adriana often visit with their baby). She appears genuinely happy, and seems to love everyone, just as everyone loves her, and her entrance hall is always traipsed over with muddy footprints and wet leaves, chaotic with toddler shoes and lunch boxes and mis-matched mittens and shed petals of flowers and the bustle of dogs. I think of her belly laugh, her jolly face, to ward off despair whenever I see that other woman, that obese, slovenly, gray-haired and gray-faced woman who lives all alone and drags herself through the house, dressed in a dirty pink robe and dirty pink slippers, sighing wetly, mumbling poems under her breath, never failing to twist my heart with pity. I do not know her story, but I can see death in her stark, empty eyes—a child's death—and I turn away every time, horrified and ashamed for some reason.

There may also be a Mrs. Caldwell who is moving away—though, strangely enough, neither she nor Paul is organizing the move; it is only the children, much older now, who come to the house, arriving in somber groups of two and three. Maggie and Celia, I notice, have been crying, Emma is white-lipped as she speaks to Eugene on the phone, giving him details of some funeral arrangements, asking when his flight from Bucharest is due to land, and I overhear Rich consoling George as they stand in the doorway surveying the boxes. For the entrance hall has been fill-ing up with boxes upon boxes in the past few weeks—boxes of por-celain, boxes of silver, paintings wrapped in cocoons of padded paper, precious plates buried in crates of packing peanuts, con-tractors and realtors coming and going, two electricians carrying the dining room chandelier trussed up like a slaughtered boar on a pole between them. As the movers shuttle in and out on moving day, the double doors stand open for hours at a time, and hour after hour I sit in the hall, revising the packing list in my head (I

have resolved to leave the notebook and the pens behind) and staring outside, at the rectangle of the gray November sky above the
movers' heads, at the waving of the oak tree's naked branches.
When the final boxes depart, I feel relieved to be rid of all that
useless stuff at last, but a bit depressed too. I catch a glimpse of a
"For Sale" sign stuck in the lawn outside, and then the doors close,
and the house stands empty and dark, a winter draft from below
the doors blowing a dead oak leaf across the filthy floor. To the
left, then to the right, then to the left again, flutters the leaf. I
wonder if it has my name written on it, and attempt to smile at the
thought; but I do not get up to look. The lights of the grand chandelier above me no longer come on, for the electricity has been
turned off; I can sense the long winter night moving in.

The old panic takes hold of me roughly.

How would I know, I think wildly, if I were not myself, but
one of these other apparitions instead—and if so, how would I
know which one? How would I know if I were only a footnote
in a story that has gone on without me—if some other, braver
woman has not led an entirely different, wonder-filled existence
in my name, never even setting foot in this house, never even
coming near all this? How would I know if I were the ghost of
someone long dead within these walls, unable to leave, trapped
here as punishment for my waste of a life—as failed at death as I
was at living? And if this really is some kind of purgatory, how
will I know when I am forgiven for my sins, when I am allowed to
leave it all behind?

But quickly I push these dark thoughts away. Because of course
I am going to leave, I am going to leave just as soon as Christmas

is over. In the meantime I continue whittling down my list—I
have decided to take nothing but Celia's one-eared bunny and the
volume of Annensky, and soon the volume of Annensky seems
superfluous too, as I find I remember his poems with perfect clarity, even as I can no longer recall a single line of my own. I recite
his words for hours, for days, for months on end, sitting in the
entrance hall, looking at the closed door.

Do you not imagine sometimes,
When dusk wanders through the house,
That here, alongside us, lies another plane,
Where we lead entirely different lives?

It is not a bad way to spend one's time. It could have been so
much worse. This morning, for instance, I heard a siren wailing
outside. The next thing I know, the doors are being flung open,
and two men in white burst in, a stretcher between them, and
disappear at a run inside the house. I sit in the darkened entrance
hall, waiting for them to return. After a while they walk back
across the hall, slowly now, bent under the weight of the body on
the stretcher. I glimpse a limp strand of gray hair, a dangling pink
slipper, a hanging fold of a dirty pink robe. I do not look closely;
I do not want to know what the matter is with her. I just whisper
a quick prayer for the poor soul, and feel grateful for having been
spared, and, as I hear the ambulance start, say to myself: There
but for the grace of God go I.

The men in white, I notice with a sudden jolt, have left the
doors standing wide open. I look at the glorious blue sky of April,

or is it July—the light pouring through is radiantly clear, a luminous invitation. I realize that I do not, after all, need to bring Celia's bunny. As I stand up and walk empty-handed toward the shining rectangle of light, I think of all the secrets, all the marvels of the world I am about to see.

Part Five

The Future

THE END

Acknowledgments

As ever, I am deeply grateful to Warren Frazier, my agent, and Marian Wood, my publisher and editor—without their friendship, judgment, and faith in my work, none of this would have happened. Thanks are also due to everyone at the Penguin Group who helped make this book a reality, especially Ivan Held, for all his support; Alexis Sattler, for assisting with so many details; and my indefatigable copy editor, Anna Jardine, who spared me many an embarrassment, among them the militant image of an elderly professor rifling, rather than riffling, through index cards. I would also like to thank Alexander Hollmann for his artistic input, and my first readers and oldest friends, Olga Levaniouk and Olga Oliker, for their immensely helpful insights—I couldn't wish for better readers, first or otherwise.

Finally, special thanks go to my family—my mother, Natalia Kartseva, who was always there for me, and my children, Alex and Tasha, who became so delightfully curious about all the stages of making a book. Eleven-year-old Alex helped with designing the sketches, six-year-old Tasha made a sign—"Do not disturb, I need time"—for my office door, and both of them tolerated their share of Chinese takeout dinners and pizza deliveries while I was busy describing the culinary accomplishments of Mrs. Caldwell. Thank you for letting me write, most of the time—and for making me happy, always.